Tod Benjamin left Palmer's School in 1953. National Service in the RAF was followed by fifteen years in retail management. A change in career led to twenty-five years in the chemical industry and world-wide travel.

From the age of fifty-nine, Tod played winter golf in Florida and began to write. A damaged back meant the end of golf and more concentration upon his writing. His first success came with the publication of a memoir, followed by his first novel at the age of eighty. Then, he set about creating *The Stoker Trilogy*. The first book, 'Charles and Charlie' was published by Austin Macauley in 2020. 'The Tally Man' is the second of the series and Tod is currently writing the final instalment, 'The Soldier'.

Tod Benjamin

The Stoker Trilogy, Book II
The Tally Man

AUSTIN MACAULEY PUBLISHERS™
LONDON • CAMBRIDGE • NEW YORK • SHARJAH

Copyright © Tod Benjamin 2022

The right of Tod Benjamin to be identified as author of this work has been asserted by the author in accordance with section 77 and 78 of the Copyright, Designs and Patents Act 1988.

All rights reserved. No part of this publication may be reproduced, stored in a retrieval system, or transmitted in any form or by any means, electronic, mechanical, photocopying, recording, or otherwise, without the prior permission of the publishers.

Any person who commits any unauthorised act in relation to this publication may be liable to criminal prosecution and civil claims for damages.

This is a work of fiction. Names, characters, businesses, places, events, locales, and incidents are either the products of the author's imagination or used in a fictitious manner. Any resemblance to actual persons, living or dead, or actual events is purely coincidental.

A CIP catalogue record for this title is available from the British Library.

ISBN 9781398459946 (Paperback)
ISBN 9781398459953 (ePub e-book)

www.austinmacauley.com

First Published 2022
Austin Macauley Publishers Ltd®
1 Canada Square
Canary Wharf
London
E14 5AA

My sincere thanks to Peter Turnill, the editor of 'Fishtail' (Magazine of the Velocette Owners' Club) for the guidance on early motorcycles; to my niece Amber Cook for her guidance on things medical; and to Major Peter Williamson for his assistance in matters military.

Above all, thanks to my beloved wife Suzi for being the first reader and for declaring the book worthy of an all-night read!

Chapter One
A New Career

It was in the dark economic atmosphere of 1931 that twenty-year-old Charles Horace Stoker sacrificed the security of the Enfield solicitors, Cavendish, Brigham, Mabey, for the unpredictable world of commerce. Charlie Stoker was introduced to Collick's department store in January of the year.

The Wall Street crash of 1929 had caused immense economic suffering worldwide. Ironically, Great Britain was not at first affected as disastrously as many other countries, having already been in depression since 1920. Nevertheless, by the end of 1930 the impact of the collapse upon the British economy had become fierce. Exports had halved in value and unemployment had reached an all-time high. It now accounted for more than twenty percent of the workforce.

As throughout the preceding decade, London and the South-East was suffering less than other regions of the country. Many people in the north and west, seeing their businesses and careers threatened by the damage to the coal and cotton industries, moved south in search of better opportunities.

The Collick Estate recognised a potential for gain from this trend, and in 1928 established a construction company to build detached and semi-detached houses on land purchased cheaply in the leafy areas to the north and north-east of London. Charlie and Margret Stoker now lived in one of these houses.

The Estate's wealth was widely spread, and in two quite separate domains. Lord Roderick Collick personally presided over the estate itself with its six managed farms, plus four large farms in Hertfordshire not within the estate, and two further estates, in Scotland and in Yorkshire.

His brother, the Hon. Stephen Collick, oversaw an assortment of industrial enterprises, split into four divisions. Firstly, there was a newspaper and its associated businesses, including a large printing works and a precision engineering company. The construction company formed the rapidly growing second division. Thirdly, there was a tea plantation in Ceylon, and finally, there was the textile division: two textile mills in Yorkshire and a department store in London. The mills produced high quality woollen cloth but had been experiencing hard times for several years and were struggling to remain solvent.

With the exception of the department store, the day-to-day operation of all the businesses was delegated to highly qualified and well-established management teams. It was from these that the family received the bulk of its income.

The department store, however, was regarded by the confirmed bachelor as his own pet operation. Together with the mills, it had been handed down from his mother's family; but it was his father, Lord Collick, who had wasted a great deal of money and time renaming and extending the store, and building a grand façade to the front.

When, shortly after the Great War, the old man's health began to fail, he handed Stephen the reins. He charged him with ensuring that his dream of a store as grand as the famous West End and Knightsbridge businesses would be established in the East End of London.

Unfortunately, Lord Collick's ailing health coincided with the ailing state of trade in his grand emporium, and after a few years of struggle Stephen concluded that the East End of London demanded a different sort of business. It needed a department store for all people. It must be a store that met the needs of those without the resources to purchase its wares, while still catering for the more opulent residents of Leytonstone, Ilford and Stamford Hill.

He decided upon a system that incorporated the luxury of visits to his imposing store with the age-old trade of the tally man. To implement this plan, he appointed a sales manager, who was tasked with setting up and training a team of salesmen-collectors. They would sell goods to customers by encouraging them into the department store to choose merchandise, or by carrying stock to sell to them in their own homes. The sold goods would be paid for by regular payments over a period of twenty weeks.

Each salesman's responsibilities would be threefold: to keep his customers' accounts active and healthy by collecting the weekly payments; to repeatedly sell more goods to perpetuate the accounts; and to open new accounts.

* * *

On a Sunday at the end of January, Charlie and his wife Margret had travelled from their new home at Chigwell to lunch with his mother and her friend the Hon.

Stephen Collick at Mrs Stoker's house in Amhurst Road in Hackney. After lunch, leaving the ladies to chat, Stephen Collick drove Charlie in his shining red Lanchester motor car to the Collick's building in Whitechapel Road.

The building was comprised of five floors: basement, ground level and three upper floors. Bypassing the impressive frontage, Stephen unlocked the staff entrance door and took the lift to the top floor. In the comfort of his office there, he explained his proposal to the young man. It was, he said, a very long-term plan.

In a noticeably tense tone of voice, he reminded Charlie that when they had first been properly introduced, some eighteen months earlier, he had mentioned his conviction that Charles Stoker's son should be granted the opportunity to build the sort of material success denied to his father. Since that day, he had come to know Charlie well and to recognise in him much of his father's character.

"He would have been proud of you, Charlie. You have his build, his looks and his strength of character."

He looked admiringly at the young man for a moment, then continued, his voice again tense.

"Today, before I begin to explain what I have in mind, I have to insist that what is said here, what will be agreed in this office this afternoon – indeed, our very presence here today – must never be spoken of outside these walls; nor ever referred to in a casual conversation."

He paused for reaction and acknowledged Charlie's slow nod of the head with an inclination of his own.

"At that first meeting," he continued, "you expressed your hopes of building your father's shoe business. You said that what you had enjoyed most of all there was talking with the customers. In the intervening period, you have endured a great deal of stress and have been compelled to make life-changing decisions.

"Today, I intend to give you the opportunity to make another decision: to learn about not only shoes but the much wider world of commercial business. Only by understanding fully the many aspects of an organisation could a person properly attempt to run the show. And that is what I desire for you, Charlie. I want you to learn how to manage this business from the bottom to the top.

"I am, as you know, a bachelor. I am wealthy, and much of that wealth I owe to the extraordinary work of your father. I have now reached the point in my life when I have just two dreams – two ambitions. They are to establish this department store as the retail beacon in the east of London that my father envisioned; and to retire in twenty years' time knowing that what will then exist will continue to thrive under your guidance. Only then, will I feel my debt to your father is paid. Only then, can I die at peace."

The two men were facing each other in comfortable matching chairs either side of a coffee table on which a tray held a decanter, two sherry schooners, a silver cigarette box with matching table lighter, and an ashtray. On the wall to Charlie's right, above the fireplace, was the portrait of a thin-faced man with a Prince Albert moustache, in black waistcoat and jacket with an upstanding collar and bow tie. The tiny plaque beneath the frame was indecipherable from where he sat, lips slightly apart, struggling to absorb what he was hearing.

The room became very still when Stephen Collick stopped speaking, but eventually Charlie said, "Excuse me, sir, this is all a bit overwhelming. May I smoke a cigarette?"

Collick was at once his usual warm self. "Of course, dear boy, help yourself and I shall be delighted to join you. Shall we enjoy a sherry, also?"

Charlie lit and inhaled. Stephen Collick lifted the decanter and filled the glasses. He also took a cigarette from the box. They smoked and sipped silently, the older man quite content to wait until his protégé was ready to speak.

Charlie drew another lungful of smoke and breathed out slowly, fighting to control his whirling thoughts. He had huge respect for Stephen Collick. He much admired his amenable manner, to say nothing of the man's generosity. But this… this was a move of another order completely. When he had calmed himself enough, he said:

"I remember you talking to us about your debt to my father, and Mum said that you'd told her years ago there would always be a job for Charles Stoker's son, but I naturally thought it would be in the print works, like my dad. Partly, I thought that was why I was doing a physics course."

"If that were what you really desired, Charlie, I should have accommodated you. I have seen, though, that that is not where your heart lies. It is not where you see your future."

Stephen smiled his shy smile. "Neither, I now understand, do you see it in the legal profession." The smile became a chuckle.

"No, not that!" Charlie grinned briefly. "Mr Collick… Stephen, Sir… you are… this is… this is quite unbelievable. As you can see, sir, I'm struggling to say something coherent. I'm told I tend not to show my feelings, and I don't usually say a lot, but today I can't stay quiet."

He drew a deep smoke-filled breath and crushed the cigarette into the ashtray.

"I have to confess I don't understand how you can have that sort of faith in me. After all, I'm only twenty, and all I've achieved so far is to make a bit of a mess of my life. Yet you've made Chigwell possible for Margret and me, and now you're mapping out a future that I have no right to expect. The only thing I can say for certain is that I will accept whatever terms you lay down, and I'll drive myself to the limit to succeed and never to let you down."

"You won't let me down, Charlie Stoker. I don't think you will ever let anyone down. You are your father's son and you have, in addition, your mother's sound common sense. To have you at my side will give me the greatest happiness of my life. Let us shake hands on it."

He stood up, almost six feet tall and slim; Charlie did likewise, inches taller and broader in the shoulders. Stephen stepped around the table and grasped the young man's hand. Then he pulled Charlie to him in a close hug and held him there for some seconds.

"We shall build an empire, you and I, Charlie Stoker," he whispered. He gently released the embarrassed young man and said, "Come, sit. Let's have another sherry, there's more to be said."

They settled back into their seats and with refilled glasses toasted the future. Then Stephen adopted his serious face once more.

"Charlie," he said, "as you have no doubt already concluded, I am a man of conviction. I rather lack a forceful personality, but I do have a great inner drive. What I am about to tell you, I have told no other person, ever. I am going to tell you a little of the past, and why, as far as the rest of the world is concerned, this afternoon's meeting is not taking place.

"I was not blessed with the happy childhood you may have imagined. My father, Lord Collick, was a hard man, a ruthless man, who had inherited two large estates and other associated assets, but was in financial difficulties when his first wife, Mary, the mother of my half-brother Roderick, died in childbirth. Very soon afterwards, in 1882, he married Elspeth, my mother. She was the only child of a business associate, a Yorkshire industrialist, Reginald Battersby. Lord Collick married her solely for her wealth, and he used the marriage to forge deeper links between the two business empires.

"He was furious when in 1884, while I was still a baby, grandfather Battersby died, leaving most of his fortune in trust with my mother for me when I should reach the age of majority. Nevertheless, my father soon managed to take control of most of my mother's affairs. He contrived to act as administrator of the trust.

He also proceeded to abuse and to bully my mother until he drove her to an early grave in 1902. For the last eight years of her life, when I was away at school and university, she, a mild and gentle person, found it necessary to live alone in a separate house on the far side of the estate to obtain a modicum of peace. That house, Parklands, in which she died, she left to me and it remains my home."

"I was always referred to as her boy rather than their son, and as it gradually became apparent that I had inherited mostly Battersby characteristics – a mathematical mind and an inclination to read a great many books – my father and my half-brother both treated me more and more as an outcast. Their attitude changed only when I came of age and received my inheritance."

"At that time, the print works, a major component of the family estate, was running under the direction of my uncle, Sir Arthur Collick, who had recently retired from the army after thirty-six years of service. A far more level headed person than my father, he had assumed control of the printing works in 1901."

"Uncle Arthur was a wise old bird, the two brothers being as different as chalk and cheese. His disciplined guidance was to prove of great benefit to me when I commenced working there after graduating from university in 1904. He made my father recognise that I was now not only a major shareholder, but also the one member of the family most intellectually capable of protecting the interests of the estate. Thereafter, my father began to treat me with a grudging respect, but with little affection.

"So, you see, the Collick Estate's industrial interests, the newspaper, the printing works, the mills, the construction company and this venture, grew principally from the Battersby fortune. This store began life as Battersby's, built by my grandfather to sell the textiles from his Yorkshire mills." He raised his arm to point at the portrait above the fireplace.

"That is his portrait. It was hanging at Parklands but I prefer to see him here. He left this store to my mother independently of the other family businesses and she bequeathed it to me. My father changed the name during the war, when he formed his misguided concept of a rival to Harrod's. When he handed me the reins he was just beginning to realise his error. He was already a sick man and he feared the business would fail. He instructed me, as the financial brain of the family, – he used the term derogatively – to sort it out. He died nine years ago, believing to his dying day that I would have to close the store and sell the property."

He paused for a moment.

"But I am getting ahead of myself. Back to 1904. I had always been what is generally called a loner, even at university; and at Clerkenwell the only person with whom I formed a close association, my first really close association with anyone, was the works engineer, your father, Charles Stoker."

"Charles, a brilliant engineer, was everything I admired in a man. We were of similar ages, and from the very first, we became friends. He had the most wonderful laughing blue eyes and he used to explain to me with a fervour his ideas for the development of processes and equipment. I was able to calculate the financial implications of his proposals for the company, and together we formed plans for the business that I would press upon my uncle until they were adopted. And they always were, and the business grew."

"Charles was constantly suggesting bold innovations in the use of old machinery. He made possible the development of new markets for the company. We spent a great deal of time together and I grew to love him, Charlie, and to live for the hours I was in his company. I was a lonely young man. My mother, the only person ever to show me love, had died a few years earlier. I had never had a friend of my own, and here was this bubbling blond engineer who seemed to see everything, from our very first meeting, as I did. I was emotionally overwhelmed by him. He instinctively understood my need for love, and he respected and returned it in his gestures and in his natural all-encompassing warmth."

"Then, he met Millie Cowper. I watched, as everything I felt for him I could see him feeling for her. I was jealous of your mother, to whom I had barely been introduced. I was envious of the love they clearly had for each other – I myself have never been able to enjoy such a contentment with another person – but I could see that Charles was joyously happy and contented. Not that his manner toward me ever altered."

"My uncle made him works manager in 1911, but the extra responsibility changed him not a bit. He was still the same bubbling, sparkle-eyed colleague and confidant. Inevitably, though, through time, with increased workloads, a wife, his home, and then the birth of his child, a little distance did grow between us. I was pained, and when the opportunity came for me to work elsewhere within our operations, I took it."

He downed the last of his schooner of sherry and raised an eyebrow and the glass towards Charlie. The invitation was met with a shake of the head and a polite smile that said nothing of what the young man was feeling. His own sherry poured, Collick resumed:

"Then came the war and service. When my uncle made his suggestion about the Royal Flying Corps, Charles of course jumped at it. He saw it as both his duty to his country and an opportunity to make new discoveries. He went off to France and I went to headquarters. We remained in contact for some time until, a year or two later, I was sent to Palestine. When I returned, I had become a very rich man in absentia. That wealth has continued to grow ever since – but you know about that, Charlie."

Charlie stared blankly across the table, not sure what he was hearing, or why. After a moment, he shrugged.

"I suppose so," he said slowly, "but what I don't see, Sir, Stephen, Sir, is exactly why you've told me all this personal history. I'm embarrassed to be hearing all this about your private life. I can certainly see, now, why you said what you did about the secrecy of this meeting, and I fully understand about learning the business. That's one thing, but it doesn't mean I should know all this about your private life, does it? You've told me things that are too personal. It doesn't concern me. It's none of my business."

"It is, Charlie, because I am making it your business."

The tone was firm but not unkind. Stephen Collick continued:

"While your father was alive, I was compelled by his edict to watch your family from a distance. After he died, I have engineered matters so that I have been able to come closer to you. Your mother, a person always worthy of great respect, has since become a dear friend, something quite rare for me; and now you have blossomed into a youthful version of the man I loved. I have no one else to care about in my life, Charlie, and I do not want my property or my work to be wasted on, or ruined by, the Collick family. I want to be able to pass on whatever I have to you, to Charles Stoker's son, and that is why you have the right to understand why I feel as I do."

Charlie gestured toward the silver box and looked enquiringly at Stephen Collick. Stephen, smiling, lifted the lighter. Charlie took another cigarette. He lit it and, head lowered, spoke at little more than a whisper:

"You said you became very close to my father. You grew to love him, you said. What exactly did you mean? Did you mean you were…" – he hesitated, unsure how to express such a relationship – "… you were lovers?" He drew deeply on his cigarette in an attempt to hide his embarrassment.

Stephen Collick's face bore the look of a concerned parent. "Love is a multifaceted diamond, Charlie, never to be confused with carnal lust. Carnal desire is mere fleeting gossamer. I loved your father, but ours was not a gossamer relationship."

Charlie pondered over that, aware of the evasion within it. As for carnal relationships, he himself had good experience of that and of its consequences. Moving to a less sensitive subject, he said:

"My head's in a whirl, sir, Stephen. Allowing for all you've told me, I still can't understand how you can have such belief in me. How do you envisage me learning, I think you said: 'to manage this business from the bottom to the top'?"

Stephen's smile became comfortable again.

"I am very glad you asked me that. That is the other reason for the secrecy of this meeting. All the staff employed at this store are well aware that I am who I am, the bachelor brother of Lord Collick. They assume I am an instrument of the Collick Estate. I have never discouraged this assumption and have always encouraged a rather forward-looking policy of promotion on merit for all staff. It has been emphasised that the opportunity is there for any member of staff to rise to the very top of the tree, should they show themselves to have the necessary qualities. To date, though many aspire to higher levels, I have seen no sign of that potential. Very few men are blessed with the talents to run a company, Charlie."

"You, however, do have those qualities, but if I were now to introduce you as someone chosen to succeed me, it would completely defeat what has been built. It would destroy the faith and the dreams of many. No. Quite simply, Charlie, you must be just another young man starting at the bottom of the ladder with the determination and ability to rise to the top. You will reach the top of the tree because you are the man you are, and not for any other reason. Whatever post you are appointed to will accord you exactly the same privileges as any other member of staff in a similar position."

"I shall appear somewhat remote until you reach the level of authority with which I communicate directly. I shall at no time indicate any preferential sign of personal acquaintance. My secretary will mention to Mr Fortescue that your name has been passed to her as someone looking for a career, a not unusual occurrence. He, the personnel manager, will invite you for an interview. You will take it from there, and I shall proudly watch you climb the ladder.

"The only other matter of concern is that of income. You must accept the lowly wage offered by Mr Fortescue and you will be paid in cash, each Thursday. There can be no exceptions to the rules."

"However, privately and quite independently of your wages from Collick's, an account will be opened in your name at Martin's Bank in Bishopsgate and a payment will be made into that account by Maxwell and Thrape, my personal solicitors, on the first day of each month. This private income will allow you to meet your obligations at Woodside Way."

He paused, at once assuming his usual diffident air as he switched from managing director to family friend. "Now you understand how I see the future, Charlie. What do you think? Are you content with that?"

Charlie licked dry lips. The Hon. Stephen Collick was like a chameleon. He appeared exactly as he needed to appear at every moment. His smile came and went like a flash of lightning. Yet, always, integrity and honesty oozed from every pore of the man.

The elegant aristocrat had confided his love for the young man's father. The more Charlie listened to and talked with him, the more he appreciated how his father might have responded to that love. Indeed, his own feelings toward Stephen were by no means merely a sense of gratitude. The man exuded kindness, warmth and sensitivity. His diffident sincerity cried out for reciprocation. Charlie was unsure exactly how to respond, but he realised that the starting point must be to grasp the opportunity presented to him.

"Yes, sir," he replied, "I am content."

Chapter Two
The Stockroom Boy

The house at Chigwell was in a beautiful setting in a quite rural area. It was conveniently situated for the train to Collick's, a journey of about forty minutes, but it lay a full ten miles – most of an hour's cycling – from his mother's house in Amhurst Road, from the Northern Polytechnic, or from his friend Bobby Bruce's home, in Harringay.

To make things easier, the two friends made new arrangements for their weekly swim. Walthamstow Baths, more or less halfway between them, became the new venue for a new time, six o'clock on Wednesday evenings. For Bobby, it was no problem. The journey was easy by motorbike. When Charlie had invited him to view the house before it was completed, he had driven his friend on the pillion of his totally refurbished BSA Model L.

8 Woodside Way stood in a plot of a quarter of an acre. The front garden was bounded on two sides by decorative stone pillars, linked by a curved brick wall, four to six feet high. A pair of wooden gates led via a sweeping paved drive to a brick garage attached to the side of the house, and to the front door of the already structurally completed, visually striking house.

A panelled fence separated the property from the next plot, to the left. To the rear was a large rectangular garden, at the bottom of which stood two oak trees. A picket fence marked the boundary behind the trees. Beyond that was open woodland. On the right of the property, next to the garage and separated by another panelled fence was the two acres of land that was to become the paddock for Margret's horse.

Bobby, who lived with his parents in a small terraced house in Harringay, had been bowled over by the sight of the property. The house, he stammered, was 'f-fabulous'. But the surrounding plot was, he admitted, 'a m-m-mess'. He insisted on helping Charlie to convert the building site from a wasteland into a proper garden.

Bobby Bruce had no compunction about taking time out to work for Charlie Stoker. The two had become firm friends as students at the Northern Polytechnic. Now self-employed as a mechanical engineer, he was still in the early stages of building his business.

He had established a customer base with a number of local tradesmen but was spending a considerable amount of time searching for work or experimenting with bits and pieces of equipment. He had built a detachable and easily disassembled sidecar to take his fiancée Daphne in the gleaming model L. He had also constructed a simple low-sided wooden platform that fitted on the same chassis to carry equipment, engines and parts.

It had been easy, therefore, to carry almost everything they would need for their task and a fortnight before the move from Enfield, the two friends had set about what Bobby called 'cultivating the g-great w-wilderness'. Any extra equipment or hands they needed were readily available through the goodwill of the construction company's works foreman, whose men were still working on the other houses. The men had been greatly encouraged by Charlie's provision of a lunch basket and a barrel of beer.

At the end of a week, the site had been cleared front and back. Two paved paths now gave some definition to the flattened rear garden, and a wooden garden shed, erected in one corner, was reached by a short linking path,. Patchy grass lay between the paths, having defied the builders' efforts to kill it, but it could not be called a lawn. The front garden, cleared of debris and levelled with new topsoil, lay quite bare, awaiting seeding.

* * *

Two weeks later the Stokers had moved into their new home. The four bedroomed house was an extravagantly spacious home for the young couple. It was furnished in an attractive, if somewhat spare, art deco style. There were three reception rooms and a large kitchen. From the wide hallway, with its magnolia walls and oak parquet flooring, a staircase led via a landing with a large window looking out to the rear of the house to the four bedrooms and the marble finished bathroom.

One reception room and two of the four bedrooms had been left completely unfurnished for the time being. It was explained to visitors that they wanted to take their time and not rush to furnish them in a manner they may later regret;

but in fact, the new Stoker home was designed so that it could, if necessary, be divided into two self-contained residences.

Margret had packed all her clothes, books and personal odds and ends for the move to Chigwell, but she deliberately took nothing whatsoever that would specifically remind her of the Mabey family home. Intent upon a clean break from its painful memories, the only exception she made was for her horse, Tempest. The beautiful 15-year-old black mare was still being kept at the stables at Enfield but would be brought over to Chigwell as soon as possible.

In truth, Margret was not much put out by the upheaval. Delighted to be able to cut free from Clay Hill, she cared little about the furnishing of a house beyond the basic requirements. In addition, she regarded the house at Woodside Way as no more than a weekend home, at least while she remained at university. Her room at Clare Market would remain her main base.

From there, contact with Charlie and Jennifer was a simple matter. She saw Charlie at weekends, of course, and travelled with him to the city each Monday. During the week she could easily meet Jennifer, who was in the final year of her pharmacy course at the Northern Poly. The journey from there to Clare Market was a short one. Thus, she was in regular contact with the only two people in the world about whom she really cared.

For Charlie, life was a far more serious matter. As he stared blankly through the window of the morning train to Collick's on a dark February morning, he reflected that fate had transformed his life from carefree college boy to working shop assistant. Even more significantly, he was a married householder owning a property that, but for his incredibly generous secret monthly allowance, would be far beyond his means to maintain.

That was what he had committed to via a marriage ceremony, a mortgage contract and a contract of employment. He smiled ruefully to himself. What the hell! Charlie Stoker would not default on his responsibilities.

The job interview at Collick's had gone more or less as expected. Having completed a form with his personal details in the waiting room, Charlie had been ushered in to meet the personnel manager, Mr Fortescue. A stiff, rather formal little man with a narrow, waxed moustache, Mr Fortescue spoke punctiliously in a voice little above a whisper. He reminded Charlie of his childhood and of his grandfather Ockie, the old bookkeeper Horace Cowper.

After a brief examination of the completed form and a two-minute interview on the details, Mr Fortescue confessed there were one or two vacancies in the store at that time, one of which was in the footwear department. In view of Mr Stoker's background, he was pleased to offer him an immediate start in that department. His wage would be one pound and fifteen shillings per week for a probationary period of three months. Thereafter, on successful completion, he would become a permanent member of staff and his wage would be increased accordingly, to two pounds per week.

The offer accepted, Mr Fortescue explained earnestly and precisely how the great machine of a department store worked. Opening hours at Collick's were from exactly 9.00 am to 5.00 pm daily from Monday to Saturday. That is, except Wednesday, the half-day. On the half-day the doors closed at 1.00 pm. Sunday was, of course, a day of rest. All staff were granted a thirty-minute break for lunch, which was usually taken in the restaurant provided for them at the rear of the third floor. Staff were required to be in place behind counters five minutes before opening time and to remain in place until all customers had vacated the building. In practice, the little man confided seriously, most staff members considered their hours to be from 8.45 am until 5.15 pm.

To complete his well-practiced lecture, Mr Fortescue ended the interview with a word or two about general decorum and a promise that a fine young man such as Mr Stoker would be given every encouragement to rise through the ranks. He then introduced the new man to the Store Manager, Mr Gossett.

Henry Gossett presented a contrasting figure to the little personnel manager. He was a tall, confident man, slightly corpulent, with a round face and a ready smile. He had been at Collick's since Lord Collick's time and was highly respected throughout the building. He greeted Charlie with a firm handshake and the comment:

"Hmm, you certainly make an impression, young man, I don't have to look up to many of our employees!"

He led Charlie on a tour of the store, visiting each department and pointing out special features, such as the newly laid out customers' coffee shop on the ground floor, before introducing him to the thin-faced manager of the footwear department, Mr Healey.

Charlie was tickled pink at being set to work in the footwear department, where the familiar and comforting smell of leather pervaded the atmosphere. He was less pleased to find that his job, as he discovered from the surly Mr Healey, was to be the department's stockroom boy. He was to fetch and carry shoes to and from the stockroom when so instructed. Between times, he was to re-box, clean and generally refresh shoes returned by the salesmen-collectors from their 'appro' stock. This consisted of goods selected by the field force and carried to be sold to their customers 'on approval'. Unsold stock was returned fortnightly and a fresh selection taken, although agents were at liberty to add to their selection at any time.

There were two footwear salesmen in the department, George Beefington, a young man of about Charlie's age and a much older, careworn-looking fellow in spectacles, the senior sales assistant, Mr Kirkly. They were kept occupied in dealing with customers and clearly regarded themselves a grade above the stockroom.

Charlie applied himself to his tasks with his usual shrugs, grins, and relaxed, competent ease. At over six feet tall, the fact that he was able to reach the high shelves without a step-ladder speeded up the delivery of stock to the sales staff and helped him to gain their approval. The apprehension that had greeted his arrival soon vanished and he was accepted as a colleague. George Beefington was delighted to find someone to share a joke with as well as to get support from, and old Mr Kirkly quickly came to rely on Charlie's efficiency and intelligence.

Mr Healey's office was a cubbyhole by the side of the stockroom, from where he watched all activity like a hawk. He recognised at once that Charlie was someone of promise, and after a few days, he asked the new man to relieve George Beefington for his lunch break. When a prospective customer wandered into the department and addressed him, Charlie was transported back to the happy days in the cobbler's shop. For the first time in what seemed a very long time, he was filled with the joy of doing what he believed he was made for. He had smiled the full Stoker smile and gone to work...

As the train approached his station, he prepared himself for another day. Another day at the very bottom of the pile as stockroom boy in the shoe department. His remarkable benefactor, the man who had put him in this position, had complete faith that he would rise to the top. He smiled grimly to himself. He was determined to reward that faith. He would succeed in this new career, driven by his belief in his own ability, and by his trust in the judgement of Stephen Collick. He felt a rush of excitement on entering the building. It was time to put more shoes in boxes.

* * *

With Margret choosing to live at the college residence all week, Charlie opted to stay with his mother at Amhurst Road, just a ten-minute cycle ride from Collick's, rather than journey to and from Chigwell each day. This was an ideal arrangement, enabling him to enjoy sleeping in his old room and to renew the comforts of a mother's attention. It was a harsh fact that, magnificent though the Chigwell house was, the atmosphere was cold. A house needed love.

For Millie Stoker, it was wonderful to have her son home again. Since his marriage to the strange, outspoken Margret in the previous April, he had been living at Clay Hill, the Mabey family home at Enfield, until the new move to Chigwell. Living with the Mabeys had been, in her mind, a situation predestined to disaster, if not the particular disaster that had occurred. Now, by Stephen Collick's extraordinary beneficence, Charlie was at ease again in a new environment and able to move forward.

Arriving at Amhurst Road in the evening and leaving early each morning meant that Charlie rarely saw Billy or Sally Walters in the basement shoe repair shop. They had invariably closed for the day when he reached the house. Just occasionally, though, Billy could be found working late, to finish jobs needed early the next morning, and the two would enjoy a chat about anything and everything.

Billy had inherited an accordion from his grandfather and according to Millie Stoker spent what little spare time he had practising on the instrument. This had always fascinated Charlie, but he had never actually seen or heard Billy play. They had known each other a long time, but Billy was always eager to talk of how the business was thriving, and how well things had worked out for him and Sally. Two years older than Charlie, Billy always regarded the younger man with a certain amount of awe. When he had first started working as an apprentice, he had been an inch or two taller than the cobbler's 13-year-old son. Now, they were both married men and Charlie towered six inches above him.

Billy's respect for and loyalty to the Stokers was unshakeable. He always treated Charlie with the utmost respect as Mrs Stoker's son and, more significantly, as the son of the major. Major Stoker had taken him on seven years earlier as a 15-year-old lad, and the dour, troubled, but always kind man had taught him the cobbling business. Three years later, it was the tragedy of the major's sudden death that had precipitated Billy into the management of the shoe repair shop, a huge step upwards for the young cobbler.

To Charlie, Billy was one of the best. He thought it ironic that Billy Walters, a married man and the manager of the business he himself had dreamed of building, found it so difficult to regard himself the equal of Charlie Stoker, the stockroom boy in a shoe department.

* * *

For a few weeks, on Tuesday evenings, Charlie cycled to Clare Market to spend time with Margret. They enjoyed a pint and a pie at the Old Wheatsheaf, in the same saloon bar in which they had discussed Margret's pregnancy and Charlie had proposed marriage, a long year earlier. Margret had settled back into her routine as if nothing had changed. She had resumed her studies and re-established her supremacy over the other students, treating them with the same disdain as ever.

Like Charlie, Margret rarely felt the need for company. But, whereas in his case, casual contact with people was invariably a pleasant, if inessential, experience, for her it usually caused sparks to fly. Margret sought conflict as a bee seeks honey. She was always ready to fight the world, and she usually fought dirty. Her sharp mind, combative nature and whiplash tongue were enough to win most arguments; and the rare few she lost usually ended in a slammed door or a bruised body.

There were only two people with whom Margret rarely felt at war. Charlie had earned his unique place in her world partly by his remarkable ability to appear completely oblivious to her outbursts. He was the only man for whom she had ever felt respect rather than disdain. The mere sight of him, with his shrug, his cigarette and his twinkling hint of a smile, calmed her as no one else could. She had been scarred by men throughout her childhood and had grown to treat them all with contempt; but, as far as it was possible for her to care for any man, God help her, she loved Charlie Stoker.

Most weeks they were joined by Jennifer Lacey, who would bring all the gossip from the Northern and fill the evening with her chatter. Jennifer was the one other person whose company Margret ever craved. Usually, when she arrived Charlie would finish his pie, his pint and his smoke, then depart, leaving the ladies to their conversation.

From the age of five, Margret had had only one close friend. Introduced as daughters of fellow officers in 1915, she and Jennifer had quickly become inseparable. Jennifer, a beautiful, quick-witted child and the younger by several months, had been overawed by the precocious Margret. Wherever Margret led, Jennifer had followed, and the arrangement suited them both until the younger child began to show too much of the other's influence by her antisocial behaviour in her own, warm family home. Contact had thereafter been considerably restricted by Mrs Lacey until her eldest daughter had rediscovered her former manners.

The families still met occasionally, however, and the depth of the girls' feelings for each other did not change. When Jennifer began to study for a pharmacy degree at the Northern, and Margret went to the London School of Economics, they were once more within easy reach of each other.

Charlie had known Jennifer longer than he had known Margret. He had met Jennifer, Bobby and Daphne Hipstead on his first day at the Northern. All four had studied physics in their first year and they had become friends, spending their lunch breaks and spare time together. With his new friends, Charlie had quickly learned the pleasures of smoking and drinking, delights denied to him during his somewhat sheltered life as the only child in a house where neither were permitted.

Jennifer was a brunette very conscious of her beauty and always eager to impress in any company. She had become an active member of nearly every group and club at the Northern, dragging her friend Daphne with her. Daphne was a quiet girl who worked in the Lacey's chemist's shop in Highgate. She had taken the less demanding two-year Ph.C. course at the college, but closely followed Jennifer's every lead in social activity.

It was only when she began to appreciate Bobby Bruce's attentions that she grew in self-confidence and stepped out from under Jennifer's umbrella. The lackadaisical Charlie had also allowed himself to be dragged into all of Jennifer's activities initially, although he too had withdrawn from most of them as the year progressed.

One universally popular student activity was the Friday social evening at the Victoria Tavern, opposite the Northern on Holloway Road. It was there that Charlie had first tasted beer. It was also where he had first met Margret, at the camera club's Christmas party, held in the saloon bar. Charlie had watched as Jennifer, with her slim cigarette holder held at shoulder height, her glass of shandy untouched in front of her, sat wide-eyed in admiration of her tall, thin, friend, who downed several pints of beer during the evening while delivering cutting comments and withering stares around the table.

Charlie had never seen a lady drinking beer before. He had assumed they drank wine, cocktails or half pints of shandy. Although surprised, he was not offended by the sight. After all, he himself was just discovering how good beer was. It did occur to him later, however, that his mother might have been more than a little upset had she been told at that time.

* * *

Wednesday evening was swimming night, always eagerly anticipated by both Charlie and Bobby. They invariably swam numerous lengths of the pool, either in bursts or in long uninterrupted spells. Both had become strong swimmers in the last couple of years. Bobby often moaned that it was boring and tiring and he was going to pack it up; but then in the next breath he would say something like:

"But it's g-good exercise and you f-feel great when you g-et your breath back!"

Mostly, this earned no more than a shrug from Charlie. Occasionally, though, there would be a riposte:

"Well, if you swam a bit faster, you'd keep up and get through it quicker!"

In fact, although Charlie was tall and well-built, Bobby was probably the stronger swimmer. It was of no consequence. Swimming, for both of them, was not a competitive exercise. The pleasure was in the satisfaction that came from the exertion and the comradeship of the whole evening's experience. The evening was rounded off with something to eat and a pint or two at a local pub.

It was over a pint of brown ale in the pub next door to the Walthamstow baths that Bobby told Charlie of his change of plans. Proud to have been Charlie's best man a year earlier, Bobby was now planning his own marriage. Daphne Hipstead, his fiancée of a few months, was earning a decent wage as a pharmacist, and was saving her money ferociously. They had hoped to marry in the following September, but common sense was dictating that they wait a little longer. Bobby's motor engineering business was still in its infancy, and time was needed to build it further. It was already more than covering his costs, but he was determined, he insisted, not for the first time, that he would not be dependent upon his fiancée's income for their future.

"We are aiming for A-A-April next year instead. It m-akes much more sense than r-rushing things this y-year, doesn't it?"

Charlie nodded and Bobby added anxiously, "B-but you'll still be my b-best man, won't you?"

Charlie nodded again, grinning. "Yeah, I'm not planning on running away, Bobby."

A relieved Bobby drank some ale and changed the subject. It was early in March and the daily newspapers were full of reports of the pact agreed between the viceroy of India, Lord Irwin, and Mohandas Gandhi. Many British officials in India, and politicians in England, were outraged by the idea of a pact with a party whose avowed purpose was the destruction of the British Raj, but the deal was done, Gandhi, known by his followers as Mahatma Gandhi, was the activist leader of the

Indian independence movement against British rule. Only recently released from gaol, Gandhi had agreed to suspend all civil disobedience in the country in return for the release of political prisoners and the repeal of the salt tax, which banned any salt production not supplied through government depots.

Bobby screwed his face up. "He's a f-funny sort of bloke, that Gandhi, ain't he? He's a Lincoln's Inn lawyer, but he goes around in that old w-white shirt thing. 'E's odd!" He paused momentarily. "B-but you've got to admire the way he f-fights for what he believes in, and for his people. He wants self-rule for India but I shouldn't think they could run the country without us, d'you? They'd all be f-fighting among themselves for ever!"

Charlie shrugged.

"Actually, Gandhi's a pretty remarkable bloke," he said. "I read that he's a very quiet man who took a vow of non-violence. But he helped us fight the Boers in South Africa. Because he didn't believe in violence, he formed an ambulance corps. He recruited a load of Indians. They were medically trained and also trained to serve on the front lines. They carried wounded soldiers for miles from the front line to a field hospital because the terrain was too rough for the ambulances. He was given a medal by the Queen."

"C-Crikey! I d-didn't know that," said the incredulous Bobby. "Well maybe he could run the country after all!"

The room was quite small, with tables placed the length of the bar, each with a few chairs, and an upholstered bench running along the wall, rather like the Victoria Tavern in Holloway Road. When they had entered the pub, the only occupants were two men seated at the first table. Neither friendly nor familiar faces, they had abruptly stopped their conversation when the boys entered, and had sat glowering sourly while the friends ordered at the bar. Only when they had taken their pints and sat down at the table farthest away did the two, in low tones, resume their conversation.

At about nine o'clock, near the time the two swimmers usually went home, three more men entered the bar. They joined the pair by the door, dragging empty chairs across the room and crowding around the end table. One of the three, a red-faced young man in a loud-checked suit, noisily bought a round of drinks for all five before noticing there were other people in the bar. He rather sheepishly nodded towards the two friends, then sat down and entered, head lowered, into a long, whispered conversation with the rest of the group.

The conversation halted as the boys passed the table on their way out, and heads were kept carefully averted. As soon as they were outside the door, Bobby burst out, "W-wasn't that Alec Cha-chapman with that group? W-with that s-suit on?"

"Yeah, it was. He didn't want to be recognised, though, did he?"

"N-no, definitely not. He was h-hiding his face! I d-dunno exactly what they were whispering about, but I'm sure I heard one of 'em say 'ef-f-----ing commies!' Did you hear that?"

"No, but it's none of my business, Bob." Charlie shrugged dismissively. "I only met that Chapman once, when he was at the camera club party the year before last. I was unimpressed then. He's a bit of a lout, I thought. And this lot looked a bit rough, didn't they?"

Chapter Three
Reality

When, in later life, Charlie thought back to the year 1931, his memory was of a quite unreal period of his life, a time when he had felt he was living two lives. Working in the department store from Monday to Saturday and sleeping in his room at his mother's in Amhurst Road was one life. The people with whom he came into contact every day were just like the people who had always been present in his life. It was a comfortable world. His daily routine was as he had anticipated as a boy, and he was attending an evening class each week at Holloway Road, having been persuaded by the principal to spread the final year's course over two years.

The short weekends at Chigwell, though, placed him in a quite different world, one far less comfortable for the young man. There, he was a man of property with a wife, a fine house, and socially obligatory Sunday lunches once a month in the cold atmosphere of the Mabey household at Clay Hill.

It was interesting, even exciting, for a time, so long as it remained a novelty. Charlie was, after all, only twenty years of age and Margret twenty-one. But once their settling in period was over and the house required less attention, it became obvious to both that their lives had little in common.

Margret had set herself firmly against any attempt to have another child. She had no interest in her husband's work or the people he worked with, and she had no time for swimming or cycling. She spent much of her weekend grooming or riding her mare, Tempest, and showed no inclination to involve herself with their neighbours at Woodside Way. Her only relationship was with the local stables, whose staff cared for the horse during the week.

There was one social activity the couple did enjoy together in those first months. Every Saturday evening, a game of cards with Daphne and Bobby was accompanied by a few drinks and a lot of laughter. Bobby was one of those remarkable people who never forgot a joke told to him. Whether gleaned from the visitors to his Harringay workshop, picked up from the wireless, collected from a pub bar, or recollected from any odd moment long passed, a glass or two of whatever was on hand would invariably act as a magic key. The stammer would vanish, the eyes sparkle, and out would pour a stream of hilarious tales, silly stories and often wildly exaggerated remembrances that had the whole room rolling with laughter.

But a few social hours on Saturday evenings, no matter how pleasant, were hardly enough to build a life around. Even tending the garden ceased to be a necessary function for them. A weekly visit by Alf Binney, the Mabey's gardener, was all that was needed for its upkeep. The garden's simple layout meant that little further attention was required. Alf's services had come as an unexpected act of generosity from Herbert Mabey, who persisted for some time in harbouring the hope that Charlie would reverse his decision to leave the Enfield office.

This, of course, was something that Charlie had no intention of considering. More and more, as that first year passed, he gained comfort from the atmosphere of the department store. As far as most of the staff there were concerned, he was a young married man who lived, it was assumed, somewhere in Hackney. Always a man of few words, he avoided becoming too closely attached to any one individual, and he never divulged details of his private life.

Despite this reticence, he had from the very start become popular with colleagues in all departments. His winning smile, his enthusiasm for work, and his all-round competence saw him progress with ease from job to job and from department to department.

Charlie's height and big frame ensured that he was always easily visible in the department store, but what quickly gained him a reputation as a person of quality was his ability to remain emotionally detached when called upon to deal with any of the minor crises that occurred regularly in the various departments. Dealing with difficult customers became a speciality. Always disarming, with his Stoker smile and empathetic shrug, he was a rock of calm and dependability.

One Friday afternoon during those first weeks in the footwear department, Mr Healey and George Beefington were for some reason not on the floor at the time, and Mr Kirkly, a man of nervous disposition, was striving ineffectually to deal with a wildly irate customer, a large woman adorned with expensive jewellery and a silver fur coat.

She had slammed a boxed pair of shoes onto the counter, claiming that the shoes in the box, the shoes she had taken home the previous day, were not the same as the pair she had tried on in the store. She had particularly liked the fit and the style of that model and now demanded that he find her the correct pair, size five.

Mr Kirkly had taken the box into the stockroom to compare with existing stock and had checked the shoes and the paperwork with Charlie. There had been no error. Size five had been asked for and size five supplied. Mr Kirkly had returned to the floor and tried to explain, but he was quickly silenced. The woman ranted at the poor salesman, calling him stupid and inconsiderate and threatening to report him for inefficiency, insubordination and dereliction of duty.

While she was still in full flow, Charlie approached from the stockroom with a box of shoes in his hand.

"Excuse me, Mr Kirkly," he said, eyes shining, "But I think I may have discovered what happened."

He turned to the fur-coated customer, endowing her with a huge smile. "Would Madam care to try this pair?"

Mouth open, she stared up at this young Adonis with the blue eyes, allowing him to lead her to a chair on the showroom floor.

"Allow me, Ma'am," said Charlie in a low voice, reaching to remove her shoe. He took a shoe from the new box and placed it caressingly on her foot. "Now, how is that?"

He stood back, encouraging her with a sweep of his arm to walk on it, but she remained seated, waving her foot coquettishly from side to side.

"Yes, that is perfect! This is the one I tried yesterday. Thank you, young man, I knew I was right!"

"Of course, Madam. They must have been placed inadvertently in the wrong box. These things happen from time to time. Please forgive us. Is there anything else Mr Kirkly can help you with today?" He waved Mr Kirkly forward to resume control of the matter and disappeared back into the stockroom.

As soon as the customer had left, Mr Kirkly rushed through the stockroom door. Charlie was grinning, and the old salesman was nearly in tears of relief and gratitude.

"Thank you, Mr Stoker, thank you from the bottom of my heart. I was absolutely terrified of her!"

"It was no problem, Mr Kirkly, She needed size five and a half, and I just over-stamped the size inside the shoe. Her feet could never get into a five!"

"But you were so smooth. You stopped her in her tracks!" Mr Kirkly took a deep breath. "I honestly don't know what I would have done. Thank you again, Mr Stoker."

Charlie's eyes were twinkling. "I've told you before, Mr Kirkly, my name's Charlie. With respect, you age more or less with my dad, and he was Mr Stoker. I'm just Charlie."

"Oh, no, that would not be right, not in the store, Mr Stoker. We must maintain the store's decorum." The nervous little man wiped his glasses with his handkerchief. "But please, let me buy you a half-pint of ale across the road when we close."

Charlie had acquiesced with a shrug as the senior salesman fled back to the sales floor.

The Three Kings public house, just across the road from the store, was a favourite haunt of many of Collick's staff members. The lower paid staff, the cleaners, porters, canteen workers, and one or two sales and office workers, all crowded into the public bar; but senior salesmen, the supervisors and the managers visited the more salubrious saloon bar.

Charlie did not care which of the bars he was in. As his circle of friends in the store expanded, he found himself drawn more and more into their social life, particularly when that involved imbibing a few pints of ale. Whenever he had the time, he would cross the road, play dominoes or skittles, or listen with a smile to the bar room chatter of his colleagues, before returning to his mother's for supper.

* * *

For Millie Stoker, life in 1931 was busy and enjoyable. It was also comparatively stress free for the first time in many years. She was now financially secure and socially active. She devoted most of two days each week to the church, assisting Father Peter in his pastoral work, visiting the sick or organising church events. At other times, she was busy managing the house at Amhurst Road.

The two flats on the upper floors were let to reliable tenants and were maintained well; and Billy and Sally now required very little supervision in the basement cobbler's shop. They were making a good living from the business and providing a steady income for Millie; but, careful bookkeeper that she was, she continued to check all the paperwork every week.

Her friendship with Stephen Collick continued to give both parties great comfort. Stephen's life had always been a lonely one. His business commitments gave him little free time, but outside of his work, his life had offered him nothing. Unsurprisingly, he held very dear his newly established link to the Stokers. He ensured that he found time each week to make contact with Millie. In her, he had for the first time in many years a true friend, an acutely intelligent and utterly trustworthy confidante.

Their meetings often took the form of Saturday lunch or Sunday afternoon tea. That might be at Amhurst Road or anywhere within an hour's drive. Then, as time passed, Stephen asked Millie to assist him whenever he felt obliged to entertain guests at Parklands, his home on the Collick Estate, a service she happily rendered.

Occasionally, Charlie would join them for Sunday lunch at Amhurst Road, usually with Margret, and on such occasions, Millie was delighted to witness the relationship between the two men.

Charlie clearly regarded Stephen differently from other people. Only with Stephen did the young man seem to lose his mask of casual detachment. His eyes shone and he chatted eagerly. Stephen responded just as enthusiastically and Millie saw them as she had seen her husband Charles with Charlie. Somehow, Stephen, that remarkable bachelor, had filled the terrible void that had existed in her son's, and indeed in her own life.

When Charlie was not present, his name was often mentioned in conversation, but Stephen never spoke of the young man's progress at work. On the one occasion that Millie asked how Charlie was doing at Collick's, Stephen replied:

"I have no idea, Millie. I don't expect I shall have any direct contact for a year or two yet. I am sure he will be gaining good experience in the store. He is a fine boy, and for now, it is good for him to enjoy life and to learn. Please understand, as far as the business is concerned, I see Charlie as a long-term investment. He is, perhaps, rather like a personal pension fund. When saving for a pension, one sees no return for one's money for many years. In due course, we shall all reap the reward."

Millie changed the subject, angry with herself for raising it. Within the Collick's empire the two men existed in different worlds, and it was clear that Stephen intended it to remain thus.

* * *

Jennifer, carefully trimming Margret's hair during an evening visit to Clare Market, casually asked how Charlie was getting on at work. Margret replied that she had no interest in Charlie's day to day life at that place. She always asked him, when he arrived at Chigwell on Saturday evenings, how his week had gone but Charlie's usual reply, "Oh, not bad, it's all good experience," ended the conversation. Occasionally they would talk about an incident or conversation that had been particularly memorable, but not often.

"Don't you care much about his career, Margret?"

"Career? What career? Shop work? Putting shoes in boxes, sweeping the floor and standing behind a counter? Taking orders from idiots all day long? That is a career? I fail to see where Charlie is heading at the moment. I can understand anyone not wanting to work with my family, for God's sake, but the law does at least represent a decent career path for a person! And yet he seems perfectly happy in that department store. He has utter faith in Stephen Collick, who, I must say, has always appeared to be a man of honour. But I am not convinced. Not that it is my concern, of course. We have decided upon our routes to the future and, whatever transpires, we shall remain friends."

Jennifer was shocked by Margret's dismissive tone; she concentrated upon the scissors. Deep down, though, she felt a wicked sense of satisfaction. She had always known things would be like this. Margret could never settle for being a dutiful wife, even when her husband was Charlie Stoker.

Chapter Four
Laura and Aitch

World depression followed the 1929 Wall Street crash and, in Great Britain, took its greatest toll in 1931. The Bank of England reported a run on the pound, forcing the government to act. Under pressure from both its Liberal allies and the Conservative opposition, the Labour government appointed a committee to review the state of public finances. In July 1931, Sir George May's committee urged large cuts in public spending, in public sector wages and in unemployment benefits.

The proposals caused a massive split in the Labour Party and by the summer, the weak two-year-old government had collapsed. A National Government was put in place to run the country, formed by a Conservative-dominated coalition but with the Labour leader, Ramsay Macdonald remaining as Prime Minister.

Public service wages were cut by ten percent and income tax increased by ten percent from four shillings and sixpence to five shillings in the pound. Even so, before the tide could be turned, the gold standard had to be sacrificed and the pound was devalued by almost thirty percent.

Remarkably, conditions in the south were not unbearable. The London County Council decided to establish huge new housing estates in London's outer suburbs. In places like Becontree to the east, and Bellingham, south of the Thames, new homes and airy living space was provided for countless families previously crammed into inner city slums. Employment was at the same time provided for great numbers of construction workers in London and the Home Counties.

Wages, though, were low everywhere. Money was still scarce but people had to furnish their new homes, and it was in this economic environment that Stephen Collick's unique vision of a luxury store for poorer people proved to be such a success.

The new estates provided an ever-growing natural customer base for the furniture, curtains and bedding that abounded at Collick's, and the twenty-week interest-free rolling credit facility offered by the salesmen-collectors to all their customers was a godsend to young families on small incomes. The building was always full of activity with its many departmental staff busily presenting stock to a steady flow of customers, and most mornings to salesmen-collectors re-stocking and placing orders.

Mr Gossett, having noted the improvement in performance of the footwear department in the months since the arrival of young Mr Stoker, decided that Charlie would be the person to boost business for the drapery department. Things there were not going as well as he thought they should. Mr Healey was summoned and informed that the young man was to report to Mr Barker, the textiles manager, at once.

This news, despite the protestations of Mr Healey, who had come to regard Charlie Stoker as his personal property, brought only a shrug and a nod from the young man himself. He had no experience in fabrics but was keen to learn about everything in Collick's. If measuring curtains was his next challenge, then so be it.

Reginald Barker had responsibility for the fabric department and the nearby linen department, where he had his office. A tall, narrow-faced man of about fifty, he carried himself in military manner and with the same self-important bearing as Mr Healey, the shoe buyer. Both had been with the store since Lord Collick's days and the two could often be seen conferring in whispers in either of their offices.

Charlie duly presented himself and Mr Barker looked him up and down suspiciously from his desk before nodding approval.

"I have received a good report about you, young man. You have made quite an impression in Mr Healey's department. You look like a strong chap too and that can be a great asset in drapery. Mr Carratt, the senior assistant over there, has been off sick for some time."

He paused and half mumbled, "I don't expect we shall see him again." He sniffed, then resumed his authoritative tone:

"The two women over there are managing, but not well. The senior one, Mrs Dekker, the Polish Jewess, she knows fabrics and will teach you all you need to know. I shall introduce you."

Without further discussion, he rose from his seat and marched across to the curtain counter, where two women were busy measuring cloth. Briefly, he introduced Charlie as a new departmental assistant and instructed the older woman to teach the new man all about fabric. Then he marched off.

As in footwear, Charlie made an immediate impact. Interdepartmental gossip had already told them of his enthusiasm for work, and his physical size was once again significant. Lifting and measuring bolts of cloth was hard labour for Mrs Dekker and Annie Appleton, the two diminutive departmental assistants who toiled at it day after day. For the blond giant with the twinkling eyes who now joined them it was effortless work.

Curtain fitting was a service available to customers, and a curtain fitter, Harry Cottington, had been employed to both measure and fit. The development of the outside sales force, however, meant that most measuring jobs were now passed to the salesmen-collectors. Harry still fitted occasionally, but the reduced workload saw him transferred to the building maintenance team.

The fabric department did retain the sewing room, though, where customers' orders were fulfilled by two machinists. Charlie, with his experience on the leather machine at Amhurst Road, was disappointed not to be called upon to actually sew, but this was not the shoe-repair shop. These were different machines, lighter and faster.

He discussed the different features with the machinists and his engineer's mind quickly enabled him to be of use whenever there was a hitch. It also meant that Charlie learned thoroughly what could or could not be accomplished for customers.

Mrs Dekker was herself a skilled machinist, but she had opted to work on the sales counter. She enjoyed the social contact, and spent much of the time giving customers the benefit of her knowledge. Always willing to accept extra work, she machined curtains at home in the evenings when the department was overburdened.

Barely five feet tall, square-built and dark-eyed, she was a Polish Jewish immigrant who had lived since 1920 with her husband, a tailor's presser, and their four children in Smithy Street, just a few minutes' walk from the store. She spoke good English with a strong continental accent. Her knowledge of fabrics was considerable and she spent a great deal of time explaining to Charlie the subtle differences between similar-looking cloths: their qualities, their appearance with and without linings, recommended usage and other snippets. She emphasised repeatedly the importance of adding enough cloth to allow for all the pattern repeats when measuring and pricing curtains. The new recruit soaked up her words, acknowledging with nods and shrugs.

The other assistant, Annie Appleton was a rather dowdy young spinster who lived with her aunt in Bethnal Green. She was a willing girl, if a bit slow in thought and movement. Charlie gained the impression she spent a great deal of her time star-gazing, although according to Mrs Dekker her gazing was mostly doe-eyed at Charlie.

This opinion was met with a dismissive Stoker shrug, but was, in truth, an observation that could have been made of most of the female staff. Charlie, as at every point in his life, had made an impression on them all. With his height, broad shoulders and ever-present, if often quizzical, smile, his appearance was always of a young man who was going somewhere in life.

One other person in the store stood out from the crowd as much as Charlie. Laura Matthews was the senior assistant in the china and glass department. Just nineteen years old, Laura was tall, a willowy brunette with bright eyes, a sharp brain and a quick tongue. Her father had been the china and glass buyer in a West End store until his sudden death a year or two earlier.

Through the good offices of Henry Gossett, an old friend of her father's, she had been given the opportunity to work in the equivalent department in Collick's. Laura was an instant success. Knowledge accumulated from her father since childhood, together with her brimming self-confidence, made her within a short time quite indispensable to Wilfred Gant, the buyer. As head of department, he quickly came to regard Laura as his protégée and successor, and on Friday evenings she was encouraged to enjoy a gin and orange under his protective fatherly gaze in the saloon bar of the Three Kings.

Laura was particularly adept at handling the salesmen-collectors, playing up to their advances with fluttering eyelids and giggles. But she never allowed anyone to overstep the mark: any attempt to do so was met with a sharp look and a cutting reprimand. She and Charlie soon recognised each other's qualities and became good friends. Laura quite clearly hoped that the friendship may become a more serious affair, but the Stoker smile and shrug were the only answer and the perfect counter to her suggestions, innuendos and loud peals of invitational laughter.

* * *

The Lacey pharmacy at Highgate was a thriving establishment. Lionel Lacey was a sincere and conscientious man who had built his chemist's business to the point where it required two or three people to be on hand most of the time. Daphne Hipstead had been working full-time as a pharmacist for a year now, but while both girls had been studying, whenever they were not available he had scraped by with just one other unqualified assistant. It was much to his relief that his daughter Jennifer re-joined them as soon as she completed her final examinations at the Northern Polytechnic Institute.

Jennifer then awaited her examination results in a state of anxiety for some weeks, in spite of her father's insistence that she had nothing to worry about. With his ever-present cigarette waggling up and down in the side of his mouth, complete with the half inch of ash that seemed always to droop but not drop from his cigarettes, he assured her emphatically that she was a far more knowledgeable pharmacist then he had ever been.

  His confidence was soon proved to be fully justified, and a certificate for Jennifer Lacey, with the letters BPharm attached to her name, was proudly added to the dispensary wall. The achievement was celebrated by a Lacey house party to which the original group of four as well as many other friends and family were invited. Charlie shrugged and smiled his way through the evening, to all appearances his usual relaxed self. He opted to spend most of the time in the garden rather than in the house, however, where the memory of his previous party visit was all too easily recalled.

He happily sat through another session of Mr Lacey's rambling reminiscences in a deck chair on the terrace, and he thoroughly enjoyed the Jameson's whisky pressed upon him. But this Charlie was three years older and very much more worldly wise than had been the young man in December 1928.

* * *

The academic year finished, Jennifer regularly visited Margret at Chigwell on Wednesday afternoons. Margret, who had also taken her finals in June, obtained First Class honours in the B.Sc. (Econ.). This result she accepted nonchalantly: it was no more than she expected. However, while awaiting the results she had begun, somewhat to her own surprise, to take a belated interest in the house. With Jennifer's assistance, some warmth was added to the décor: flowers, a few occasional tables, small draperies; vases and other ornaments were spread about. Together, the little extras did the job, and the house was brought to life through the summer.

  Charlie arrived at weekends and, impressed by the girls' efforts, felt obliged to make a contribution. Unsure of what to do, he telephoned his mother for help. Millie suggested that some decent garden furniture would be nicer than the two wooden chairs and the upturned tea chest that adorned the patio outside the French doors of the sitting room. A few days later a wrought iron table and four matching chairs magically appeared at the house. To these, Charlie added two garden loungers that he found in Collick's furniture department.

Celebration of Margret's graduation was more muted than Jennifer's. The regular Saturday card evening was enlivened by a few bottles of champers, enjoyed with newspaper-wrapped fish and chips collected on Bobby's BSA from the fish shop in the village.

* * *

It was in the Three Kings that Charlie had his first proper conversation with Harvey Harrington, the manager of Collick's outside sales force. Lean of build, with a strong, weathered face and thinning brown hair, Harrington's demeanour was in total contrast to that of the pompous department heads in the store. Easy-going and friendly in manner – he was known to his acquaintances, including many customers, simply as Aitch – Harrington commanded respect from all. An ex-captain in the Northamptonshire Regiment, he had, in seven years, built the sales team from one young recruit to the present force of twenty-eight salesmen-collectors. His position in the company was now parallel to that of Mr Gossett, reporting directly to Stephen Collick himself.

On a Friday evening early in August, Charlie, now moved from drapery to the furniture showroom, had joined Laura Matthews and Mr Gant for a drink in the saloon bar. They were accompanied, as they crossed the road, by a flash of lightning and a thunderclap, precipitating a torrential rainfall.

"Crikey, we just made that in time!" exclaimed Laura, making a bee line for one of the empty tables in the room. "I wonder how long *this* downpour will last?"

"There's been an awful lot of it this summer, hasn't there?" agreed the china buyer. "We get a few warm sunny days then more thunderstorms. I think it's that Dogger Bank earthquake with that tidal wave. It has upset the balance of the weather."

Charlie thought it was just another summer storm. He shrugged non-committally and smiled.

"What will you drink, Mr Gant?"

"No, no, young man, you sit down with Laura, I'll fetch the drinks. A pint of brown ale?"

"Thank you, sir. That's very kind of you."

The buyer turned towards the bar, almost colliding with Aitch Harrington, one of a rush of people scurrying in out of the storm. The saloon was becoming crowded, and Aitch, having removed and shaken his soaking grey fedora, was intent on being ahead of the throng at the bar.

"Oh, hallo, Wilf, are you buying?" He grinned wickedly at Gant. "I'll join you, if I may. What are you having?"

"No, no, Aitch, this is my round but, indeed, please do join us. Will it be a pint of stout?"

"As ever, Wilfred. D'you need help or shall I just join the lovely Laura?"

Wilfred Gant laughed. "Away with you, Aitch. You know I can handle anything in glass!"

Harrington patted him on the shoulder and eased his way across to the table where Laura was sitting with her back to the bar. He placed his hands on her arms and squeezed gently, whispering into her ear at the same time.

"Oh, Mr Harrington, you are incorrigible, behave yourself!" she giggled.

"May I join you?" He asked, having already sat down next to Laura. He grinned at Charlie. "You are young Charlie Stoker, aren't you? I believe we've spoken once or twice, but I don't get into the departments too much, these days. How are you enjoying life? I mean in the store, not with the delicious Miss Matthews here!"

"I'm very happy, sir, thank you. I love the busy atmosphere and working with all the people in the store."

"They tell me you're pretty good with the customers, too, eh?"

"Well, they're just people, sir. I like meeting people, and mostly they come into the store because they need something. If we can help them find what they are looking for, it's good for them and for us."

Harrington nodded and made no comment. Wilfred Gant arrived with a tray of drinks and passed them around before settling himself into the empty seat opposite Aitch.

"Cheers, all!" he called.

All four raised their glasses. "Cheers!"

"Have you had any dealings with this young man, Wilfred?" asked Aitch. "He's a thinker. We don't get too many of those in Collick's."

Gant coughed and placed his gin and tonic on a beer mat. "Well, not really. You should perhaps ask Laura, she is on the floor much more than I, and Charlie is Laura's friend." He smiled at Charlie apologetically. "Of course, we have spoken, but I know him simply as a member of staff and a very polite young man."

"Charlie and I understand each other," said Laura with an arch smile. Aitch raised an eyebrow. "But not in that way, Mr Harrington!"

There was general laughter and the next quarter of an hour passed in light-hearted chatter. Then Aitch said, "Let me get the refills. Charlie, would you help me carry them?"

"Of course, sir!" Charlie rose to his feet and followed the Field Sales Manager to the bar.

As soon as they moved away from the table, Harrington asked, "Have you thought about being a salesman-collector, Charlie? I think you are the ideal type of chap; you know?"

"Well, not really, sir. I think it may be a great move later on, but there's still loads for me to learn in the store."

"Yes, yes. How old are you, son? I see you're married." He nodded towards Charlie's ring finger.

"I'll be twenty-one in November, sir," Charlie replied, embarrassed.

"Bloody hell, is that all? You look a lot older!" Aitch looked hard at the young man. "Have you got kids?"

"No, sir, we lost him."

"I'm sorry, son. That's sad. It happens to so many, it seems. But you're very young, you've got plenty of time."

"Yes, sir, I'm sure you are right."

"I'm sure so, son."

He broke off to deal with the barman, then turned to Charlie again.

"Listen, your age is not necessarily a disadvantage. You are a particularly bright chap, and mature. I need young men like you. Obviously, Henry Gossett will want you to stay with him through the autumn rush to Christmas," he said pensively. "How about I have a word with him and we look to move you into the field in January? What do you think?"

Without hesitation Charlie replied: "I think that sounds like a good idea, sir."

"Good, then that's what I'll do. Now, you take two of these and I'll carry the other two."

* * *

Although Charlie believed a degree in physics and maths to be irrelevant to his career plan, he had made a promise to his mother, and at the commencement of the new academic year in September 1931, he arranged to attend two evening sessions each week at the Northern. One evening had not been enough to cover the syllabus fully, and he was determined to complete the degree course this year.

The second evening class was on Tuesdays, which put an end to his visits to Clare Market. Margret had returned to college for a fourth year, having been invited to spend a year as a research assistant to Professor Robbins. She had been toying with the idea of studying for a law degree but had decided instead to commit herself to an academic career in economics. The house at Chigwell was again empty from Monday to Saturday each week.

Despite his youth, Charlie was enjoying more responsibility in the department store. Having spent four weeks as a furniture salesman, he was moved to the men's department, where the assistant manager, Alistair Peabody, a loyal employee who had injured himself moving boxes of merchandise, was absent and expected to be off for several weeks. At Collick's, established staff were assured of job security, providing any justifiable absence was not for too long a period, so Charlie had the opportunity to learn about yet another department.

In truth, while he contentedly shrugged and smiled his way through each day, he viewed the last four months of 1931 as merely a period of waiting; until he could do what he regarded as a real job, joining the outside sales force. He eagerly anticipated his foreseeable future as a salesman-collector. It was much more the life he had always wanted, more like the fulfilment of his boyhood wishes. He would be his own master, building his own business, making his own choices about what to do and how to best serve his customers.

After the conversation about his career with Aitch Harrington in August, he had begun to think about the best way of actually getting around as a salesman-collector. Only supervisors qualified for company motorcars and he could not realistically afford to buy his own automobile, like one or two of the more far-flung travelling men. Most salesmen walked, carrying a suitcase, or often two, but he was sure he could do better than that.

He could fit panniers to his bike, of course, but it would severely restrict the stock he could carry. It would also be difficult to keep stock looking neat and presentable. He decided the best idea would be to do as Bobby had done with his B.S.A., to rebuild an old motorbike and attach a trailer.

During the year, Bobby had encouraged Charlie to learn not only to ride a motorcycle, but also how to maintain one. Charlie's practical mind and willing hands made him an ideal assistant, and helping in the workshop in his spare time had taught him to appreciate the pros and cons of different models. Bobby promised to look out for a bargain that they could work on.

Although Charlie's physique and bearing made him appear to others much older than his years, he had been born only in 1910, and his twenty-first birthday fell on a wet Friday in the November of 1931. That was the day he achieved his majority. He was from that day a citizen with the right to vote.

It occasioned a celebratory drink, and as soon as the store closed, he was marched by Laura Matthews across the road to the Three Kings, where he found himself surrounded by an enthusiastic group of colleagues singing a birthday greeting. Collectively, they had bought him an initialled silver tie-pin as a birthday gift. It was presented with a flourish by Laura and celebrated by all with much chinking of glasses. Charlie, much moved by the show of affection, said a few words of thanks and shook many hands. Nevertheless, as soon as he was able to extricate himself without offence, he cycled to Amhurst Road, where his mother had promised to prepare a special birthday dinner.

To his surprise and delight, on entering the first-floor sitting room, he found not only Stephen Collick and Margret, both of whom he had expected to be there, (he later learned to his astonishment, that Margret had taken the afternoon off from college to assist Millie and the loyal Florrie to prepare for the evening); but also Billy Walters in a smart new dark grey suit, with his wife Sally; Bobby and Daphne; a stunningly dressed Jennifer Lacey in red chiffon with a white petalled spray attached; and the Reverend Peter O'Rahilly. With huge smiles on their faces and champagne goblets held high, they burst into song, singing "He's twenty-one today!"

It was the first time in Charlie's memory that champagne had been served in that house, and certainly the first time in many, many years that the place had been full of people laughing and joking and enjoying a party together. The ever-calm Millie, her face unusually flushed, stood by the tray of champagne. She handed a goblet to Charlie and then, to his amazement, carefully raised one to her own lips.

For one of very few occasions in his life, Charlie found it almost impossible to hide his emotions. His deep blue eyes widened and his cheeks coloured. There was a momentary tremble of the lips and a long deep breath before the full Stoker grin emerged. It was a moment Charlie would never forget, one to cherish for the rest of his life above all the happy memories of that weekend.

The dinner party was a gloriously happy occasion, but it proved to be not the only surprise. There were of course gifts: Margret had presented him with a lapis lazuli blue Parker Duofold pen and pencil set, inscribed with his initials C.H.S. Father Peter had brought a presentation bottle of a single malt Scotch whisky; Billy had hand-crafted a pair of fine leather boots, for winter cycling, he said; and Jennifer had also bought a cycling accessory, a pair of heavy leather cycling gloves. Charlie accepted all the gifts with his usual smiles and shrugs, with hugs of gratitude, and with pecked cheeks for the ladies.

Then his mother said:

"Charlie, this is a wonderful evening, and words cannot say just how happy I am for you. Unfortunately, though, there has been one small hitch. Stephen and I had together planned a surprise present, but it will now not arrive until tomorrow. Fortunately, Mr Gossett, the store manager, has granted you a day's leave of absence tomorrow, and you and Margret will be staying here tonight. Stephen has arranged to collect the parcel and bring it here in time for lunch, so your birthday celebration will continue for two days! And Bobby, the only other of your guests to be free, has agreed to join us again."

Bobby, cheeks florid beneath his ginger mop, nodded fiercely. Having enjoyed the champagne to his usual excess he sat holding Daphne's hand, flopped in his seat with a silly grin on his face.

Chapter Five
The Tally Man

The following day found Charlie drawing deeply on his cigarette and staring at his smirking friend, who leaned lazily against the workshop wall.

"How the hell did you manage to do this without me knowing?" he asked, delighted at what he saw, but shocked that he had been taken so completely by surprise. "It must have taken months of work, yet I never had a clue."

Bobby just grinned, smug with the satisfaction of his achievement and with Charlie's reaction to it.

"Do-d'you want anything changed, anything at all?"

"No. It's perfect! It's fabulous, Bobby," then, with a shake of his head, "you're a bloody genius!"

The object of his admiration was a sidecar of beautifully polished oak, set on a base frame of painted steel. With a sleek pointed nose and a slightly curved top, it had been designed to carry stock. A five-lever mortice lock with a stainless-steel handle secured the lid to the box. It had been designed and built by Bobby himself.

The previous evening's dinner party had been a rollicking success, but it was the events of Saturday morning that had left Charlie speechless. Breakfast had been late and leisurely after a night through which he had shared his room and his bed with his wife for the first time in nearly a year. There had been no attempt at passionate arousal but they had been comfortable together, friends with no need for pretence.

At a little before midday, Millie Stoker, spying the red Lanchester rolling to a stop at the kerbside, had moved quickly to welcome Stephen Collick. They did not re-enter the front room, however, becoming involved in a whispered conversation at the front door. To Charlie's surprise, he heard Bobby Bruce's voice as well as Stephen's. Then his mother, from the door, said: "Charlie dear, would you mind coming to assist at the car for a moment? I'm afraid you are needed."

When Charlie reached the kerbside, he found Millie, Stephen and Bobby standing in a group behind the Lanchester. As he approached, they stepped aside to disclose, hidden behind the motor car, a sparkling new Velocette KSS motorcycle, a blue birthday ribbon tied on the handlebars.

"Happy birthday, Charlie," said Millie quietly.

For the second time in less than twenty-four hours, Charlie was overwhelmed. He stared at the shining machine, at his mother, at Stephen, and finally at Bobby. He was quite lost for words, although when questioned about the matter later by Margret, who had followed him out and was standing behind him, he said he was simply absorbing the moment, one of the happiest of his life.

Eventually, Charlie had climbed onto the saddle. Under Bobby's guidance, he tested the controls and fired the engine. Bobby suggested they take it for a short spin and they rode, Bobby on the pillion, from Amhurst Road to the workshop at Harringay. There, the bespectacled motor engineer had unveiled the sidecar.

Charlie stroked the polished surface of the box. "Tell me, Bobby, how *did* you manage to hide this from me?"

"Well, I b-built the s-s-sidecar in my dad's shed. The b-ase frame has been standing in sections at the b-ack of the w-orkshop among the bits and pieces. I p-put it all together on Friday."

Charlie inhaled deeply and exhaled the smoke slowly, sending circles like haloes, or, as Jennifer Lacey called them, angel rings hanging in the air.

"You are some man, Bobby, you really are," he said, crushing the burning cigarette end with his foot.

Expressions of strong feelings were alien to Charlie Stoker. He recalled the one occasion, after the loss of the baby, when he had felt a truly powerful bond, when he had shed tears in a tight embrace with his mother. Now, as he stared across the workshop at his somewhat scruffily dressed friend, he realised that he felt closer to Bobby Bruce than he did to anyone in the world with the exception of his mother.

"You know I don't like gushing much, and I may never say this again, Bobby, but you are a very special guy, and I'm proud that you are my mate."

He concentrated on wiping a speck of dust from the sidecar, taking care not to look up. Thus, he avoided seeing the tears of happiness in his friend's eyes.

* * *

If in later life Charlie Stoker was to recall 1931 as an unreal period, then 1932 was the year when he came to believe he was on the right road to the future.

Despite the government's abandonment of the gold standard and its subsequent actions to boost the economy, unemployment in the country still rose for the next couple of years. By 1932, it had reached twenty percent, although the figure was considerably lower in London and the southeast. The south was the principle home of new developing industries. The large-scale electrification of housing, public transport and industry brought new products such as electric cookers, washing machines and radios within the reach of many people; and the industries which produced these desirables prospered. Nearly half of all new factories opened in Britain between 1932 and 1937 were in the Greater London area.

Nevertheless, finding employment was often the difference between starving and living a decent life. The basic wage of a salesman-collector was poor, barely enough to live on. Only by boosting his income with sales commission could a man earn enough to get by. But it was a job, and in 1932, for young men of presentable appearance with sharp minds, that meant an opportunity. Successful salesmen built themselves a good living, but a great number failed to last the course. The turnover rate was high.

At Collick's, by 1932 a salesforce of twenty-eight men had been established, most of whom were building their incomes well under the careful guidance of Harvey Harrington and his supervisors. The force was split into three groups, with a supervisor to each group. Harrington had decided that a supervisor should not control more than ten salesmen, so when that number was reached a new group was formed and another supervisor appointed.

In what proved to be a stroke of good fortune for Charlie Stoker, he was invited to join the salesforce in February of that year. Round 3, in Group C, had become vacant a few weeks earlier when, on a routine check, discrepancies had been found in a number of account books. The previous salesman had been a man named Herbert Tebbin. Charlie remembered him as a rather dull, surly man, not the usual chatty sort. However, he had been in the job for over a year and had been thought to be developing quite well until the discovery that he had been stealing money from his customers and from the company. He had been dismissed at once and handed over to the authorities. He spent six months in gaol for his efforts.

The supervisor, Mr Spafford, had taken personal charge of the round for two or three weeks to clear up all the queries and to ensure that the affected customers were recompensed and happy. Only when Spafford was completely satisfied that everything was, in his own words, 'hunky-dory' was the new man, Charlie Stoker, given his opportunity.

Charlie, in preparation for it, completely re-organised his personal living arrangements. Now that he owned the Velocette, it took little more than twenty minutes to reach either Collick's or his mother's house from Chigwell, so it was no longer necessary to live two lives. The daily journey to work on the KSS was a trip of pure joy. Regardless of the weather, he felt a sense of freedom and power like nothing he had ever imagined. The roar of the engine, the thrill of the machine's acceleration, the exhilaration of the wind rushing through his hair as he sped along the open road, all charged him with adrenalin for the day ahead. He moved his things out of his old bedroom at Amhurst Road and settled permanently in his country house.

Except for odd occasional outings, his bicycle was now not much needed, and he made a home for it in his garage. He screwed two strong hooks to the wall six feet above the floor and placed the frame upon them. The Raleigh hung there, looking forlornly down at its motorised successor and at the shining oak sidecar resting on its painted frame by the side.

* * *

Unlike the department store with its Monday to Saturday working week, the salesman-collectors worked from Friday to Wednesday. The wage earners in most households received their weekly pay on Fridays, and in a great number of cases it would be spent by Monday. Consequently, the bulk of weekly collections from less affluent customers needed to be made on Friday evenings and Saturdays. Mondays, Tuesdays and Wednesdays were less feverish in activity but generally accounted for only a third of the week's takings. Thursday was the travelling man's half-day and in the course of that morning, every salesman was required to report to his supervisor, to take care of his round's weekly administration, to collect new stock and to attend Mr Harrington's weekly sales meeting.

Ivor Spafford, supervisor of Group C, was a man of slightly more than average height, of military bearing, quiet voice and sober manner. He was a very private man. On his eighteenth birthday, in 1915, he had followed his father into the army to serve as a clerk with the Army Service Corps. Posted to the Infantry Base Depot at Étaples in north-west France, he rose to the rank of sergeant before being demobilised early in 1919, a young man prematurely aged by his experiences, and haunted by his memories.

Mr Spafford had been a very early member of Aitch Harrington's sales team, having joined in 1924 following five years in the fire brigade at Leicester, his home town. A meticulous man, he was rarely seen without a small notebook in his jacket pocket into which he entered a constant stream of notes and reminders for subsequent action. His voice had a naturally authoritative tone. When addressing people, he looked them straight in the eye, speaking precisely, clearly, and always politely.

Charlie first reported to the basement to take up his new post on a Monday morning, and on arrival he was instructed to stand next to Mr Spafford's table and to watch the supervisor's morning routine: the examining of each man's weekend work. Sales tickets were countersigned or rejected according to the supervisor's judgement of the particular account. Rejection meant that a salesman must revisit his customer and either recover the goods or take another payment, sufficient to meet the company's terms, before re-presenting the sales order. Failure to do either would leave the salesman charged with the cost of the goods. As Charlie watched, two orders were rejected from a cluster presented by a ruddy-faced chap named Darbyshire, to the man's obvious, but unexpressed irritation.

After an hour or so, a short, thickset fellow in a dark blue suit, with a narrow forehead beneath shiny black hair, brought his weekend's work for approval. He addressed only his supervisor but acknowledged Charlie with a smile of recognition. Most of the salesmen were acquainted with Charlie from his time in the store, and several greeted him with nods or the odd words as they passed.

On this occasion, Mr Spafford formally introduced the man to him as Walter Habisch, the salesman with whom he was to spend the next three days. Charlie was to accompany Habisch, now established as a successful salesman on Round five, on his Monday to Wednesday rounds, before being introduced by Spafford himself to the customers of Round three from the Friday.

In his late twenties, Walter Habisch was a man whose face presented a picture of shy anxiety until the moment he smiled. Then the warmth of his nature shone forth. He had migrated with his young wife Esther to England from Czechoslovakia some five years earlier and spoke an idiosyncratic but fluent English with a strong continental accent. As soon as his supervisor's inspection was over, he hurriedly collected his required stock for the day and, with Charlie by his side, prepared to set off.

Habisch was one of the salesmen who found it convenient to select his customers' orders on a daily basis. All his rounds were within walking distance, no more than a mile or two from the store. Most of his business was gained by customers visiting the store, but he carried special orders and a small amount of selling stock in a leather suitcase.

"You got a raincoat? A hat? Iss not nice out there today," he said, concerned, as he buttoned his own coat.

"Yeah, in the staff cloakroom. I won't be a minute, I'll meet you by the door," replied Charlie.

It was a misty, damp February day, not quite raining but necessitating raincoats and scarves in the chill, wet London streets. Charlie reached the staff entrance door to find Walter standing outside, a leather satchel hanging from his left shoulder, and holding his suitcase in his right hand. Although solidly built, he stood only five feet seven inches tall. Charlie towered above him.

"I seen you lots inside," said Walter, assessing him. "You're some big guy!"

Charlie shrugged. "Yeah, but I don't know much. I'm eager to learn."

"Thass okay. I show you how I do it. You watch. Then Mr Spafford, he teach you everything. He's a top man. First, today we go to Mile End."

Charlie said, "I've got my motorbike combination out front. Shall we use that instead of walking, this weather?"

"You gotta motorbike? Thass nice! Okay, today we go on the motorbike. But tomorrow we walk. Today we go a bit further, issa long walk. Tomorrow is easier."

They walked to the front of the building where the KSS was parked, and Walter gasped.

"Thass yours?" Iss beautiful!"

Charlie opened the lid of the oak box and placed Walter's suitcase inside.

"Wait a minute!" The little Czech was excited. "We got all that space; we can make some good business. We get some stuff to sell. Come!"

He almost ran back through the front door of the store, Charlie following more slowly. With flying visits and urgent commands to the fashion department, the shoe department and menswear, Walter collected and hurriedly transferred his new stock to the sidecar. Then, his small-brimmed hat jammed onto his head, he mounted the pillion behind Charlie and they set off.

Each round at Collick's began life with its own specific area, often just a few streets, but customers' movements, new calls and salesmen's working habits tended to change its shape with time. If a good customer moved home within travelling distance, the salesman would make an effort to retain the business. It became common for rounds to overlap. Sometimes two salesmen would even discover they both had customers at the same address.

Walter Habisch's Round five was one that had retained its compact shape. All his customers lived between Stepney and Mile End. As soon as they reached the first call, Walter explained that there were only forty-three customers to visit on a Monday. They were mostly good customers who paid their bills each week without needing chasing. Charlie asked if many customers did need chasing for their money and Walter frowned. "Depends how you look after them," he replied. "Most people's nice. You good to them, they're good to you. Iss easy."

Charlie nodded,-his eyes pensive.

After just three or four calls at which the weekly payments were collected without more than a few sociable words, Walter adjusted the contents of his case and carried it into the home of a well-established family, the Dansons. Having instructed Charlie not to speak, he introduced him vaguely as a man from the office. They were made welcome by Mrs Danson with a cup of tea and a slice of home-made fruitcake before Walter opened the case. With the lid wide open, he produced a pair of sheets that were lying on top of some men's clothing. The sheets had been ordered the previous week and were accepted with thanks by Mrs Danson, who handed Walter her payment books and weekly cash.

In the silence as he diligently made the entries in the books, Mrs Danson eyed the case. After a while, she said: "Ooh, my Bill needs some new socks. I can't darn them anymore; he's gone right through his bottoms at that foundry!"

Walter looked up with a beam. "Thass okay, Mrs D. I gotta couple pairs there just fit him. I put 'em on this ticket, eh?"

"Oh, thank you, Mr Haybish, you're so good to us."

"Iss my pleasure, Mrs D. You're good customer. I take an extra shilling, okay?"

"Yes, of course. More tea?"

The rest of that day and the next two followed a similar, comfortable pattern, with the silent Charlie happy to watch the little master at his work. Only once was there an unpleasant moment, later on the Monday afternoon. They knocked at a house in Limehouse and the door was opened by a burly man wearing a navy boiler suit and a look of alcohol-fuelled ill-temper. The man glared at Walter, seemed about to speak, then looked up at Charlie and closed his mouth. He turned and stamped back into the house, calling out scathingly, "It's your little Jew bloke for yer!"

The woman of the house quickly appeared with her payment book in hand, flushed with embarrassment and apologising for her husband. Walter acted as if he had heard nothing, smiled his shy smile and collected his money. Afterwards, when Charlie asked him if he experienced much of that sort of attitude, Habisch replied:

"Y'know, for Jews iss never far away. We used to it. But here, in England, we breathe free most of the time. Iss only the occasional oaf is bad. On continent, with Slovaks and Bavarians and Austrians, iss much worse."

Charlie nodded and lit a cigarette, watching the little man out of the corner of his eye. Walter busied himself with his books. Charlie blew a smoke ring and said: "Oaf?"

Walter looked up, grinning. "Yes, oaf! Schlemiel! You see! I learn good English!"

Charlie exhaled slowly, shaking his head from left to right, wisps of smoke dispatched all around. He shrugged his acknowledgement with a grin.

* * *

Whether Charlie Stoker's appointment to Round three had been a considered one by Harvey Harrington or purely fortuitous because of the Tebbin business was never disclosed, but Ivor Spafford was without question a perfect match as his supervisor. Charlie found the whole training experience massively rewarding. For Spafford it was a delight to work with a trainee who was clearly destined to succeed.

The choice of Walter Habisch for Charlie's initiation had been the supervisor's first shrewd move. The time spent with Walter Habisch proved immensely valuable for the new man. The Czech, with his shy, almost diffident manner, had clearly established a remarkable relationship with his customers. Almost all treated him as a family guest for whom they had the utmost respect. Yet he was as sharp as a needle when the moment arrived to make his case for a sale or to request an extra payment.

The supervisor's qualities were completely different, yet just as successful. Mr Spafford, with his military bearing and polite formality, at once established a business-like relationship with customers, always with respect but never leaving any doubt as to who was in control of the meeting.

Charlie himself often gave the appearance of being slightly casual, as if his mind were elsewhere, but he also missed nothing. He watched, listened and learned much from both men. The relationship between supervisor and recruit quickly became one of trust and mutual respect. When calling on customers they formed a formidable pair. Their imposing presence often caused apprehension for whoever opened the door, but the initial ice was easily broken by the Spafford courtesy and the Stoker smile.

Round three, one of the original rounds, had been in existence for seven years and had changed hands a few times. Consequently, it had become more widespread than Round five. On Friday and Saturday, the customers were predominantly in Whitechapel and Bethnal Green; on Monday, Shoreditch and Haggerston; and on Tuesday and Wednesday around Victoria Park and Old Ford, out as far as Hackney Wick. This suited Charlie very well. He was able to take his lunch with his mother on Mondays, and to complete his weekly paperwork at Amhurst Road on Wednesday afternoons before meeting Bobby for the Wednesday swim.

Chapter Six
Bobby, Daphne and Elsie

Religion was a concept Bobby Bruce found complicated – a confusing world he preferred to stay away from. With his severe speech impediment, something not always well tolerated by other impatient youngsters, his childhood had been difficult much of the time, although life at home had always been comfortable with his loving, hard-working parents.

They, if asked, would have said they were good Christians. They visited the local parish church spasmodically, they had sent their son to Sunday school regularly, and they supported the church fetes loyally; but they lacked the commitment for weekly attendance. Nevertheless, they expected their son to find a nice girl from a familiar Anglican background and to marry in the church at Harringay.

Daphne Hipstead's background was quite different. Her grandfather, Abraham Lypszyc, a Jewish schoolteacher, had come to England from Russian Poland in 1886 with his sick and pregnant wife, Devorah. Their son, Daphne's father, David, was born in London in the same year. Devorah was unable to have any further children and she died in 1898, when David was twelve years old. Abraham, struggling to come to terms with his situation and believing he was acting for the best, arranged for the boy to stay with cousins in Stoke Newington. David was unhappy with the decision but bowed to his father's will.

Abraham maintained regular contact with his son but their relationship was never again easy. On reaching the age of twenty-one, David changed his name from Lypszyc to Hipstead. He then obtained a position as a clerk in the offices of Hornsey Borough Council, where he met and two years later married, Hester Atwell, a pretty Welsh girl who worked in the same office. Hester was from a Calvinist Methodist family, and their wedding in a Methodist church intensified the bad feeling between David and his father. For over a year there was almost no contact between them, but with the birth of Daphne, in a terraced house in Crouch End in 1910, the possibility of being estranged for ever from his son and his granddaughter was enough to persuade Lipszyc to swallow his pride and to accept the situation.

Daphne grew up with a Calvinist Methodist mother and an agnostic father, a shy, intelligent girl with brown eyes, doted upon by a Polish Jewish grandfather who repeatedly reminded her that she was the spitting image of her sorely missed grandmother.

During the early months of 1932, Bobby Bruce was quite often in need of the Stoker smile's calming influence. Although in company a cheerful chap, Bobby was a born worrier. He preferred to avoid life's complications. Complications meant stress, and he was not good at handling stress. He felt blessed to have found a perfect partner in Daphne, but the business of preparing for their wedding was full of complications that involved them both.

The most effective de-stressing activity he knew was the weekly after-swim with Charlie, the one person to whom he could unload his worries with confidence.

"I'm getting myself into a state about this b-b-blooming wedding!" he moaned.

"Nothing to it, you enjoyed mine!" retorted Charlie with a shrug, lighting a cigarette.

"Yeah, and I'll p-probably enjoy mine if I l-live long enough to g-go through with it."

Charlie grinned. "Calm down and drink your beer, Bobby. You'll be alright. You're always alright when it matters. What's wrong today?"

Bobby hung his head, then moved it slowly from side to side. He sighed.

"Charlie, I j-just want it over. I didn't want a church wedding. Daph doesn't want a church wedding. Daph's family don't really care, 'cos they're a m-mixed lot anyway. But my m-mum and dad have set their h-hearts on it."

"What does Daph say about that?"

"She says if it makes them h-happy, we should just go along with it. Her p-arents will arrange a reception for f-family and close friends at the Community Hall near where her dad works."

"Well, she's right, isn't she?" Charlie blew a cloud of smoke. "What's the problem?"

Bobby's head dropped again and he spoke without looking up.

"Last month I booked the Registry Office at Islington Town Hall for 28 April, but my mum says that wouldn't be convenient for people bein' a w-weekday and it would mean too much t-traipsing about for everyone. She's made an appointment for us to see the vicar at H-H-Harringay next week to plan for the second Saturday in May, the week before Whitsun. I d-don't like m-meetings like that."

Charlie's eyes were twinkling. "You're an idiot, Bobby, you know that, don't you. Cancel the booking at Islington and go and see the vicar. Do you need me to hold your hand?"

Bobby looked up, stared for a moment then grinned sheepishly. "N-no. D-Daphne can do that. But I'll n-need you to hold me up at the church in May!"

"The only thing that matters is that you and Daphne know what you're doing and agree. You two were made for each other. Forget all these irritations, you've got a whole life to look forward to together."

Charlie inhaled the last of the cigarette and squashed it into the ashtray. He lifted his glass.

"One more?"

"Okay." Bobby removed his glasses and began to polish them with his handkerchief. "I love you, Ch-Charlie, you know that, don't you?"

Charlie gave him an old-fashioned look. "Yeah, well just keep it between us, eh?"

* * *

Millie Stoker's birthday happened to be in the last week of February, and Charlie and Margret were invited, along with Stephen Collick, to enjoy Sunday lunch at Amhurst Road as a small celebration. The young couple were beginning to forge very separate lives, with Margret busily researching at L.S.E. and virtually living at Clare Market. But this was a visit she was quite happy to make with her husband. She always enjoyed spending a few hours with Charlie's mother, whom she regarded as 'no fool', an accolade of the highest order when accorded by Margret.

Stephen had offered, through Millie, to collect the young Stokers from Chigwell on his way to Hackney and to take them home again later. Their house was only a short distance from Parklands and the offer was gratefully accepted. Stephen duly arrived at Woodside Way on the Sunday morning, driving, to Charlie's surprise, not the red Lanchester but a brand-new wine-coloured Armstrong Siddeley 15/6 saloon.

"It's beautiful," said Charlie. "Is it replacing the Lanchester? Or is it in addition?"

"I was having considerable problems with the gear box of the Lanchester," replied Stephen somewhat mournfully, "and so, although it was a wrench, I decided it must go. This vehicle is of similar size but should prove to be more reliable. It has a pre-select gearbox, a new development that makes driving more comfortable. The company is making aeroplane engines as well as motor cars, so they should know what they are doing!"

"It certainly looks good," replied Charlie.

The drive to Hackney proved that the new motorcar was also a joy to ride in, the new gearbox providing smooth gear changes with no noisy grinds or bumps.

Margret had arranged for a large bouquet of flowers to be delivered to Amhurst Road and the blooms were on full display when they arrived. Millie was delighted, of course, and welcomed them with sherry in the sitting room.

Lunch, traditional roast beef, was an altogether pleasant and relaxing experience. Stephen had brought two bottles of claret for the table, obviously with Millie's approval, and Charlie was discreet enough not to mention the subject. He simply enjoyed both the wine and the idea that his mother's hard prejudice against alcohol appeared to have softened considerably.

Stephen Collick, always a fine raconteur, told a few amusing tales and led the general conversation. Then, after the meal, Millie engaged Margret in conversation in the dining room while the two men repaired to the sitting room to enjoy a cigar.

It was the end of Charlie's fourth week as a salesman-collector and he was taken a little by surprise when Stephen said:

"How is your work going, Charlie? Are you enjoying yourself?"

"Yes, very much. This month I have taken over Round 3, under Mr Spafford."

Stephen smiled. "So, I noticed. Your name appeared on the weekly report lists this month. You have done well to reach that position so quickly. Good show!"

"Thank you, sir. Not that I've really done anything, except watch Walter Habisch and Mr Spafford."

"You could do much worse, Charlie. I am told that Mr Habisch goes about his work in a very professional manner; and Ivor Spafford is a most reliable man. You just continue to follow his lead and you will make sparks fly, I have no doubt!"

"I hope so." Charlie shrugged. "That's what I intend to do, sir."

"How about your studies? Are you still persevering?"

"Yes, sir. I quite enjoy the classes. They take my mind off work, but I shall have to put in some extra study time before June's exams."

"Is there anything I can do to ease your load?"

"No, definitely not, sir. I shall manage. The exams hold no fear for me."

Stephen slightly inclined his head but did not reply.

They were joined by the ladies. As it was her birthday, Millie announced that she would decide what was to happen. They were to play whist, the ladies against the gentlemen. "And, of course, gentlemen being gentlemen, I expect the ladies to win!"

Stephen replied that he suspected the ladies would not require any gentlemanly concessions. Charlie just grinned. To see his mother so happy and chatty was a source of enormous comfort. He surveyed the room. Stephen, Millie, Margret and himself. This happy group was as near as Millie Stoker would now get to a family, he mused.

Without a doubt, his mother still hoped to see grandchildren. Charlie had never told her of Margret's determined stance on pregnancy. Had he said nothing because he still hoped that his wife would change her mind? That given time, the pain of their tragic loss of eighteen months earlier would have receded to a different perspective? That the natural female urge to have children would come to the fore? Or was it simply that he clung to the forlorn hope that she would satisfy his own deep desire for a son?

* * *

Bobby Bruce and Daphne Hipstead were married on the afternoon of the second Saturday in May in front of the new marble altar at St. Paul's Church in Harringay, where Bobby's parents were respected members of the congregation. It was not an ostentatious affair but there was quite a large gathering of people at the church.

Daphne, wearing a simple white wedding dress and carrying a bouquet of red roses, looked radiantly happy, her dark hair lustrous against her naturally pale skin. She was attended by her maid-of-honour, Jennifer Lacey, stunning as always and smiling brilliantly, and two young bridesmaids, the bride's cousins, aged six and eight, up to town from Swansea with their parents, Daphne's uncle, Hester's brother Clive Atwell and his wife Mfanwy, known as Miffy.

Bobby had been suffering a fit of nerves when Charlie reached the Bruce's house in the morning. His stammer had become so intense that he was quite unable to put a sentence together. Charlie's firm handshake and languid grin seemed, however, to act as a magic potion; and with the added bracer of a large glass of whisky, he quickly regained control of his excitement. Everything thereafter went without a hitch, the groom barely hesitating over his marriage lines at the church.

Afterwards, a total of about sixty people enjoyed a relaxed wedding supper and ball at the Crouch End Community Hall. The guests included, for the most part, the extended families and family friends of the bride and groom, plus Margret and Millie Stoker, the Hon. Stephen Collick, Lionel and Sarah Lacey, and a number of the happy couple's friends from college.

Speeches were kept to a minimum. David Hipstead thanked everyone for attending and expressed his joy at seeing his daughter so happily partnered. Bobby replied in a controlled speech of surprisingly few words in which he thanked the Hipsteads firstly for the wonderful day, then for being such great people, and above all for producing Daphne, the most perfect bride he could ever have dreamed of.

The third and final speech was from Charlie, the best man. Having complimented everyone on how spiffing they all looked, he read a couple of well-wishing letters from absentees, then explained how Bobby, Daphne, Jennifer and he had first met at the Northern and come to be friends. Holding a glass in one hand and a cigar in the other, he detailed how, until he met them he had been an innocent. They had conspired to seduce him, he explained. Jennifer had forced cigarettes upon him, Bobby had forced alcohol upon him, and Daphne had forced Gilbert and Sullivan upon him. And he wanted to take this opportunity to thank them all from the bottom of his heart! He concluded by stating that Bobby was a man who deserved the best, and in Dorothy he had found it.

As soon as he had finished, four local musicians, whose leader was a friend of the Hipsteads, began to play popular music for dancing and Bobby and Daphne took to the floor to general applause. Charlie, now relieved of duties, joined Margret at a table shared with his mother, Stephen, Lionel and Sarah Lacey, and Jennifer. After a short time, the four older people began to dance a lot. Margret and Jennifer chatted together, mostly making small talk of no interest to Charlie, who sat, content to watch the goings-on with a whisky and a cigar.

Bobby, however, was keen to show off his handsome best man, and rushed to introduce Charlie to those of his and Daphne's families who had not met him previously. Among them were the bridesmaids' parents, Clive and Miffy Atwell. Clive, a clerk in the employment exchange in Swansea, complained in a strong Welsh accent and a whining tone that he had used a week of his annual holidays to attend the wedding, and to show his two daughters some of the sights of London.

"That's nice," replied Charlie, ignoring the tone. "I'm sure they'll enjoy that. I'm sure you'll all enjoy that."

"Mmm, I hope so." Clive glowered morosely. "You see, London is a different world like from Wales. There's no depression here. Here, everywhere is busy and active. Life seems to have a purpose here. Down there, man, life is dying. The only place is busy is where I work. They queue up all day, there, hoping to get some dole money. Hoping to get fifteen shillings to live on! They know they can't get work. There is no work! There's thousands of willing workers but no work. That's what's happened and that's what we live with. And if, like myself, a man has a job, then they cut his wages. And that was a Labour government! A Labour Prime Minister! I work now for a pittance!"

"Now, that's enough, Clive, stop you, now. This is a wedding, not your soap box!" Miffy Atwell spoke in a sharp whisper that was quite enough to silence her husband. She turned to Charlie.

"You must forgive him; he's been having a difficult time. He needs the rest. By the end of the week, he will be a different man."

Charlie smiled and shrugged.

* * *

Finishing his pie and beans at a busy café off Bancroft Road a few days later, Clive Atwell's outburst remained vividly in Charlie's memory. The newspapers had for a long time been full of reports about the depression and its effect upon the industrial regions, but what he saw in his everyday life changed very little from year to year. Poverty was always hovering nearby. There were always people struggling to find the wherewithal for their daily bread; it was a hard world for so many people.

Occasionally he saw street scenes and skirmishes – his mind flashed back to *that* day in 1926. But most of the time people found a way to manage, to get by. His customers were, for the most part, the same ordinary people as their cousins that lived in South Wales or Northern England. It was hard to believe that life was so different there from here in London. People worked long hours for low wages. Sometimes they found themselves out of work; but there was always another job to be found, if one really looked. Wasn't there?

He paid for his lunch and continued to his Wednesday afternoon calls. The third of these was the Philpotts, loyal customers since the very early days. There were three account books in the house, one for Mr, one for Mrs, and one for Elsie. Mrs

Philpott opened the door as usual, giving Charlie a warm welcome and leading him into the front room to enjoy a cup of tea that, as always, he was happy to accept. Wednesday being her afternoon off, Elsie was at home. Whenever the weather was particularly inclement, Mr Philpott might appear too, but on this occasion he was at work. Mr Philpott was a window cleaner.

Mrs Philpott was a chatty, buxom woman of about fifty and Elsie was the youngest of their three daughters. She was twenty-four years old and the only one who still lived at home. Her two sisters were both married and had moved out of the area.

Having now been a salesman-collector – a tallyman, the term generally used by the public – for four months, Charlie had grown accustomed to having eyelids fluttered at him. He was, after all, six feet three inches tall, broad-shouldered and in possession of a devilish smile. He took all the come-hither looks and suggestive remarks in good part, dismissing them with shrugs and smiles and clouds of cigarette smoke.

Elsie Philpott, though, presented a different problem. Quite short, with a pretty face and a well-rounded figure, her chatty, eager to please nature and ready smile made her well suited to her job in the local baker's shop. She was engaged to a local lad, Wilfred Tattle, the brother of her long-time friend Lucy. The couple were planning to marry the following year. Wilf was two years older than Elsie. He worked for the council as an assistant mechanic.

Unfortunately, Elsie had become besotted with Charlie Stoker. She saw him as if through a pink cloud, rather as if he were a Hollywood film star descended upon them. Mrs Philpott would chat away about the week's goings on, as she did every week, and Elsie would sit with heaving breast, watching Charlie's every movement, hanging on his every word and becoming tongue-tied when required to join the conversation. Whenever her mother left the room, she ran out rather than have to speak.

This situation was not one that Charlie could handle comfortably. It was certainly not something he expected from a woman of twenty-four. After all, she was three years older than he. On this visit, Mrs Philpott, as usual, appeared not to notice her daughter's embarrassment. When she went to make tea and Elsie made to follow her, Charlie decided that he must attempt to normalise the relationship.

"Just a minute, Elsie," he said, "Do you mind if I have a word with you?"

Elsie instantly turned the colour of a beetroot. "Oh! Oh… Um, yes, yes, of course." She stood stock still.

"Shall we sit down?" suggested Charlie.

"Oh, oh, yes." She dropped onto an upright chair near the door.

"How about over here, so we don't have to shout," said Charlie with a smile, indicating the sofa with his arm.

"Oh! Oh, yes, alright." Elsie propped herself on the edge of the sofa next to the armchair in which Charlie was sitting, visibly shaking, with her hands clasped tightly in front of her.

"You see, Elsie, I've been thinking about you," he said, meaningfully. "You seem to be nervous of me, and that's not right, that's not how it should be."

Elsie's hands were pressed ever more tightly.

"I've not been in this job too long but I want to succeed. I want to be able to feel good, and I can only do that if I make my customers feel good. I want to be able to help all my customers, and that means you too."

He shrugged, and Elsie twisted her fingers.

Charlie pressed on, "See, I don't usually talk about myself, 'cos I think my customers' needs are more important than my private life. But I'm just an ordinary bloke who's got married young. I have to work hard to pay my way and I don't let myself stray, even when I'm tempted. I know it would be easy to be tempted with you, but I can't, I'm married – and you will be next year, won't you? I don't know Wilf, but I'm sure he's a good chap and it wouldn't be fair to let him down, would it?"

Elsie shook her head vigorously while continuing to squeeze her fingers. Charlie went on:

"What I would like, though, Elsie, is for us to be friends. If we're friends, I can help you to fill your bottom drawer and make life easier for you and Wilf when you get your own place. For example, you've got your own account for clothes and things. Why don't we start another card for you and Wilf after you're married? Then, you can reduce the payment on your clothes card to, say two bob, and use the rest to save up on the new card for your home. What do you think?"

Elsie's hands were still clasped, but her frown became a nervous smile.

"Yeah, Charlie, I think that would be good." Then, more excitedly, "And I'll get Wilf to add to it so we can save more."

She suddenly jumped up and hugged him. "Ooh, Charlie, but you are a smasher!" She planted a kiss on his cheek and ran out of the door.

Chapter Seven
The Changing World

The winter of 1932/1933 was one of immense significance for the whole world. The years of depression that had created unemployment and misery for millions of people worldwide now brought about massive political upheavals. In America, the Democrat candidate Franklin Delano Roosevelt achieved a landslide victory over the sitting Republican, President Hoover, with his promise of a new deal for the people and an end to the economic misery. To a great extent, Roosevelt was to keep his promise, but elsewhere it was a different story. In Germany, with parliamentary rule disintegrating as National Socialist Fascists fought Communists in the streets, the National Socialist leader Adolph Hitler was appointed Chancellor, promising to restore order to the country.

Meanwhile, in Chigwell, Charlie Stoker pulled the morning paper from the letter box as usual before starting his day's work. Now an old hand as a salesman-collector – he had been fully nine months in the job – he was probably unique in being the only tallyman in the country with a degree in physics; a matter of great satisfaction to him and to Margret, and of immense pride to his mother.

He spread the paper on the table and read:

'With unemployment reaching two and three-quarter million, two thousand five hundred workers, mainly from economically depressed areas such as the South Wales valleys, Scotland and the North of England, have marched to London to present a petition demanding the abolition of the Means Test and the Anomalies Act.'

Remembering Clive Atwell's bitterness at Bobby's wedding, he read on: *'The Means Test was introduced by the government in 1931 together with a reduction of ten percent in unemployment pay, as part of the attempt to cut costs in the economic crisis. In order to qualify for a weekly payment, or "dole" as it is commonly termed, a worker must pass the Means Test, and the sum paid to each family is based upon* this. As part of the test, officials visit families in their homes to assess whether they are entitled to help. This involves establishing not only what income the family receives, but also assessing the value of their possessions.'

Charlie stopped reading. Over the months on his rounds, he had heard a multitude of moans about unemployment and the dole. He let them go in one ear and out of the other – just excuses for non-payment. But for some unaccountable reason, these cold words struck home with him. *The value of their possessions?* Surely that was not right? He had been brought up to believe an Englishman's home is his castle. Surely, such a measure was offensive and demeaning? It highlighted the problems faced by so many ordinary people every day and the callous harshness of such intrusions into their private lives. He recalled Atwell's words: '*You see, London is a different world, like, from Wales. There's no depression here. Down there, man, life is dying.*'

It was as if only now did the penny drop for him. He finished his bowl of cereal, then returned his attention to the newspaper. The article continued: '*The marchers have been prevented from presenting their petition containing a million signatures by a force of seventy thousand policemen, mobilised by order of Prime Minister Ramsay MacDonald's National Government to stop the petition reaching parliament. Mounted police have been used all across central London to disperse the demonstrators. Seventy-five people have been badly injured.*'

Charlie stood up, letting the paper fall onto the table. "And how many of them were innocent bystanders, like my father?" he exclaimed in a burst of fury to the empty house.

In the silence that followed his outburst, Charlie lit a cigarette. He calmed and lectured himself. He was surprised at himself. It was not like him to lose his temper. No, it was not. In fact, he could not recall the last occasion. It was not in his nature, he told himself. No, it wasn't, he agreed.

So why had it happened? He glanced again at the paper and knew the answer. It was the bit about policemen being mobilised to deal with demonstrators – exactly as they had been when killing his father on *that* day. He took a deep breath. Six, nearly seven years had passed since the General Strike, yet it seemed to Charlie in that rather bleak moment that nobody had learned a thing.

He made an effort to put the matter to the back of his mind and to concentrate on preparing for his working day. It was a Wednesday, swimming day. That always brightened the week. By the time he met Bobby for their swim, the black cloud had passed from over Charlie's head. Nevertheless, he mentioned the matter to his friend over the evening pint.

"It was in the H-Herald too," said Bobby, "and w-we actually saw some of the marchers. It was a r-ragged bunch that I saw. They wouldn't have needed much p-policing."

Charlie blew smoke rings.

"Have you heard any more from Clive Atwell?" he asked.

"N-no, we've not seen them since the wedding. I think Daph's mum keeps in touch but we don't hear. I b'lieve, in the f-amily, he's reckoned to be a bit of a misery."

"From what we're reading, Bobby, he's got plenty to be miserable about, spending every day doling out his fifteen shillings to those poor beggars!"

Bobby looked sharply at Charlie. He did not speak for a long time, busying himself playing with two halfpennies around his beer glass. Then he said,

"N-not like you to get passionate, mate."

Charlie shrugged. "Some things matter, Bobby. What's going on is not right. So many people starving while others live in luxury. It's not right."

* * *

The boys had parted from the pub agreeing to arrange a Saturday card night for the following week. The lives of the Stokers and the Bruces were beginning to develop different priorities, and the Saturday evening card game at Chigwell had ceased to be a regular weekly event. Once married, Bobby and Daphne, who were both from close-knit families, often found themselves with other more pressing social commitments. This week they were attending a family dinner with grandfather Lypszyc. They still retained their enthusiasm for the card evening, though, and it remained a popular, if more occasional social evening for them.

For Charlie, it was always a fun evening, but he was happy to go along with what others wanted. Since Friday and Saturday were his two longest working days, he was quite content to spend Saturday evening quietly making up his accounts for the weekend, and then perhaps enjoying a glass of beer or two at the village local. Margret, if she were at home, usually joined him. She was always keen to enjoy a pint.

Increasingly, though, Margret was not at home. She had so enjoyed her experience as a research assistant that she had accepted the invitation to serve a second year. It was probable that after that she would be offered a position as a lecturer. Meantime she was increasingly drawn into activities at the college. Never slow to voice her opinion on most subjects, she had been a member of the Students' Union – often a vociferous one – since her first year, and was an enthusiastic member of the debating society. Now in her fifth year, she often found herself asked to remain at Clare Market at the weekend for some college campaign or other. The most recent of these was to become a voice for 'the right to roam'.

A keen walker, she sometimes travelled with groups of enthusiasts on protest rambles. Access to most of the beautiful uncultivated open country across England was prohibited to the ordinary population, being preserved for the landed gentry to enjoy hunting and shooting without disturbance.

This was seen as ridiculously unfair by many of those excluded from enjoying the beauty spots and the walking routes that criss-crossed the land. Earlier in the year, several hundred people had engaged in civil disobedience in the form of a mass trespass on moorland of the Derbyshire Peak District. A number of the trespassers were arrested and jailed for several months, but their action sparked a movement among ramblers and country lovers everywhere in favour of access to areas of open country. The movement was eagerly taken up by students at universities throughout the land and 'the right to roam' became a rallying call for trespass marchers.

Whatever Margret's arrangements, however, she invariably found time for Sunday lunch at Amhurst Road. She cared about that relationship. It was the one regular family event at which she clearly affirmed her commitment to her marriage. With Millie Stoker, she became almost another person, showing affection and always being respectful. Charlie found it fascinating to compare the Margret who accompanied him to Hackney with the sharp-taloned vixen he saw on their rare visits to Enfield.

"So, tell me more about 'the right to roam'," said Millie brightly as they enjoyed the roast.

Stephen Collick coughed. Charlie grinned and said:

"Are you sure you want that lecture just now, Mum?"

"I don't presume to lecture your mother, Big Boy!" snapped Margret sharply. "She devotes enough of her time to helping the needy. She needs no lectures from me about people's suffering."

"Good for you, Margie." Charlie's wide grin matched Margret's glare.

Stephen coughed again, then smiled round the table and said, looking at Charlie:

"Please, children, do not hold back from saying what you think! Although it may perhaps surprise you to hear that I am actually in favour of action to allow responsible access to the land. I agree in principle with that young man recently gaoled, that Rothman fellow, the leader of the Kinder Scout Trespass. What was it he said? I think it was: *'After a hard week's work in smoky towns and cities, we go out rambling for relaxation and fresh air. And then we find the finest rambling country is closed to us'.*"

"I believe he is right. The public deserve to have a right of way across restricted open country – providing they do not abuse that right. If it can be shown that they cause no damage, I believe they should have their paths. And Lord Collick agrees with me. There are now paths clearly marked for public access on all Collick Estates."

"Paths!" Margret fired the word like a bullet. "It's not just paths people need! They are not on a trek, they need space! They need the freedom to wander over the land. They should have areas to spread out in, areas for children to play! Space to relax and to enjoy the countryside's glory!"

She ceased as abruptly as she had exploded and the room was suddenly silent. Four knives and forks hung in the air. Charlie caught Margret's eye. She laughed sheepishly.

"Forgive me, everyone, I do not mean to be rude but I tend to get carried away. The fact is we need so many more to think as you do, Stephen. What Lord Collick has done is a start, but so much more is needed."

Stephen acknowledged the uncharacteristic apology with his usual grace.

"I admire your passion, Margret," he said. "Do carry on the good work. But here, remember, you are among believers!"

"Have some more beef, Charlie." said Millie with a laugh, bringing the conversation to the safety of the business in hand.

"Delighted to oblige!" said Charlie, grinning.

* * *

Daphne Bruce took very seriously her responsibilities as a wife, but she was also deeply committed to her work. By 1933, Lacey's Chemist's shop was always very busy and required the presence of at least four staff, two in the shop and two in the dispensary, nearly all the time.

Daphne enjoyed working in the chemist's shop and knew that she was highly regarded by Mr Lacey. When she had completed her course at the Northern and became qualified to manage a dispensary, Lacey had told her that he regarded her as management potential. Exactly what he had meant was not made clear but Daphne had felt it was not her place to press the matter. Nevertheless, it gave her a gratifying feeling of security in her job.

What Lionel Lacey actually had in mind was expansion. In 1918, after his traumatic experience in a field hospital during the war, he had bought the empty premises in Highgate and opened the village chemist's shop with a grand vision. He wanted two things: firstly, to use his knowledge to promote good health and happiness in as many people as possible; and secondly to build a business, a business for his family to inherit and to further develop. To this end, he worked long hours, day after day for fifteen years, first to establish himself locally, and then to build the business to the point where he could afford to expand beyond Highgate and to allow his son to slowly take the helm from him.

That had been his dream. Unfortunately, by 1918, Sarah, his wife, had only managed to produce three girls in succession. When later that year she gave birth to a boy, whom they named James Lionel, it seemed to Lionel Lacey to be a sign from God that his dream was destined to come true.

By the end of the twenties, however, he had come to realise how wrong he had been. James, at twelve, showed absolutely no interest whatsoever in the family business. Conversely, the boy had apparently inherited all his mother's musical genes. He was considered by his music teacher to be astonishingly advanced for his years and without doubt headed for a career as a concert pianist.

On the other hand, Jennifer, the first-born, a girl, had blossomed not only into beautiful womanhood, but also into a natural shopkeeper. Customers warmed to her brilliant smile, and she thrived on the boring but necessary day-to-day tasks of stocktaking and replenishing the shelves with the many items required for a dispensary and the sales counters. In addition, she had earned a first-class degree in pharmacy. It would be she that would take the reins in due course.

After a year or two of watching Jennifer and Daphne more or less running the day-to-day business, Lacey decided the time had come to expand beyond the Highgate premises. He was forty-eight years old; he had reached the point in his life when he felt the need to end the drudgery of being tied to the dispensary for six days each week.

He intended to actively seek, within the next couple of years, a second site in a nearby borough where he could install Jennifer as manageress. Then he would promote Daphne to become the senior pharmacist at Highgate, thus freeing himself to oversee both businesses without being tied to either dispensary.

Only then would he be able to enjoy the luxury of slowly reducing his working hours. He would have more time to sit with his wife Sarah, listening to his son playing the piano. He would have more time to listen to his wireless and to play his treasured records on his old Decca gramophone, with a glass of Jameson's in his hand. Or perhaps he would splash out for one of those new radiograms?

Perhaps, then, the horrific memories of his years in France, of the blood and the mindless slaughter, memories he had habitually used the Irish spirit to mask, would at last recede.

* * *

Daphne unwrapped the soggy contents from its newspaper outer and sighed. "When will you remember not to put vinegar on the chips in the shop, Bobby?"

Margret finished slicing and buttering a loaf of bread before handing plates out one at a time for Daphne to apportion the food for the four card players. "That's men for you, Daphne. You should know by now that you can't trust them for anything important!"

"Oh, I know! But really, Bobby, bless him, tries so hard to please that I try to overlook these little mishaps."

"You're too damn soft for your own good! I would squash him!"

"Yes, I'm sure you would! But we are very different people, Margret. I prefer to deal with it in my own way. I shall get my message across in due course, rest assured!"

Margret laughed. She placed her freshly re-filled wine goblet on a tray with two plates of cod and chips.

"Well, it all goes down with a bottle or two, anyway, I don't suppose we shall notice the difference!"

"I suppose." Daphne agreed with a non-committal smile.

They carried the food into the dining room, where two hungry men awaited them at the table.

"That smells g-greaat!" said Bobby with a big grin.

Charlie, moving quickly to the door, said, "I'll fetch some more beer, we seem to have emptied that one. Can I get you another gin, Daphne?" he asked.

"No, thank you, Charlie. I've made some tea. It's under the cosy in the kitchen."

Charlie vanished and returned with a large bottle of brown ale. They settled down to eat.

"It seems a long time since we d-did this. I've m-missed it!" said Bobby, swallowing a mouthful of chips.

Charlie nodded, a quizzical expression on his face.

"I suppose we've all been busy," said Margret, "I certainly have. Charlie and I have hardly seen each other since Christmas. I have been either in town or away most weekends this winter, but I expect Jennifer would have told you that, Daphne. She told me how busy you have all been at Highgate."

"She may have mentioned it at some time, I don't remember, but we have been extra busy. We have taken on another assistant. Mr Lacey spends a lot of time away from the pharmacy now that Jen and I can cope. I think he is planning some new venture but he has not said anything yet. We shall have to wait and see."

* * *

The year 1933 ended sadly for the Collick family with the death of Stephen's uncle, Major-General Sir Arthur Collick, at the age of eighty-five. The distinguished man had been in poor health for a few years, and his passing was not unexpected; but it was nevertheless met by Stephen with considerable distress.

Sir Arthur had been, in his nephew's eyes, the backbone of the Collick family, and throughout Stephen's life, the old major-general had been the only Collick to show him any real affection. When his mother had refused to live any longer under the same roof as his father, it had been Sir Arthur who had attempted to calm the waters. He had visited her and had listened to her; and he had walked across the estate's fields with young Stephen, talking about history and life.

When Stephen had graduated at university, it had been Sir Arthur who had seen in him the ability and who had guided him in gaining the experience, to be able to control the family's vast commercial interests. The two bachelors had remained close to the very end.

For Millie Stoker, the death of Sir Arthur brought mixed memories. She remembered the austere, moustached gentleman to whom she had first been introduced by Charles at the printworks' annual ball, and she recalled him in his late seventies, in full military dress at Charles's memorial service. These were warm memories, but she also remembered that it was Sir Arthur who had encouraged Charles to join the Royal Flying Corps. Unreasonable though she knew it was, no matter how hard she tried, she could never quite forgive that.

Chapter Eight
Rousing the Rabble

Astride his Velocette KSS, a woollen scarf around his neck and goggles tight on his face against the wet wind of a chilly spring morning in 1934, Charlie Stoker was a much more worldly-wise man than the novice who had first become a tallyman only two years earlier.

1933 had been a turbulent year for most of the civilised world, with unemployment levels at their highest ever. By 1934, the numbers of unemployed were at last beginning to drop, but it was quite clear to all newspaper readers that the three great powers were dealing with the problem in completely different ways.

In America, President Roosevelt had ended prohibition and injected a huge volume of money into the economy to ensure that his 'new deal' created better working conditions, and more employment opportunities for millions of people. There was an atmosphere of optimism.

In Germany, Hitler and his Nazis were ruthlessly quelling all opposition to their newly established one party National Socialist state. Anyone considered to be not of 'pure Aryan blood' was in danger of being arrested, beaten up, sent to a concentration camp, or even summarily executed. The driving force was anti-Semitism, but in the firing line along with Jews were the physically or mentally disadvantaged, Romanies, anybody whom the Führer's bloodhounds considered of inferior blood, and, often, simply anyone displaying an opposing political view.

The menacing atmosphere was causing a frightening exodus from the country. Many were fleeing to the USA and some to Great Britain, where on the whole they were welcomed compassionately. Sadly, though, there were a considerable number of people in these islands who seemed to see merit in many of Hitler's ideas – an attitude influenced by the apparent success of Mussolini's Fascism in Italy. In fact, just a month or two earlier, Oswald Mosley had held a rally in Birmingham for his British Union of Fascists. It was attended by ten thousand people, including nearly three thousand members of the B.U.F. Some among them wore the new B.U.F. uniform of black shirt and leather belt – this copied from the Italians.

The significance of Mosley and his ideas had been a subject for discussion over lunch at Amhurst Road at the end of February. Charlie and Margret had joined Millie Stoker and Stephen Collick on the occasion of Millie's forty-fifth birthday.

Margret had introduced the subject, suggesting that, in the opinion of a number of the economists at the London School of Economics, the economic programme proposed by Mosley was sound. His book, '*A Greater Britain*' had been compulsive reading among many of her colleagues and she herself had been impressed by it.

Having completed two years as a research assistant, Margret now held a position as a junior lecturer in economics. She still maintained, in her conversations with Charlie, that she really wanted to teach mathematics, but she had felt unable to turn down the offered position, a two-year placement.

"Are you saying, Margret, that you believe this Fascist movement has a future in this country?" queried Millie. "Do you really believe that black-shirted militias are a good thing, a thing to be encouraged in England?"

"No, of course not! But I don't consider the uniform to be significant. It is the economic argument that I find appealing. The idea of a corporate state uniting workers and leaders in a massive movement for growth."

"Under Mosley? I don't think that would be very wise," interposed Stephen. He sipped his wine and patted his mouth with his napkin. "He certainly has a most persuasive tongue, and is no doubt a clever devil; but politically he has never been a man to be trusted, has he? He's been Conservative, Independent, Labour, and Fascist, all in a dozen years! I remember being struck by something he wrote, I think it was something like '*Among Conservatives there are many who are attracted by the Party's tradition of loyalty, order and stability, but who are, none the less, repelled by its lethargy and stagnation.*' I agree, but surely, the answer is to work to eradicate that lethargy and stagnation from within the party and the democratic system. Setting up a one-party state must be anathema to all free thinking men."

Margret laughed unexpectedly.

"You've read the book! I forgot, you are an economist as well as a businessman, Stephen. But you must admit he makes a powerful economic argument."

"Powerful, certainly, but tasteless, I think. What does the man in the street think, Charlie?"

Charlie shrugged.

"From what I see," he replied, "they fall into three groups. On one side, there are the communists and their admirers, dreaming of a worker-controlled state and trying to create chaos in our democracy. On the other side are the black-shirted layabouts, the ones with chips on their shoulders; the ones who are easily bought; who always think the grass is greener in the next field. They hate the commies with their up the workers cries, so they rush to join the fascists – so long as there is easy money there. In between are most of the population, people who keep their heads down and hope that others, the ones in authority, will do the right thing."

"Charlie!" Millie was shocked. "You're becoming a cynic!"

Charlie shrugged. Margret said: "Obviously, some of me is rubbing off onto him."

* * *

Charlie had always been a quick learner. He soon realised, seeing the ruthlessness of the competition and the gullibility of many of his customers, it was sometimes necessary to use imaginative methods to retain and build his customer base. He asked questions in the right places and learned well from the answers, with the result that twenty-four months into his tallyman's career he was in control of a business nearly twice the size of the one he had inherited. He was now collecting in the region of £50 per week from his customers.

This dramatic success meant that he was now regarded by Ivor Spafford, his supervisor, as a prized possession. On Thursdays, he was held up by Aitch Harrington as a model for all salesmen to emulate: "If young Charlie can do it, you can all do it!" the sales manager declaimed each week from his position on the raised dais at the front of the salesmen's room.

A not unnatural consequence of this recognition was that the majority of salesmen had come to treat Charlie more and more with a certain amount of reserve. In the case of the more open-minded and a number of the newer men, this was coupled with admiration and respect – which his physical presence tended to attract at all times regardless; but there was, equally, a small number in whom jealousy had imbued a sense of grievance or antagonism.

There was also a third group, the group in which Charlie now found himself, the elite group of salesmen quite unaffected by his performance. These were the half-dozen or so top men, men who had themselves experienced that same adulation and who set the targets for others to chase. These were the men Charlie found to be the most likeable of all: chaps like Horace Darbyshire, Walter Habisch and Jack Grieve; men free of the anxiety of possible failure but at all times earnest and conscientious in their weekly planning and operation.

His own weekly routine had not changed a great deal. He had increased his total customer base by about fifteen percent, but that added up to no more than half a dozen extra calls on any day. Greater growth had come from his original customers. A number of homes that had held one or two books now had three, four, or even five as more family members were discovered, or teenagers had grown to become wage earners.

Such a case was the Cutter family. Mr and Mrs Cutter lived in a terrace house in Armagh Road, Bow. Mr Cutter was an assistant to the buyer at a local timber company and Mrs Cutter was a pleasant woman of about Charlie's mother's age with whom he enjoyed a cup of tea and a toasted crumpet on Tuesday mornings. That was until it became necessary to change his calling time to 1.00 pm in order to catch the individual family members on their lunch hours. From that time onwards, Charlie was invited to lunch.

The Cutters had two daughters, Cecilia, known as Cissie, aged twenty-one, who was a clerk at Lewis Berger's paint factory at Homerton, and Sarah, known as Sally, who had been only fifteen years of age when Charlie first saw her, a slight, shy girl with striking blonde hair. She was employed as a junior assistant at the clothing factory in Mare Street.

When he had first known the family, there was just one account book in the house. Mrs Cutter had paid one shilling per week without ever missing a payment. By the middle of 1934, however, there were four separate accounts paying a total of twelve shillings and sixpence per week. The main family weekly book was now worth five shillings. Mr Cutter, very conscious of his position as a white-collar worker, kept his own clothing account on which he paid a florin per week. Cissie paid four shillings – she was hoping to marry the following year and her boyfriend, a young shop assistant named Harry Bateson, was paying half of her account. They were building a credit balance for when they should need it – a sort of bottom drawer to be! Then, when Sally turned eighteen in June of 1934, Charlie was pleased to open an account for her for another one and sixpence per week.

Charlie had not seen Sally since before her sixteenth birthday – she had always remained at the factory for her lunch. When, aged eighteen, she suddenly appeared at the house one Tuesday, he received an enormous shock. The person he saw now was not the shy, slightly built girl he remembered, but a quite astonishingly beautiful young woman with golden blonde hair and big blue eyes. With much of her shyness gone, Sally greeted him with a broad, open smile that showed how pleased she was to see him again.

Charlie had always considered Jennifer Lacey to be one of the most beautiful women he had ever seen, certainly the most stunningly beautiful person of his own acquaintance; but Sally Cutter had an extra dimension. It was quite extraordinary. Her beauty was every bit a match for Jennifer's, but there was something more. There was a glow about Sally: she exuded an aura of warmth, of humanity, and – and this was what caused Charlie's shock – of desirability.

Sally only stayed for about fifteen minutes on that occasion before rushing back to work, but in those fifteen minutes she created turmoil in the tallyman's mind. He left the house soon after and moved on to the rest of his day's work without ever quite getting Sally Cutter out of his head.

He rode back to Chigwell, completed his bookwork and made his supper, accompanying his lamb chop and chips with a bottle of brown ale. Charlie was a man of exceptional self-discipline. On working nights, the bottle of ale was all he allowed himself. On this night, though, having cleared up the kitchen, he poured himself a large whisky and dropped heavily into his favourite armchair. He needed to think.

He had learned well from his parents and had trained himself to live by a set of rules, of standards that others might find restrictive but which to him were comfortable. He enjoyed drinking but avoided excessive bouts. He enjoyed being with people but was equally content with his own company. He knew he was attractive to women but he never felt tempted to stray. He was a married man and that was that. That he lived in a sterile marriage was a strictly private matter, never to be discussed, not even with his mother.

He was quite untroubled by the celibate life he had chosen. He experienced no sexual urge in his day-to-day life because he did not allow himself to contemplate it. Deep within him, there still burned the forlorn hope that Margret would change her mind and would give him a child; but his rational brain told him she had no interest and would never have any interest in giving birth.

He sipped the whisky and lit another cigarette. Not for the first time, he reflected that most of his life had been an exercise in self-control. Rarely, had he felt that self-control to be under threat. He did not allow himself to feel really tested. That is, he had not before this day, before he saw Sally Cutter.

Concentrating on his burning cigarette and blowing concentric smoke rings, he resolved to put her from his mind; but the picture of her sudden, stunning appearance could not be wiped from his head. She had knocked him so off balance! He, casual, detached Charlie Stoker, with his shrugs and grins, always in control of every situation; he had been completely discombobulated by the smile of this 18-year-old blonde.

* * *

The following evening, Wednesday, Charlie swam with Bobby as usual. The blonde image still lingered in the back of his mind.

"W-what is it, Charlie? You've got something on your mind, I can tell."

"No, I'm alright, just a bit tired."

Bobby stared across the table at his friend. They had enjoyed a good swim and were now relaxing with a couple of pints of ale. He took a mouthful.

"Charlie, this is me, B-Bobby. We've been mates now for six y-years and I know you. Something's wrong. S-something's worrying you."

Charlie opened his cigarette case and proffered it. Bobby took one and they both lit up. Charlie blew a huge cloud of smoke above his head. He shrugged.

"No, I'm okay, honest, Bobby. It's just something happened yesterday that I can't seem to get out of my head."

Bobby took another mouthful of ale. He did not speak but held Charlie's eye determinedly across the table. There was silence until Bobby couldn't bear it any longer.

"W-well, go on!" he said, exasperated.

Charlie laughed. He said:

"It's nothing, mate, really. I saw a girl yesterday I hadn't seen for a couple of years, and when she walked in, she took my breath away. I can't forget the sight and the shock it gave me when she smiled at me. You know, the change in two years. She was a skinny shy teenager the last time I saw her. Now, she's absolutely beautiful. I mean it. It made me blink. I've never seen anyone who affected me like that, ever." He shook his head. "You know me and girls, Bobby. I can take it or leave it. I don't get excited about women, any women."

Bobby duly acknowledged the fact.

"Yeah. You're always so r-relaxed about everything. That's why I could tell you had s-something on your mind."

"Well, I shall have settled down before next Tuesday, you can be sure. It won't be a surprise the second time! Anyway, enough about me, how's life at Harringay?"

Bobby sighed. "W-we're doing okay. The work's c-coming in pretty well now, and Daph's busy as ever as well. Old Lacey is planning a new place, I think she said s-somewhere in Southgate. J-Jennifer will run it and Daph will be running Highgate under the old man."

He scratched his head. "Everything's changing, Charlie, isn't it? The world's changing. Daph's dad was going on the other night about M-Mosley and his Blackshirts. He said Mosley's trying to bring fascism to England like Hitler with his Nazis in Germany and M-Mussolini in Italy. It c-couldn't happen, could it Charlie?"

Charlie shrugged. "Yeah, it could, Bobby, but it won't, not here. There have always been troublemakers who achieve popularity for a while, but they get more publicity than they get real support. The rump of our country believes in democracy and the Empire. As a nation with responsibilities all over the world, we always do our best to act with honour and to honour our commitments. The people of this country won't be swayed by rabble rousers, whether fascist or communist."

Bobby wiped his glasses. "I expect you're right. You always seem to have th-thought things out better than me. I think the thing D-Daph's dad worries about, though, is the constant g-going on about immigrant J-ews, the anti-s-semitism. He says it rubs off on people; he s-says he sees it at work a lot now, people making sly comments and inn-nuendos that they didn't do in the p-ast."

Charlie shrugged. He crushed out his cigarette.

"Yeah, that's what I meant. That's the rabble being roused."

* * *

Lionel Lacey had owned a small Austin car for a few years, but late in 1933, he had exchanged it for a Wolseley Hornet four-door saloon. The new vehicle was, he felt, one that would comfortably serve a dual purpose. Fitted with the new synchromesh gearbox on all but first gear, the Hornet was an up-to-the-minute, finely engineered vehicle that would comfortably carry the Lacey family on holidays or outings; but it would also enable him to transfer stock and equipment between Highgate and the new pharmacy he planned to open.

In the spring of 1934, with a tip-off from a member of his Freemasons' Lodge, he found exactly what he was looking for. Just being completed was a small development of a block of flats above a parade of new shops opposite the newly opened London Underground station at Bounds Green. Local planning demanded that one of the premises be filled by a chemist's shop with a pharmacy. Recognising that the tube station was sure to become a focal point for the growing number of residents in the area, Lacey eagerly met that demand. The site lay only a little more than three miles from Highgate Hill, near enough to be serviced but far enough to have a different customer base.

Thus, September brought a dramatic development in the life of Jennifer Lacey. Her father's plans for the business were finally put into effect and Jennifer found herself in complete charge of Lacey's Chemist, Bounds Green. Of perhaps even greater significance was the fact that, at twenty-four years of age she also became the owner of her own home. The flat above the shop was more than adequate for one person, having two reception rooms, two bedrooms, a kitchen and a bathroom.

Margret visited her friend as soon as she moved in to give the building her nod of approval. Because of the size, Jennifer explained, she had briefly considered inviting someone to share it with her; but the thought of sharing her home with a stranger or one of her staff was not something she was prepared for. She would leave one bedroom empty until it suited her to furnish it, she thought.

Margret firmly approved of that.

Chapter Nine
A Crack in the Façade

"I don't think I shall apply for another position at L.S.E. when my two years are up next summer."

Margret and Charlie were relaxing with coffee and newspapers on the rear patio at 8 Woodside Way. It was a beautiful Sunday morning late in September at the end of a summer of unpredictable weather. It was also the first weekend in over a month that Margret had remained in Chigwell with her husband.

Margret's relationship with her father and brothers remained as icily hostile as ever. The young couple had attended a few Sunday lunches at Clay Hill during the three-year period but for the most part, they were happy to keep their distance from Enfield. Indeed, Charlie had rarely seen any of the Mabeys since the move to Chigwell. Margret had maintained regular contact with her mother by visits when the men were all away or, more often, by telephone and occasional meetings for afternoon tea at Lyon's Corner House, near her college.

Life as an academic suited Margret well. She had already made a strong impression on both students and staff at the college. Her exceptional intellectual qualities had earned her much respect, and her sharp, intolerant manner had created instant enemies. Her self-confidence irritated a number of people, but most learned quickly that it was wiser to avoid argument with Mrs Stoker. Arguments caused only pain, and that, invariably, to the other person.

Aware of this, Charlie found her statement surprising. Nevertheless, knowing Margret as he did, he allowed himself just a quizzical smile.

"Well? Ask me why!" Her tone demanded a reply.

Charlie shrugged and drew on his cigarette. "You'll tell me when you are ready," he said. He blew a smoke ring.

"You are so bloody infuriating, Charlie. You will never rise to the bait. We have been married for four years and you *never* (she spat the word) rise to the bait!"

Charlie let her words hang in the air before replying.

"Is that what you really want? Me to rise to your bait? Like your family?"

"Touché!" She was immediately conciliatory. "No, not really. I love what makes you different from other men. You are quite remarkable in your self-control, your restraint, but I know that's why this works. The truth is I am a loner, Charlie. You know that, but then, so are you. We are a couple of loners, a couple of oddities, each with much to give to the world but without the wherewithal to live comfortably within it."

Charlie put out his cigarette, crushing it with care into the heavy ashtray on the table between them.

"I'm not sure I agree with that," he said deliberately. "We are living the life we agreed upon. It is not the life either of us would have chosen but it is what we had to do. So far, it's worked well. We have both achieved all we could have hoped for in four years. Perhaps we have reached the point when we have to make new decisions. Tell me, why do you want to leave L.S.E.?"

Margret did not reply at once. She emptied her coffee cup and placed it back on its saucer. She sat, staring down the garden. Eventually, she said:

"I have lived and breathed that place for six years, next year will make seven. That's nearly a third of my life. I need to get out, Big Boy. I feel cloistered. I want there to be more to life than those walls. I want to experience some of the wide world everyone at the college jabbers about. I think I may apply for a position at a French university."

Charlie nodded.

"That's an interesting idea. I should think it would be a good experience, but hardly one we could share. I'm rather stuck here for a number of years."

"Yes, I know."

She spoke quickly, continuing to stare ahead. "But it's not as if we are really living together here, is it? I only see the place the odd weekend, and then you are away all-day Saturday. It's what I just said. We're a couple of loners."

"No. I am not really a loner, Marg. Yes, I can cope. I can probably cope better than many people, but I should prefer a more conventional life. I should be quite happy to do as others do. I should like to have children and watch them grow up."

"Oh God, no! I can't do that, Charlie."

She turned to look at him. "You know I can never go through that again. You know! Yes, I used to like romping, but that pregnancy killed any inclination I may have had to enjoy sex. I freeze up inside at the very thought of it. I know it's hard on you, but the situation will never change."

She picked up Charlie's cigarette case and took a cigarette, leaning across the table for him to light it for her. She inhaled deeply and let the smoke roll out.

"Charlie, you know if you feel the need for sex, you don't have to feel guilty about it. I don't care with whom or how often you satisfy yourself. I don't want to lose you as a partner, as a friend. You are the only man for whom I have ever felt respect – and, I suppose, what is as near as I can get to love. You deserve better, Charlie, I'm sorry."

Charlie lit another cigarette, blowing smoke rings in the sultry air to avoid seeing the tears on his wife's cheeks. Minutes passed before he spoke again.

"If you want to spend a year in France, I see no reason why you shouldn't," he said in a level tone. "I think you should find it very rewarding. I should expect lots of letters and a good sprinkling of postcards, but I'll get by. I don't know how Jennifer would react to not seeing you every Wednesday, though?"

Margret looked up sharply, but read nothing in her husband's face beyond the simple question. She relaxed.

"My poor little pearl will have her work cut out looking after Lacey's Chemists. In any case, we are talking about a year from now."

"Yes, we are," said Charlie. He shrugged.

* * *

Stephen Collick led an active business life but he treasured the peace and quiet of his home and the contentment of time spent with Millie Stoker. When he had first asked Millie to act as his consort whenever he should entertain guests at Parklands, he either called for her himself or sent his chauffeur to collect her, and then, when all the guests had left, she would be taken back to Amhurst Road. After a number of late-night trips, however, Stephen persuaded Millie to remain at the house for the weekend on such occasions.

Millie enjoyed her weekends at Parklands. The guests entertained were mostly long-time business associates. Stephen maintained the loosest possible links with his family and with Collick family friends, but was obliged at certain times to include them in his invitations. He always encouraged lively after dinner conversation and she found some of the guests fascinating to listen to.

Sir René Laverton was unfortunately not one of them. The Lavertons, whose estate was quite nearby at Epping Green, owned a shipping company of which the Collicks, with their international trading needs, were major customers.

Lieutenant Colonel Sir René Laverton was about four years younger than Stephen, and the two men had been acquainted since school days. Laverton's parents had had dealings with Lord Collick and had been friends of Stephen's mother. Sir René had worked hard to maintain cordial relations with Stephen and over time, their relationship had become comfortable despite the difference in their characters. René Laverton was a hard-drinker and a notorious philanderer, corpulent, with a large nose and florid complexion. He was, indeed, everything that Stephen Collick was not. Although still a serving officer, Laverton planned to go into politics on his retirement from the army the following year.

Having witnessed the man's behaviour on a number of occasions, Millie asked Stephen how the two had become friends.

"You may well ask, Millie dear, but the truth is that regardless of the impression he invariably creates, René Laverton is an honourable man. That is to say, he is an honourable man in business. His word is his bond. Socially, I realise he can be irritating. He is unable to resist the temptation to drink, and drink makes him loud, tactless and often boorish. He also has a reputation for embarrassing the opposite sex with unwanted advances, but I must say I have never witnessed any behaviour of that sort. Incidentally, you may have heard, my dear, he is due to finish his army career next year. He intends to become a member of parliament. I think he will be well suited to that particular environment. Drinking and shouting are prerequisites for success."

"Stephen! That's not like you. I have never heard you utter such a comment!"

Stephen chuckled. "Perhaps I have known René too long. The truth is, he's harmless, a bit of a chump but a loyal friend; and I have had few of those in my life."

Millie smiled but said no more. Stephen poked the lone remaining log on the dying fire in the drawing room's stone fireplace. The room was still warm, the panelled wooden walls seeming to act as convection heaters, recycling the heat they had absorbed from the now dying fire. Stephen said:

"You know, Millie, you and I get along awfully well, don't we?"

She gave a little laugh. "Yes, I suppose we sort of fill a void for each other, don't we?"

He replaced the poker on its stand and raised his head, his mouth slightly open, before replying:

"Yes, we do. We make a good pair."

He paused again briefly, then said: "Do you think we should make it a permanent pair?"

"Permanent? Do you mean…?"

This time it was Millie whose mouth opened.

"Yes. I do. Would you consider being my wife, Millie?"

Millie sat for a moment, stunned. She fiddled with the sleeve of her dress as she absorbed the enormity of his words; but her reply, when it came, was from the rational core of Millie Cowper.

"Oh, Stephen dear, no. It would be an honour and a privilege to be the wife of Stephen Collick and I should very much like to say yes here and now; but I have a strong feeling deep inside that it would not be the right decision. Our relationship is a good one and I think it is strong. Let that continue and let us continue to enjoy it."

Millie rose on tiptoe to kiss, for the second time in her life, the cheek of the baron's son.

"You are a perfect and noble gentleman, Stephen. I am privileged to have you as my very best friend."

Stephen pulled her close and kissed her forehead.

"And I you, Millie Stoker," he said softly, "and I you."

* * *

By the spring of 1935, Charlie was established as one of the high earners of Aitch Harrington's sales force. He had been a salesman-collector for three years and now serviced four hundred accounts in the two hundred homes he called upon each week, producing in the region of sixty pounds per week in collections. Round three had become a profitable source of income for Collick's.

More significantly for the young man himself, Charlie was happy. He was twenty-four years of age, a physical presence in any company and a true friend to all who knew him. He loved his work and looked forward to each day. Now earning between five and six pounds per week, at least twice as much as most of the staff of Collick's and considerably more than most of his customers, his income was enough to more than meet his needs. But it was not the income that made Charlie happy. For the first time in his life, he felt fulfilled. He was standing on his own two feet, earning his own keep and making his own decisions.

His marriage, the one aspect of his life that might appear to an observer to be problematical, Charlie no longer regarded as such. He and Margret both used the name Stoker; they shared a name, a house and a few social engagements. In law, they were married, and they respected the law. The law did not concern itself with the sterility of a marriage.

In the six months since their conversation in the garden of Woodside Way, the young Stokers had simply gone their own ways. They remained friends but lived separate lives. The façade of a healthy marriage was easily maintained in public, and it was accepted without comment at both Amhurst Road and Clay Hill.

Indeed, the only thing troubling Charlie Stoker when he stopped the Velocette in Armagh Road on Tuesdays was the unease that had been affecting him for some time when visiting the Cutters. Mr and Mrs Cutler were warm, affectionate people and they recognised the fine qualities of the young man from Collick's. He was welcomed into the house almost as a respected member of the family, and he relished that acceptance. He appreciated their attitude and responded to it.

His problem lay not with Mr and Mrs Cutter. He was comfortable in their company and enjoyed a hearty lunch with them each week. Their elder daughter Cissie had married and moved out a couple of months earlier and lunch was now served for just four people. Charlie's unease stemmed from the feelings aroused in him by the close physical presence of the fourth person, their daughter Sally.

Charlie's defences against all emotional involvement were smiles, shrugs and cigarettes. They formed a wall behind which he was at ease, in control; behind which he could safely calculate every move he made. It was a wall that had been penetrated very rarely in his life, the one significant occasion being when he had visited his mother while Margret was suffering in the cottage hospital. As for sexual arousal, other than his alcohol-stimulated discovery of romping with Margret, he had never really been bothered.

In Sally's company, however, Charlie sensed a desperate need to bolster his defences. His wall was in danger of crumbling. He trembled at the knees but fought to control his feelings and to appear his usual self. He remembered Margret's words, *'I don't care with whom or how often you satisfy yourself'* but was aware that what was growing within him was not a mere need to satisfy himself. That would be a sensation he had no difficulty in dealing with. What he felt at Armagh Road was a hunger to be with and to properly know this beautiful creature.

He realised that he must mask the problem well, because no one in the family ever appeared to notice anything. He kept telling himself that he would soon regain control of his feelings and re-establish his customary emotional balance. Nevertheless, for several weeks he called and suffered. The situation resolved itself each week when Sally rushed back to work while Charlie finished dealing with the family accounts.

Of course, the matter had to come to a head, and so it did on a fine day at the end of May. Instead of rushing out as usual, Sally asked Charlie, as he devoured a large bowl of Mrs Cutter's apple crumble and custard:

"Which way are you going when you leave here today, Charlie?"

"That depends," replied Charlie with a quizzical smile. "Why do you ask?"

Sally was still working at the clothing factory, where she had obviously made her mark. Recently, she had been appointed as the office clerk in the dispatch department.

"I've got to deliver a packet of cloth swatches to the chief buyer of Hepwoods Stores this afternoon," she explained. "Seems they have to be there today and the transport manager thought the best way to do it was to send me. I can go by tube from Bow Road station, and if you're going by there, you could maybe drop me off. I'd love to have a go on that motorbike of yours."

"Sally, you cheeky thing!" exclaimed Mrs Cutter. "And, anyway, you can't go on a motorbike in that dress."

Sally was wearing a floral afternoon dress of blue rayon with a fashionable belted waist and calf-length fullish skirt. It was ideal for a business call.

"Yes, I can, Mum. I'll wear my long raincoat over the top. I can hoick up my dress and wrap the coat over my legs."

"But you're taking advantage of Charlie's good nature."

"No, she's not, Mrs Cutter," interposed Charlie quickly. "It's a pleasure to help any of my customers any time I can. I've got plenty of time on Tuesdays so I can give Sally a lift to wherever she wants to go."

"Charlie, you are too good. You deserve to do well. Would you like a bit more crumble? There's some left."

"No thanks, Mrs C, that was delicious but I can't afford to fall asleep during the afternoon!"

The meal ended, Mr Cutter left for his office and his wife and daughter took the dishes into the kitchen while Charlie made his book entries. When he had finished, he gathered his book and his case, lit a cigarette and called out to the ladies.

"I'm off now, Mrs Cutter. Ready, Sally?"

"Ready when you are, Charlie Stoker!" replied Sally, appearing rapidly from the kitchen like an eager child anticipating a treat. "Let's go."

They went out of the house together and Charlie carefully placed his case and book in the oak sidecar.

"Where exactly is the buyer's office, Sally?" he asked. "I may be able to drop you somewhere nearer. I'm okay for time."

"It's a long way, Charlie, in Chalk Farm Road over Camden way. Bow Road station'll be alright, thanks."

"How long will it take you?"

"About an hour each way. It's a bit fiddly on the tube."

"That's ridiculous! It'll be nearly six o'clock before you get back."

"Yeah, I know, but bein' out's more fun than bein' in the office."

"I can take you to Chalk Farm," said Charlie, shrugging, a light in his eyes. "We'll be there and back in an hour. You can deliver your parcel, we can have a cup of tea and a chat, and we'll still be back by four!"

"Ooh, Charlie, can we really? I've been dying to have a ride on this." She caressed the polished sidecar.

"You can sit in there if you want to, but it would be a bit hard on your rear, and you'd have to hold the lid out of your way. It's better on the pillion, but you'll have to hold on to me."

"Ooh, that's good!" Sally burst out laughing.

Charlie crushed his cigarette out on the kerb and exhaled a cloud of smoke before mounting the Velocette. Sally settled herself behind him, discreetly hitching up her dress and adjusting her coat around her legs.

As soon as they moved off Sally wrapped her arms tightly around Charlie's waist. To Charlie, it was like receiving an electric shock. A married man of upright principles, the emotions stirred in him by the woman whose arms were around his waist were not such as might lead to any casual relief. Rather, they could lead him to disaster. As he concentrated on heading for Chalk Farm Road, his rational Stoker brain warned him that what he was really heading for was trouble.

Chapter Ten
Sally

By 1935, while those parts of the country dependent upon the established heavy industries continued to suffer from the many years of depression, the situation in the south, six years on from the disaster of Wall Street, had been greatly relieved. Government measures had stimulated the creation of thousands of new homes, and transport links had greatly improved. The economy was beginning to prosper from the rapid growth of the motor car industry and other consumer led industries such as electrical appliances.

This economic upturn made Charlie Stoker's job a little more rewarding. More employment for the people of London meant more cash available for Collick's customers. Now an established and successful salesman-collector, Charlie's weekly wage had reached a level that made the acquisition of a motor car a sensible proposition.

Much as Charlie loved his Velocette, he realised that a car would be far more suitable for his work. It would enable him to carry passengers, and as he explained to Bobby over a post-swim pint, to transport customers to and from the store.

"Yeah, I s-s'pose you're right," acknowledged Bobby, "but driving a m-motorcar's nothing like riding a b-ike. S-sitting inside a b-box like that's not in the same world as riding a bike, is it? There's no f-eel to it, is there? No fresh wind blowin' through your hair, no body swerve when you take a corner – you know what I mean!"

"Yes, I know what you mean, Bobby, and I think you're right. I'd miss the bike, but I wouldn't lose it, would I? I should still use it whenever I could, just not for work or when I'm with people."

"I s'pose so. A motor car would certainly be more ff-itting for your job. It's not like it is for me. My machine's an advert for my b-business."

Charlie shrugged. "Yeah. Even you'll have to think about it when Daphne decides she wants a family."

He opened his cigarette case and proffered it. They both lit up.

Bobby said: "We won't be starting any ff-amily yet for a few years. We're s-saving for a place of our own first."

Charlie nodded, and shrugged again.

"You'll get there, all in good time."

"Yeah, could be." Bobby emptied his glass. He grinned mischievously.

"Anyway, why now? Would t-taking that pretty blonde to Chalk Farm have anything to do with you suddenly wanting a m-motor car?"

"Now, now, Bobby, you know better than that!"

Charlie had a twinkle in his eyes. He turned away to blow three perfect smoke rings.

"I know that you've mentioned her every week this m-month!" retorted Bobby.

"That's just coincidence. You know me and women, Bobby. I can take it or leave it. Have another?"

"One more."

Bobby removed his glasses and studiously polished them while Charlie collected two pints of ale from the bar. Carefully replacing his lenses, he said, soberly:

"Ch-changing the subject, Charlie, I read a few weeks ago the g-government's ordered a load of new airplanes for the RAF. They say it's in r-response to Germany's m-massive re-armament programme. Th-they're not seriously getting ready for another war, are they Charlie? Surely, n-no one wants that?"

"No, nobody wants that. But I suppose the country has to be prepared for anything. Nobody wanted a war in 1914 but it happened. I don't think anyone in their right mind wants a war now, Bobby, but Mr Hitler is doing a lot of stamping and shouting in Europe. I'm glad we've ordered the planes."

"Da-aphne's dad says that Hitler won't rest till he's killed off all the Jews in Germany, and he says the next thing we'll know is that M-Mosley will be doing the same thing here."

Charlie shrugged.

"I don't know about Germany – they seem to like strutting about over there. I expect Hitler and his Nazis will quieten down eventually; and I don't think Mosley and his Blackshirts will come to anything here, any more than the Communists will. The people of this country will never allow extremists like them to take over."

He drank some ale, then placed his elbows on the table and rested his chin on his clasped hands.

"I'll tell you a funny thing though," he continued thoughtfully, "Margret's got Mosley's book, I think it's called 'Greater Britain' or something like that, and she read a bit to me about – I can't quote it exactly but what it was saying was that British politics was failing because the system itself made it almost impossible for governments to govern. It was calling for an authoritarian state that would be above party and sectional interests."

"Authoritarian? Well, that'd be like a s-sort of dictatorship, wouldn't it?"

"Politically, I suppose. We would still have the monarchy, of course. The king would still be on the throne. I think what Mosley was describing was a sort of political autocracy with him at the top of a one-party parliament. He certainly seems like a clever devil, and Margret reckons the academics at the London School of Economics all say he talks a lot of economic sense. His ideas could create employment for millions around the country by cutting imports and producing more of our own stuff."

Bobby thought about this for a minute.

"I-I don't know about the economics, but why does he need the rabble-rousing? The army of Bla-Blackshirts? And why attack Jews? They're de-ecent people trying to live their lives."

"I don't think she said anything about the uniforms or the salutes," conceded Charlie, "Mosley obviously thinks he can do here what Mussolini's done in Italy and Hitler's doing in Germany." He paused, and sat upright. "He's wrong. It won't happen. This is England."

* * *

Charlie had shrugged off Bobby's comments about 'the pretty blonde', but the truth was that Sally Cutter was still very much on his mind.

Charlie had been married to Margret Mabey for five years and had been celibate for four and a half of those years. Remarkably, his life of celibacy had not presented the young man with any serious problems. Even the temptations of Laura Matthews had not been enough to make him stray from what he believed to be the honourable path. The glamorous tall brunette had undoubtedly been attracted to him and had made efforts for some considerable time to spark reciprocation after he started work in the shoe department, but eventually she had become resigned to the fact that Charlie Stoker was both married and unavailable.

Fortunately, for Charlie, his upbringing at Amhurst Road had taught him how to hide his emotions. To all who encountered him, Charlie still appeared as big, untroubled Charlie; but from the day that 18-year-old Sally Cutter entered the dining room at Armagh Road, his nonchalant self-confidence had been troubled. After delivering the sample swatch that May afternoon, it had ceased to exist.

Job done, they had visited the local ABC Tea Rooms and enjoyed tea, scones and a long, if at first rather one-sided, chat. Sally, exhilarated by the experience of the ride, chattered non-stop about her work, the family, including her parents' health (her mother had undergone severe abdominal surgery a few years ago and her father had chest trouble), her newly married sister Cissie, and about her own experience of life to date.

As the afternoon progressed, however, she made it clear that she was completely smitten with Charlie Stoker. He, in turn, rather than experience his usual embarrassment in such circumstances, was strangely pleased. Instead of feeling the accustomed need to extricate himself from the situation, he wanted only to remain near this woman. He wanted the afternoon to go on for ever. For the very first time in his nearly twenty-five years, Charlie was conscious of powerful emotions foreign to him.

Sally's beauty was bewitching, from the flowing blonde hair to the big, sparkling eyes; from the openness of her smile to the full, inviting lips. But what shattered all his carefully built defences was the natural warmth she exuded; the instinct to welcome; the ability to lift the atmosphere of a room by her mere presence; and the power to stir feelings within him that he had not realised existed.

But Charlie was a married man and a Stoker. He would not allow such thoughts to prevail. His kindness in making the trip to Chalk Farm Road with Sally had firmly cemented his special status with the whole family. His relationship with the Cutters had become more than merely that of salesman and customer. They were friends with whom he lunched each Tuesday.

Although Thomas Cutter, like many customers, suggested that Charlie address him by his first name, it was a mark of the respect the salesman felt for Sally's parents that he always referred to them as Mr and Mrs Cutter, or sir and ma'am.

Sally's father was a man of few words, pale of complexion and plagued with a niggling cough for which he blamed the dust at work.

Originally from Norfolk, he had come to London seeking work as a young man. Now, he held a responsible position in the timber company for which he had worked since his release from the army in 1918. Thankfully, his income, although at first meagre, had proved just sufficient for him to establish, with the constant support of his wife Charlotte, a good home in a pleasant location to bring up the girls. They had hoped to have a family of four children, ideally two of each, but after producing two beautiful girls, they had been unaccountably unable to add a third child.

Sally's elder sister, Cissie, the recently wed Mrs Bateson, now lived with her husband Harry in a small flat in Bentley Road, in Dalston. Accordingly, in addition to the Tuesday call at Armagh Road, Charlie now also visited the Dalston address each Wednesday.

Harry Bateson was a sales assistant in a local drapery store. A quiet chap, slim of build and inoffensive, he was the sort of man soon lost in a crowd. Yet, on closer acquaintance, Harry would always be found to be a man one could rely on. His father had been killed at the Battle of the Somme, when he was just seven years old. He had thereafter been raised by a loving mother and her parents.

At twenty-one, he began to court Cissie Cutter. Now, four years later, they were married. Determined to have a place of their own, the flat was as much as they could afford. They hoped to start a family in time. Then they would have to consider their next move. His job was steady and secure, if without much prospect of improvement, but with Cissie still having her position at the paint factory they were able to save for the future.

Wednesday afternoon was Harry's half day and usually it was he who handed Charlie the books and cash, although the household business was controlled by Cissie. Cissie only reached home at about a quarter to five, so, whenever it was necessary to see her, Charlie popped back later. The call was only a few minutes from Amhurst Road, where for the last year or so he had taken a late lunch on Wednesdays, his easiest day. It meant he could clear up his week's bookwork and spend a few hours with his mother before his weekly swimming session with Bobby.

Harry and Charlie were the same age and had both been born in the area, although they had never met before Harry's marriage. They often chatted together, usually over a cup of tea, discussing important topics such as whether Harry's beloved Tottenham Hotspurs had had a good week, or what the merits were of the new film releases at the Empire.

On one afternoon at the end of July, the hot topic was the robbery at that same cinema on the previous Saturday. Harry was particularly interested in the matter, he explained eagerly to Charlie, because it was their local cinema – indeed, he and Cissie had been in that very cinema the night before the robbery to see the musical,

Naughty Marietta, with Jeanette MacDonald and Nelson Eddy. Lovely film! Apparently, the robbers had been caught as soon as they left the building with the box-office takings. He thought the police must have been given a tip-off. They had been waiting outside to pounce.

"Was anyone hurt?" asked Charlie. "And do we know who the robbers were? Were they local people?"

"I don't know. I heard that Cathie, the cashier, was injured and taken to hospital but I don't know any details. The Gazette doesn't come out until Friday and that'll be full of it. All I know is what I've heard in the shop."

"I expect I'll hear all about it on Friday or Saturday, then."

"Oh, yeah, once the paper's out." Harry nodded fiercely.

Two days later, Charlie called at 34 Barlow Street, the home of Wilf and Elsie Tattle (née Philpott). Now two years married, Elsie was the mother of a little boy and was very pregnant with her second child. Her short, plump body was extremely distended, but her eager smile was as quick as ever when she welcomed Charlie. She handed him two books and bade him sit in the front room to mark them up to date while she made him some tea.

It was apparent to Charlie, however, that she was agitated, and as soon as she came waddling back in with his tea and a biscuit, almost her first words were:

"What a terrible business that was at the cinema in Dalston last Saturday! We spent all day Sunday with Alice and the boys. She was in a terrible state!"

Charlie looked up with an inquiring frown.

"Alice? You mean Wilf's sister? The dark-haired girl I met here the other week?"

"Yeah! Ooh, hadn't you heard? It was her Bert what did it. He's in gaol!"

"Oh, Goodness! I'm sorry to hear that, Elsie. No, I had no idea. I heard that the robbers had been caught but not who they were. How long is he likely to be in gaol? Will Alice be alright?"

"We don' know yet. He's been remanded in custody with the other two. They're all to be tried for robbery with violence at the Quarter Sessions next month. I think Alice will be okay, she's tough. My Wilf always says he don't know why she wasted herself on that Bert. He thinks Bert's never been no good, but Alice won't hear a word against him."

"The loyal wife, eh?"

"Ooh, definitely. Bert Pensell's always been a drinker and a gambler. He's a bookie's runner, and he's always taking chances, dodgy deals and that sort of thing.

But there's never been nothing like this – bringing shame on his family. It's not as if there's any doubt, they were caught red-handed! Whatever next, eh, Charlie?"

"I don't know, Elsie, but it won't do you any good to get worked up about it in your condition, will it?"

Elsie heaved a big sigh. "No, Charlie, you're right."

She smiled. "D'you want some more tea?"

* * *

Out of consideration for Elsie's delicate physical condition, Charlie had refrained from pressing her for any further information about the robbery. Instead, he purchased a copy of the Hackney Gazette during his journey and carefully read the report before going to bed that night. If, as Elsie had implied, the culprits were all locals, he needed to know whether any of his customers were involved.

Charlie was gifted with an exceptionally good memory, especially for faces and names. This was of particular advantage when he was being introduced to various family members or meeting new potential customers; or when re-assessing someone not seen for a long time, perhaps an unreliable character who would have hoped he was not recognised.

The paper had published the names of the three men remanded in custody and none was a customer of Round 3. One of the names did cause a raised eyebrow however. Herbert Tebbin, the man who had been sent to gaol in 1932 for cooking the books and from whom Charlie had inherited Round three, was the second of the trio named. Tebbin was clearly a bad lot. He had obviously been one of the few that Aitch Harrington had got wrong.

The newspaper report stated that Albert Pensell, whose previous brushes with the law had been only for minor offences such as drunk and disorderly, appeared to be the leader of the gang; but it had been Tebbin who had been the violent one. Tebbin had attacked the cashier and knocked her down when he thought she was attempting to frustrate them. Charlie recalled Tebbin's surly expression at Collick's and with hindsight was not surprised. He had never liked the look of that man.

The third name, Michael MacCorrigan, meant nothing to Charlie but the report in the paper indicated that he also had a record. He had served short sentences for petty thieving. Charlie locked the name away in his memory.

He thought a little more about Elsie and the Tattle family before he fell asleep. Wilf and Elsie were a happy young couple. Wilf said very little and Elsie chattered constantly, and that arrangement seemed to suit both perfectly. Wilf's two sisters were contrasting figures. Alice was a handsome, strong-featured woman with a good mind and a fiery temper, although according to Elsie she had her hands full with Bert Pensell as a husband and two uncontrollably wild young boys.

Charlie had met Alice for the first time when she had visited Elsie earlier that summer. Both Alice and the third Tattle, Lucy Tinkwell, were customers of Walter Habisch but since Alice was a Friday customer and Charlie had only seen the Monday, Tuesday and Wednesday rounds they had not met when he was with Walter.

Lucy, however, was a Wednesday customer and Charlie had seen her just that once, on the Wednesday, three years ago. As he recollected that brief contact, she had resembled her brother Wilf in being quiet of nature; a rather shapeless young mother, plain of feature and fully occupied with a new baby. Now, Elsie had told him a few weeks ago, Lucy had already given birth to her third child.

He turned out the light and slowly drifted off, a picture of the good-looking Alice in his mind's eye, but with her dark hair gradually transforming into flowing blonde locks and her deep brown eyes becoming shining blue.

Chapter Eleven
The Motorcar

On the glorious August Holiday Monday of 1935, with the sun beaming down upon them, people were crowding the beaches of seaside resorts all around the coast. Sporting events and other entertainments were recording record numbers of attendees. Unemployment in Great Britain had fallen from the all-time high of more than three million in the bleak winter of 1933 to well under two millions. Throughout the country, feelings of increasing prosperity were at last being experienced by ordinary people – feelings boosted by the fine Bank Holiday weather.

Lord Collick was spending the summer with his wife and children on their Scottish estate, and so Stephen Collick took the opportunity to invite a number of guests to enjoy the weekend at Parklands where they would have the freedom to roam over the whole estate. He naturally turned to Millie to act as hostess for the weekend and she of course agreed.

Millie had been to Parklands on several previous occasions to be a consort for Stephen but she had never stayed for more than one night. To be away from Amhurst Road for several days meant, for her, a great upheaval. She had not, since her honeymoon twenty seven years earlier, spent more than one night at a time away from her home. It was an indication of the strength of her relationship with Stephen that she did not hesitate to accede to his request.

As for the young Stokers, their house at 8, Woodside Way was, as so often throughout their marriage, deserted. Margret was attending a study weekend organised for summer visiting students by one of the senior professors at her college. The subject was: 'Political Economics – What Is an Acceptable Philosophy?' and Margret had, in her own words, been 'virtually commanded to present herself'.

By the summer of 1935, Margret had come to be regarded as a particularly dynamic speaker with a well-grasped knowledge of her subject. This high opinion of her command of economics had clearly been conveyed to fellow academics in France, for she had now been invited to spend a year as a guest lecturer at the University of Paris, La Sorbonne, commencing in October.

Consequently, Margret had spent the last week of June and the whole of July at the Chigwell house, preparing papers for her planned move to France. It was a stay from which both she and Charlie derived pleasure. They had become so accustomed to living separate lives that after just a week or two each came to realise how much they had missed the comfort of the other's company.

On several evenings, they walked down to the pub in the village to enjoy a drink in the delightful garden attached to the old thatched building. While the birds chirped their goodnights in the trees surrounding the fenced garden area, Margret, sipping a pint of pale ale, said:

"I know this sounds stupid coming from me, Big Boy, but I wish you were coming with me."

Charlie shrugged at his wife across the planked table, the hint of a smile on his face. He said nothing.

"You are the only person in the world with whom I can feel real peace, with whom I don't have to fight. You know that, don't you?"

Charlie took a deep breath and let it out slowly as a sigh.

"Yeah, on a balmy summer evening it's easy to feel at peace, but there'll be just as many bleak winter mornings in a year."

"Bastard!"

The hint of a smile became a full grin.

"That's my Margie. Another?"

"No, thank you. But you know I was being serious, Charlie. We may not have what other people call a marriage, but I treasure your friendship. When I'm alone – and I know I've never said this before – but I love you as the brother I dreamed of having rather than the animals I grew up with."

Charlie nodded slowly.

"Yes, I know, Margret. I think I've always known, and I kidded myself it would be enough. Sometimes, it is. To be honest, most of the time it is, or has been up to now."

He played with his glass of ale.

"Life only gets tough when caring ceases to be enough. But I'll always be here for you, Margie. I am not likely to forget my marriage vows."

Margret rose suddenly from her seat and began to walk quickly to the little gate that led to the road. Charlie finished his drink and followed. As he caught up with her, she swept her arm across her face and tossed her head with a sniff.

"Sorry, Big Boy. Just suddenly felt the need to move."

"Silly cow!"

"Bastard!"

Charlie took the elbow in his ribs like a man, with a slight cough.

* * *

Aware of Margret's plans for August, Bobby had invited Charlie to enjoy a bank holiday motorcycle trip. He and Daphne were travelling with a group of enthusiasts to have a beach party at Clacton-on-Sea. Charlie was inclined to accept the offer. It would be a fun day and an opportunity to give the Velocette a decent run.

However, events in the intervening days made him change his mind. Two weeks before the bank holiday weekend, Charlie had taken delivery of a brand new motorcar. He had finally accepted the arguments of both Ivor Spafford and Aitch Harrington that a motorcar would be more befitting of his position as a successful traveller.

There was no doubt that he could now afford it. Stephen Collick's generosity had enabled him to build a sound financial reserve at the bank in addition to the healthy balance from his weekly earnings. Also, it was obvious that the KSS, loved as it was, was not really suitable for social activities other than with motorcyclists. Thirdly, the Ford Motor Company had recently reduced dramatically the price of their Model Y saloon car.

The offered price of just one hundred pounds was, he decided, too good to miss. Fortunately, his garage at Woodside Way was easily big enough to accommodate the new vehicle along with the motorcycle and sidecar; and there was still working space for him at the bench on the rear wall.

Keeping the KSS was without doubt an extravagance. With the sidecar attached, it was worth almost as much as the motorcar; but Charlie was far too attached to it to consider selling. Nevertheless, he at once – and enthusiastically – transferred all his sample goods and cases from the boxed sidecar to the rear seat of the Ford.

From the moment of his first call in the new vehicle, customers remarked on, teased him about or asked questions about the new motorcar. Charlie, who, as ever, considered his personal decisions, indeed all of his life outside Collick's, as nobody's business but his own, invariably dismissed the subject with shrugs, smiles and a nonchalant word.

On the Tuesday after the purchase, he arrived at his usual time at Armagh Road. Lottie Cutter, glancing along the road as she let him in, exclaimed:

"Oh! There's a motorcar outside, I wonder who—? Charlie! Your motorcycle? Have you… is that motorcar yours?"

Charlie smiled and shrugged.

"Yeah. I thought it was time."

"Oh, Charlie, it's lovely!" She gave a little chuckle. "The neighbours will think we've got royalty visiting!"

"Hardly, Mrs C, it's only a Ford Eight!"

"Ah, but it is all so shining and new! You must be very proud of it, Charlie."

"Well, it is much more suitable for work, but I still love my Velocette."

"Yes, but this is much nicer, really, isn't it?"

"I suppose so."

Charlie followed Lottie Cutter into the dining room, where she passed him the paying-in books and excused herself into the kitchen to finish off the lunch. No sooner had he sat down than the front door banged and Thomas Cutter entered, an anxious look on his face.

"Oh, hallo, Charlie, I wondered who was here, whose motor that was out the front. Not yours, is it?"

Charlie stood up to shake hands with Sally's father, wearing a sheepish smile.

"Yeah, guilty as charged, M'Lud."

"That's a very sensible move, son, very nice. Very nice indeed. Be easier for your job too, won't it?"

"Yes, sir. You're quite right. I should have done it before, but I had grown very much attached to the 'bike."

"That's understandable. But then, life moves you on, doesn't it?"

Charlie shrugged. "Yes, it does."

After a few minutes of quiet chat as Mrs Cutter placed dishes on the table, another banging of doors signalled the flying entrance of Sally, who almost collided with her mother.

"Sorry for the bang, Mum, I'm late! There's a motorcar out—Oh, Charlie! I didn't see you there. I di—"

She stopped in mid-word and pointed a finger at the now standing Charlie, a smile forming on her face.

"You've bought the new motorcar! It's super! I love the red leather seats – I peeped inside before I came in. I didn't think you'd do it so soon."

Charlie shrugged and said, "It was the right time."

During their conversation at the ABC tearoom at the end of May, Charlie had admitted to Sally that he was being pressured by his superiors to buy a motorcar for his work. He had stated firmly that he did not want to part with the KSS.

She had said, "Being on the motorbike is great, it's exciting, but a motor car makes sense, doesn't it?"

"Yeah," he had replied, "but you can't always be sensible, can you?"

"Now, sit down everyone, food's ready," said Mrs Cutter. She proceeded to serve each of them with large helpings of meat pie, cabbage and potatoes. They all attacked the food hungrily. Once she had settled herself, Mrs Cutter looked up at Charlie and asked:

"How do you cover the Bank Holidays, Charlie? What happens to your Monday calls?"

"I get the day off on Monday and then double up the load on Tuesday. Over the two days, Tuesday and Wednesday, it's fairly easy to manage all the calls."

"What will you do with your extra day off next week?"

"I'm not sure yet. No set plan. My mother will be away for the weekend and I've been invited to go with friends on a motorbike trip, I think it's to Clacton."

"Isn't your wife home from college for the holidays just now?" asked Tom Cutter without thinking.

For a moment, warning eyes flashed around the table. The Cutters had been aware for a couple of years that Charlie and his wife lived separate lives. Beyond that bland statement, his private life was something the young man had never discussed. Now, however, he responded quite naturally, totally ignoring the heightened atmosphere.

"She has been, for a few weeks, but she's to be back at the college for Bank Holiday weekend. Some sort of summer school for overseas students, I understand."

"Well, if you're going to be on your own, why don't you come with us to Southend on Bank Holiday Monday?" said Sally brightly. "We're going by train from Liverpool Street. Mum, Dad, you and me'll make a lovely group!"

"Sally!" Mrs Cutter interjected sharply. "You take liberties with Charlie. He has his own life to lead. He doesn't need us to interfere."

Charlie had stopped eating, his knife and fork resting on his plate. "I've got a better idea," he said. "If you haven't already bought train tickets, how about I take you all in my motorcar, instead of joining the masses on the train?"

The three Cutters exchanged glances around the table, smiles on their faces, Sally's, full and happy, both her parents' slightly nervous. Lottie Cutter was the first to find words.

"Really, Charlie? Are you sure you would want to tie yourself to all of us all day on your holiday? I'm sure you had things in mind to do other than sit on the beach with old fogeys like us?"

"I'm not an old fogey, and I can think of lots of things to do apart from sitting on the beach!" Sally burst out laughing.

"Sally, you are incorrigible, stop it!" Her mother admonished her with an embarrassed smile.

Mr Cutter raised his hand to silence the women and spoke decisively:

"I think it would be lovely to go to the seaside in a motor car." He nodded towards Charlie and added, "Plus, it would give me, for once, a chance to spend a decent amount of time with Charlie. Whenever I see him, we're all in a rush to get back to work. We never have time for a real chat."

"Well, then it's settled, we'll do it," said Charlie, dazzling them with the full Stoker smile. "What time would you like me to get here? It will only take about an hour to get there once we leave."

* * *

The following evening, without explaining exactly what his intentions were, other than going out in his motorcar, Charlie told Bobby he would not be making the trip with them to Clacton.

"W-What d'you mean, you're not c-coming? You've g-got to come! You're a b-biker!" stammered Bobby.

"Yes, I know. Bobby, you know I love the KSS, but time moves us on. We have to make adjustments. My work has become the most important thing in my life, and

I have to adapt my habits to fit that life. That means motorcar instead of motorbike. That's it, really."

Bobby stared at his friend, speechless, but only for a moment.

"S-so what are you g-goin' to do?" he asked. "You're not going to w-work and you're not going to h-h-hibernate! Margret's busy at the c-college and your mum's goin' away. You're on your own!" He raised his opened palms to the sky as if seeking from God an answer to the unanswerable.

Charlie grinned. "I'm sort of working." he replied. "I'm taking some customers out for a drive."

"You're what?" Bobby's stare of amazement gradually turned into a knowing smirk. "It's that b-blonde! Y-y-you buggar! You're taking that blonde out!"

"Bobby!" Charlie straightened his back and glared down his nose. He said:

"You'll keep on till I explain, so I'll tell you now to shut you up. Every Tuesday, I have lunch with a family who live by Victoria Park. They are some of my best customers and they've become friends. I realised this week that I had the opportunity to thank them for all those lunches, so I suggested a trip in the motor."

Bobby listened, momentarily chastened, his facial expression serious as he absorbed Charlie's words. Then he suddenly exploded:

"It's the b-b-blonde's family!"

Charlie shrugged and looked away. He reached for his half-full glass of ale and bottomed it.

"One more?" he suggested.

"Hmmm!" snorted Bobby, tossing his head in irritation that the subject was now effectively closed.

Before that particular conversation, Bobby had been telling Charlie about an unexpected visitor he had received at the workshop the previous week.

"Of all people, guess who walked in last Thursday."

Charlie shrugged and shook his head.

"A-Alec Chapman! Of a-all people! I n-ever could stand him. You r-remember at that Camera Club Christmas party when we were still at the Northern? He c-cornered me at the Vic. Tavern that night and ranted o-on and on about his new AJS M12."

Charlie raised his eyebrows at the name.

"Oh yeah, and then we saw him with that group in the pub at Walthamstow a few years ago."

"That's right! In that wh-whispering huddle, wasn't he?"

"Yeah."

"W-ell, anyway, he turned up, large as life, while I was working on a van. He still looks the s-same, big, red-faced and angry, as if he's looking for a f-fight. But he strolled in the shop, wearin' a loud check suit like the one he'd had on at Walthamstow that night, just as if we was old mates. He asked how I was doing, and said he'd been meaning to get in touch for ages."

"I thought that was a bit odd, but I just said I was getting along quite well but you know how it is, you have to keep w-working. He said yeah, it was the same in butchering. Then, eventually he came to the point, he said just lately he'd been having some trouble with the AJS and a mate had recommended he come and see me about it. I'd got a good name for price and service, he said."

He paused to take a drink and Charlie nodded, encouraging him to continue the story. Bobby adjusted his glasses and went on:

"W-well, I said, I t-try to do a good job so that people can trust me and come back again. He laughed and said, 'Well, it's obviously working!'"

"He'd come in the butcher's van with his bike on a trailer, so I had a quick look at his bike and could tell it needed a lot of work, it hadn't been looked after. I told him it would be a day or two before I could do it and it was going to be expensive. He said, 'How much? A fiver?' I said I thought it would be nearer ten. He puffed his lips and said not to worry, just to telephone him when it was ready. He left me his details."

"The bike needed some expensive parts and I worked on it all day Monday. Just before I went home, I called him to tell him it was ready. He asked how much it would cost and I told him £9.5s.6d."

"He went mad on the ph-phone. He yelled, 'What? Wha' d'ya mean? I ain't made o' money! You're crazy!'"

"I was a b-bit taken aback but I explained that the parts had cost £7.10s. 6d. and I'd only charged him £1.15s for the work. He didn't argue with me but said he'd be round next morning. He slammed the phone down."

He paused again, and Charlie again prompted him to resume, marvelling, as so many times before, at how Bobby's stammer became so much less evident whenever he got involved in a story.

"Was he waiting at the door yesterday morning?" he asked.

"A-almost," replied Bobby. He smiled sheepishly.

"When he s-saw his machine, he whistled. He said it looked really good. He gave me a ten-pound note, and then he said, 'But so it should for ten fucking quid!'

"I said, 'It's a nice machine, it's w-worth looking after.'

"He agreed and said he intended to in future. I wheeled it out and we put it on his trailer. Then, as he got in the van, he said:

'You used to be keen on that dark-haired girl, that friend of wassaname Lacey at the chemists – Daphne, wasn't it? Did you ever get anywhere?'

"I said, 'We're m-married.'

"He looked s-surprised. Then he said, 'Oh, I didn't know that. She was a good-looker, for a yid, but I didn't realise you were one, you don' look it. That explains the ten quid!'

"I was so sh-sh-shocked, I f-froze and before I could say anything, he'd driven off."

Charlie frowned. He opened his cigarette case and proffered it. They both lit up. Charlie said:

"My memory had him as an ignorant slob. It seems he hasn't changed much. Still, you made a small profit on the deal!"

Bobby smiled. "Y-yeah, you're right, there's no point in dwelling on it, and he's not worth it, but," he hesitated, "y-you know, Charlie, there's s-so much of it about, now, this anti-Jew stuff."

He fiddled with his beer glass and scratched his ginger head. Charlie nodded empathetically but said nothing. Bobby continued:

"Da-aphne's dad says London's becoming an unhealthy place to li-ive in. You know, he never cared about his Jewish background when I first knew him. I didn't even know he was one till I met his father. But this last y-year or two he's begun to get upset. At the weekend, he was talking about g-getting out, going to America. He said 'p-people can live there in peace, away from the doings of e-evil scum like Mosley and Hitler'."

Charlie's cigarette glowed bright before he crushed it into the ashtray on the table between them. He said:

"They'll be okay here. All people have prejudices, and in this country they are free to express their views; but the authorities will always deal with the oafs and the trouble makers."

As he spoke the words, Charlie's mind flashed back nine years. He wondered, but did not say, 'Although at what cost of innocent lives?'

Chapter Twelve
The Kiss

As arranged, Charlie arrived at Armagh Road at nine o'clock in the morning on the first Monday in August and was warmly greeted by the three members of the Cutter family, ready and waiting with a packed picnic basket and two shopping bags full of necessities for the trip.

All three were in their Sunday best. Sally looked ravishing in a dress of light blue with pink roses. It had short puff sleeves and a belted waist. Her mother wore a similarly styled dress, but in a reddish brown with a green and yellow floral print. Mr Cutter was wearing a light brown suit with a faint check pattern, a white shirt and a green and cream striped tie. Charlie recognised with a little pride that both dresses and suit had been chosen by himself from Collick's stock.

The Ford being a two-door model, the front seats were tipped forward to enable Sally and her mother to climb into the rear compartment, where they were immediately laden with the basket and one of the bags. Then, with the seats set upright again, Thomas Cutter, red-faced and coughing, settled down in the front with the other bag.

"I see you've got the heavy one, Mr C, are you okay there?" asked Charlie.

"Yes, I'm fine, just that nuisance cough of mine. Once it starts, it keeps tickling my chest for minutes at a time. I'm okay, now."

"I keep telling him he should have a word with the doctor but he won't take the time!" called out Mrs Cutter from the rear seat.

"It's stopped, I'm fine now, Lottie. Let's enjoy the day, eh? Away you go, Charlie, start her up!"

The journey to the coast was trouble free in the glorious holiday sunshine, although, even with the windows open, it became very warm in the rear of the car. The ladies were glad to be able to stretch their legs on arrival at Southend-on-Sea and to breathe the invigorating salty sea air. Charlie was relieved to stand and light up a cigarette. He proffered his case to Mr Cutter, who declined.

Although shops in the town were closed for the Bank Holiday, all the beach attractions were in full swing. They had parked not far to the east of the pier, by the already crowded promenade. Opposite was a row of beach stalls, the aproned stall holders loudly promoting freshly prepared cockles, mussels, winkles and whelks to queues of eager customers. It was a little before eleven o'clock.

Tom Cutter stared out at the blue-grey water beyond the people already crowding the pebbled sand beach. He breathed deeply, then turned to his wife and daughter.

"I'm already glad we came," he said approvingly, "and the day is just beginning! Shall we do the pier walk before we eat? It'll increase our appetites."

"Good idea, Dad," agreed Sally. "We can leave the stuff in the motor until we come back."

"We can all walk out, but I may need to get the train back," advised Mrs Cutter, "I'm not sure I'm up to going that far nowadays."

Bags and basket locked in the motorcar, they set off, four abreast, along the promenade.

"We love walking up the pier," said Lottie Cutter, her husband nodding agreement, as on so many previous occasions. "We did it when we first got married and we've tried to do it through the years since, but this last couple of years it feels like it's getting longer and harder! Last time we came, we only made it one way and we were beaten. We had to get the little train back to the prom."

"You've let yourselves get out of condition, it's only a mile and a quarter each way!" Sally chirped.

"You wait till you've had two kids and a lifetime of cleaning up a house!" retorted her mother.

Sally laughed, looking up conspiratorially to Charlie, who shrugged and puffed smoke at her.

Mr Cutter paid the shilling for the four entrance tickets and led the way through the turnstile onto the world's longest pleasure pier. The pier was looking exceptionally bright and welcoming this summer. It was decked out with flags and bunting in celebration of its official centenary, a month or two earlier.

The party of four very soon separated into two twos, the young couple striding out ahead of the Cutter parents, Sally as chatty as ever and Charlie content to be in her company. When they were about four hundred yards along, Sally glanced over her shoulder and said:

"We'd better slow down a bit or we'll lose them! They walk slower, these days."

They halted and looked back. Sally waved and her mother waved back. Charlie said:

"It's hot today and they're a lot older than us, Sally. It's easy to forget." Then he added, "And I didn't think your dad looked well when we set off this morning. Has he been ill at all?"

"No. He coughs a lot, but he's always done that, as far as I can remember. He works hard – long hours, and he gets tired. He's always better after a break. Mum too. She was ill when I was young, in hospital with women's troubles. She gets tired easily as well, nowadays."

They carried on walking, slightly slower. Sally suddenly exclaimed:

"It's a smashing day for a Bank Holiday Monday, isn't it? And we're so lucky to be able to come with you like this, in your motor, Charlie. I'm so happy I could dance up this pier!"

Charlie grinned. "You'd be on your own, and a bit conspicuous."

She grabbed his arm and hugged it.

"No, you could do it with me."

"Not likely!"

Charlie's veto was emphatic, but he made no attempt to free his arm and they walked, linked like that, to the end of the pier. There was very little conversation but both were transported by the experience of the day and the feeling of oneness gained from the enfolded arms.

On reaching the end of the pier, they leaned against the rail to wait for Sally's parents. Charlie lit a cigarette. Sally had long ceased to chatter but when Charlie stole a sideways glance, her face was at peace and radiantly beautiful. She turned towards him.

"You know, Charlie, it's not only me who's so taken with you. You know that, don't you? Mum and Dad are too. They see you as like the son they never had, like they dreamed he would have been. That's why Mum started asking you to have lunch. She thinks you're very special."

Charlie's habitual shrug did not happen. He continued to look straight ahead, to where Sally's parents were coming gradually closer. He drew deeply on his cigarette and blew smoke rings. When, eventually, he replied, his tone was not the usual casual Charlie, it was earnest and deliberate.

"The feeling's mutual, Sal, it's really mutual. I think yours is the perfect family. When I am with you Cutters, I feel comfortable, happy in a way that's different for me. I've never had that before. I only remember fleeting moments of happiness with my mum and dad. From the age of seven, I only knew my father as a morose cripple who lived in pain, and my mother was his stern carer – there for him, not for me. To me, she was just the grey guardian. She didn't know how to show love. It was years before I really felt my mother's love. I was already a married man."

He stopped speaking and Sally started as if to respond. Charlie raised his hand quickly to silence her.

"No, don't say anything for a minute, Sally. I don't know why I just said all that, it just came out. I... I've never said any of that to anyone before. I've never given voice to those thoughts before... never in my life..."

Whatever was going to be said next by either of them remained unsaid, the gravitas of the moment swept away by the arrival of Mr and Mrs Cutter, with Lottie Cutter laughing as she declared:

"Ooh! That was lovely, but it's the train back for us, we're both done in!"

"It tells a story, doesn't it?" her husband added breathlessly. "Twenty years ago, I would walk this pier twice over and think nothing of it!"

"Well," Charlie affirmed, "that walk's certainly loosened us all up. Sitting cramped in the car for so long, you're bound to get pretty stiff. I think the train back's a good idea for all of us."

"Yeah, good idea," agreed Sally.

They headed for the kiosk by the little pier head rail terminal and Charlie reached in his pocket for the required eight pence, only to be gently pushed aside by Thomas Cutter.

"No, son. You're not to pay for anything else today. That car ride was worth more than anything I spend here."

"If you insist, sir." Charlie smiled and shrugged.

* * *

After lunch, replete with the good food from their picnic hamper and the two bottles of wine that Charlie had produced from under the driver's seat, Mr and Mrs Cutter were content to settle down and sunbathe in their deckchairs for an hour or so. At Sally's suggestion, she and Charlie took another stroll along the seafront while her parents dozed.

The sky was still cloudless but the sun hazy in its early afternoon heat. One of the many beach photographers snapped his camera at them and called:

"Lovely couple, lovely photo! Here, guv, let me take one of the beautiful lady for yer!"

Sally stopped, excited and eager, but Charlie stiffened.

"No, not now, later, with the family," he said hastily, easing Sally away to mingle with the walking crowd.

"Oh, Charlie, why not? That would have been a nice memento of the day."

"It wouldn't have been right, Sally. I'm a married man."

"You silly! What difference does that make? It's only a photo picture. We're not in bed together!"

"No, that's true." Charlie lit a cigarette to prevent himself from saying 'I wish we were'.

They resumed their walk.

"Cha-arlie?" Sally drawled his name hesitantly. "Would you mind if I bring up a serious subject? If I asked you some personal questions?"

Charlie shrugged and inhaled smoke. After a pause he said curtly, "No, go ahead."

"This morning, on the pier, we were happy and having a good time. Then, at the pier head, you started to explain something important. It was the first time you'd ever said anything about your private life and I could tell it wasn't easy for you. Then, when my mum and dad got there, you stopped and we didn't get a chance to get back to it. But I remember everything you were saying well enough. I know there's a deep sadness in you – it's part of what makes you the lovely man you are, Charlie."

She hesitated, uncertain, then rushed on.

"You've got to have seen what you do to me, Charlie. I'm mad about you. I am not the schoolgirl you first knew. I want to share your pain, to lessen it. I'm nineteen years old and I've lived a bit. It kills me not being able to help you."

They were walking slowly and Charlie did not speak. He continued to stare straight ahead.

"Why have you never told me anything about your life?" Sally persisted. "I mean your home life, your life outside Collick's. You're very clever at it, you talk about work and about your customers. You talk about your schooldays and college days, but you never say a word about your home, about your marriage" – she hesitated – "about your wife, your family."

"You know my mum lives in Amhurst Road," replied Charlie weakly.

"Yeah, so what? I know sod all else!"

Charlie halted and turned to look into Sally's brimming eyes. It was a moment come upon without warning: a moment when he knew he could not hide behind a shrug. There was only one way to deal with the matter, but how could he explain to this perfect 19-year-old beauty the mess he had made of his life? How could he tell her that he was tied for life to a woman for whom he felt nothing? A woman who had no interest in him other than as some sort of friendly father confessor? How could he tell her that he was in love with her? That she was and would be always, to him, forbidden fruit?

"Sally," he said, "I'm nearly six years older than you. I was brought up an only child in a strict Catholic family. When I was your age, I was just discovering for the first time the richness of life in the world outside. I was enjoying my student's life, drinking and rollicking, until I did a very stupid thing. I made a girl pregnant, a girl from a respectable Catholic family. My upbringing and my faith left me no choice but to marry her, and we were married quickly enough to make the whole business appear respectable."

He paused and drew deeply on his cigarette. Sally was mature enough not to speak. She knew there was more to come. She reached for his hand and squeezed it tenderly. He responded with a squeeze of his own.

"But, of course," he went on, "that appearance was totally bogus. Within a few months, after a difficult pregnancy, my wife gave birth to our son, who was born dead. After that, although physically undamaged, she swore never again to endure the ignominy of pregnancy. She made a vow never again to indulge in sexual intercourse with a man."

Sally gasped. "Oh god, Charlie!"

Her grip in his hand became limp. For a moment, he thought she might faint, and instinctively gathered her in his arms. For a confused eternity they stood, unaware of the mass of people bustling around them. Tears pouring from her eyes, Sally raised her head from his chest to look up at him. She sighed, and whispered:

"I'm so sorry, Charlie, I—"

He silenced her with a finger placed on her lips.

"I don't want you ever to feel sorry for me, Sally. Love me or hate me for what I am, for what you see, not for the mistakes that brought me to you."

He withdrew his finger and lowered his head until their lips met momentarily, tentatively. They gazed at each other, in shock, then kissed again, greedy with desire.

"I love you, Charlie," Sally whispered. "I shall always love you." Words uttered with only a vague comprehension of their enormity; and perhaps no comprehension of the even greater enormity of the reply.

"And I think I love you, too, Sally Cutter."

An ice cream parlour was open just opposite. Charlie suggested they pop in. It gave Sally an opportunity to powder her nose and to enjoy a cold drink, and it gave Charlie time to clear his head. He lit a cigarette and considered what had just occurred.

When Sally re-joined him, she was again her normal self, if with a slightly more serious demeanour. She returned straight to the point.

"What can you do, Charlie? Haven't you got grounds for a divorce?"

Charlie shrugged and exhaled smoke before replying.

"Divorce doesn't enter into it, Sal. My wife and I are both from devout Catholic families. Divorce is not something that we consider. Marriage is for life. I knew that when I married her. I knew what I was doing. I made the decision and I live by it."

"But we love each other, Charlie."

"Yes, we do, and that has to be our secret, Sally."

He tapped ash into the ashtray, then, uncharacteristically, crushed out his half-smoked cigarette. He tried to explain.

"Sweet Sally, you of all people don't deserve this, but it is the sort of lesson life dishes out when you are nineteen. In a very short time, you will have absorbed it and you'll move on. You'll meet the right person and live a normal life. As for me, this is a situation I never dreamed I should have to reckon with."

He took Sally's hands in his, leaning towards her. "We live in a society guided by rules, Sally. I was brought up to believe in and abide by those rules, whatever the cost. I've always been careful to avoid relationships with the opposite sex. To tell the truth, it's never been a problem for me, until you appeared.

"From the moment you walked in the house that lunchtime, I knew this was different. You stirred feelings in me that I honestly didn't know I was capable of. I've read all about Cupid and his arrows but I never thought he'd ping one into me! I did not marry for love and I have never until now felt the pain of love, but it has to stop here. I shall love you from a distance, Sally, but you are and must forever remain forbidden fruit."

"Charlie, but—"

"No, Sally, it cannot be! I am a married man. You are just starting out in life. You will fall in love again soon enough, and you'll be happy. I ask only to be your friend, whenever you should need me."

* * *

The atmosphere within the party had been understandably more strained for the rest of that day, but at least the older members of the Cutter family reached home tired but happy that Bank Holiday night. They had seen little change in Charlie's demeanour on his return from the afternoon walk and Mrs Cutter, if she noticed a quietness in Sally, attributed it to the time of the month and to nothing else.

Before leaving Armagh Road, Charlie collected the Collick's weekly payments, thus saving an hour from his condensed work schedule on the following day. It also created a week's space in which both he and Sally could come to terms with the emotional upheaval of the afternoon.

With Margret's study weekend keeping her at the college until Tuesday evening, the house at Woodside Way was empty when the tallyman reached home. He poured himself a glass of Jameson's and sat heavily in his armchair.

He had been firm enough in his resolve to forestall the affair with Sally at the ice cream parlour and had remained so throughout the walk back to her parents' deckchairs, despite her railing against his decision. Now though, alone with his whisky, he questioned whether he was strong enough to persist in resisting his feelings for her? Were there still to be unforeseen and perhaps unmanageable consequences of that burning kiss?

Chapter Thirteen
The Seeds of Discord

As 1935 progressed, the world steadily became a darker place. In Africa, Mussolini's fascist army overran Abyssinia and claimed the country as an Italian possession. In Germany, Hitler and his Nazi followers were holding huge militaristic rallies and passing crippling laws that deprived Jews and other minorities of their rights and of their freedom, with thousands being sent to concentration camps.

At home in Britain, on the other hand, things were considered to be more encouraging. The National Government gained a new prime minister when Stanley Baldwin succeeded the ailing Ramsay MacDonald. The economy was continuing to improve and many parts of the country were prospering. The weight of political opinion had concluded that we should not become involved in Germany's internal affairs. It was felt that Europe saw Britain as strong, and Britain's strength was sufficient to deter others from war.

At least, that was felt in some quarters. Lionel Lacey held a different view, as he declaimed to Charlie in what was usually the empty spare room of Jennifer's new flat. Jennifer was celebrating the completion of her first year in business together with her recently passed twenty-fifth birthday. The party had been in swing for a couple of hours, and between fifteen and twenty guests, including Bobby and Daphne, were happily crowding both the living room, where music was playing on a gramophone, and the kitchen. The spare room was serving as bar, cloak room, stock room and furniture store.

Mr Lacey, in his accustomed role of barman, had placed an assortment of opened bottles and empty glasses on a card table, with reserves and empties stacked in boxes on the floor beneath. Perched on wooden chairs by the table, the two men were holding generously filled glasses of Jameson's Irish whisky and 'putting the world to rights, away from the masses', as Lacey contentedly described it.

"The government is behaving like the proverbial ostrich," he insisted. "They don't want to see the danger signals. They've been content to let that megalomaniac Hitler flout all the obligations of the Versailles Treaty and to build and boast about his massive war machine. And they are doing virtually nothing – a few airplanes and a dozen tanks!"

Swallowing a mouthful of Jameson's, Lacey added, "What really frightens me, Charlie lad, is that after all we went through last time, the ostriches will let us drift into another bloody war. And nobody's trying to prevent it! No buggar cares!"

Charlie nodded and shrugged. Once the Jameson's was flowing, nods and shrugs were practically all that was required of him in his conversations with Jennifer's father; but the senior Lacey pharmacist was always an interesting man to listen to. His experiences in France in the Great War had been, in his own words, 'too bloody awful to relate without a bellyful of Irish support'.

Indeed, despite all the long monologues, Lacey's war experience remained to a great extent a secret. The scars, though, were readily apparent in the tremors of his hands and the non-stop chain of cigarettes that accompanied the Jameson's.

"I think a lot of people do care, sir," Charlie suggested. "They may not show it, and they may wish it would go away, but if push comes to shove there'll be enough willing hands and shoulders."

"Hmmh! I've no doubt you are correct, lad, but that may not be enough if no one calls that bastard's bluff! We are not properly prepared. Push must not be allowed to come to shove. That's my whole point!"

Charlie nodded. It was an argument he often heard on his rounds and one with which he was largely in accord. Yet there was a kernel in his heart that hoped the time would come when he could honour his father's memory by serving his country, as the crippled cobbler had done so nobly.

"Large gin, barman, touch of t., bit of ice!" Margret swept into the room with flushed face. She waved an empty tumbler over the table. "And what plot are you two hatching up in here?" she demanded.

Charlie shrugged; Lionel Lacey took the tumbler from her.

"Large gin, tiny tonic and ice. Certainly madam, coming right up!" He reached for the half-full bottle on the table. "When are you off, Margret? It must be soon now. Are you looking forward to it?"

"Yes, Tuesday. Don't forget, this is my going away party! Jen's birthday's only secondary, didn't you know?"

Mr Lacey raised an eyebrow. He added a precious cube from his icebox on the floor and passed the almost full tumbler to her.

"Thank you, uncle!" She made a mock curtsey and turned her attention to Charlie. "You know he's my favourite uncle, don't you?"

Charlie shrugged, eyes twinkling.

"I know you're getting halfway to blotto! Give it another hour?"

"No, I shan't go home tonight. I'll get the other halfway and stay here with Jen. I shan't see her much for a year after Tuesday and she'll need me here tomorrow. If you want to come and pick me up late afternoon, about five o'clock, it'd be nice."

"Okay, please yourself. Call me when you're ready."

Charlie turned his attention to the Jameson's.

* * *

The previous Sunday, Charlie and Margret had joined Millie Stoker and Stephen at Amhurst Road for a farewell lunch. Millie had prepared her customary Sunday lunch of roast beef, roast potatoes and carrots, cabbage and sprouts fresh from her kitchen garden, and they had toasted to the success of Margret's coming year at La Sorbonne.

Stephen knew Paris well, and he gave Margret a number of suggestions of things to do and places to visit while she was there.

"Of course," he cautioned, "I have not been there for a few years. Your friends and associates over there will no doubt guide you to many other probably more interesting establishments and sights."

Margret, concurring with eager nods of her head, made notes of the suggestions.

"I am looking forward to it immensely," she said. "The year will be a very exciting experience, and I hope a rewarding one. It is quite ridiculous that I have reached the age of twenty-five and have not yet travelled further than Ireland."

Millie had exchanged a quick glance with Charlie at that point, but neither made any comment. Neither mother nor son had ever left Britain's shores. Indeed, in Charlie's case, the only time he had ever spent more than a night away from London had been on his honeymoon trip to Eastbourne.

Three days after Jennifer's party, Charlie delivered Margret to Charing Cross station for the nine o'clock train to Dover, receiving a hug, a pecked cheek, a wave and an 'au revoir!', his reward for his considerate assistance. At Dover, she would board the ferry to France. Charlie had offered to drive her to the coast, but Margret had insisted – probably correctly, Charlie had to admit – that the train would be quicker and more comfortable.

Margret had been unusually quiet about the house on the Sunday evening and the Monday before her departure. It was not from anxiety about her preparations: she had been virtually ready to go for several days; and Charlie recognised her concern was not for him. Both knew the other would carry on as normal. He surmised, therefore, that there could have been only two possible reasons: concern about the year ahead or concern for Jennifer.

Knowing Margret, he decided that the second possibility was the more likely. The thought of the challenge ahead would excite but not frighten her in the least. Her relationship with 'her little pearl', on the other hand, was of immense importance to both women. Without the bolster of Margret's proximity, Jennifer would be, at times, he suspected, in a state of considerable distress. And although Margret had protested that she needed Charlie, he knew that in her heart her first thoughts were for Jennifer.

Charlie drove straight from Charing Cross to Collick's, where he had a word with Mrs Dekker in the curtain department about a customer sent in with Charlie's measurements of her windows to choose curtains for her sitting room. His customer, he was relieved to hear in the little Polish woman's inimitably precise detail, had been completely satisfied.

Before leaving the store, Charlie enjoyed a coffee with Laura Matthews. As always, Laura looked her impeccable best in a green silk blouse and black skirt. She greeted Charlie with a shout and a kiss as he entered her department.

"Stoker, you handsome brute, where have you been?" she cried. "You are just in time to buy me coffee!"

Charlie shrugged. "And you're as beautiful as ever, Laura. To buy your coffee is all I came in for."

"As it should be!"

They headed for the coffee shop.

"So, what is new in your life this week, handsome?" asked Laura when they had found an empty corner table. "How's the motorcar suiting you?"

Charlie lit a cigarette, creating a cloud above their heads.

"Life is always busy, Laura. You know that. The motor is fine. It has just brought me from Charing Cross, where I dropped off my wife on her way to France."

Laura was one of the very few people to whom Charlie ever mentioned his wife, a habit that had begun as a measure to stave off her advances. Now, they had a well-established friendship and understood each other's situation. In fact, Laura had herself become engaged recently to one Charles Laxford, who worked in a city bank.

"So, you had to have a Charlie!" he had teased her.

"Well, I was getting nowhere with you! And he is called Charles, not Charlie."

"So was my dad. That's why I was Charlie. I'm sure your Charles is a good chap, anyway. You know I wish you every happiness."

"We'll do very well, thank you, Charlie. But I still fancy you!"

Charlie had shrugged, palms upward to ward her off.

Now, holding her coffee cup high, Laura asked, "Why has your wife gone to France? I thought she was lecturing at L.S.E.?"

"She's been given the opportunity to spend a year at La Sorbonne."

"Wow! Leaving you alone for a year? She must be barking mad! When can I move in?"

Charlie smiled. "Control yourself, Laura, you're a disgrace!"

"I know, but that's why you love me."

"I expect you are right about that." He shrugged and lit another cigarette. Through a haze of smoke he said, "Don't ever change, Laura."

"With lovely men like you around? Not likely!" Her laughter pealed across the room.

As they were leaving the coffee shop, Laura asked:

"Have you seen Shayna Dekker this morning? Was she OK?"

Charlie frowned. "Yes, she was her normal self. Why?"

"Well, she was quite a bit upset yesterday morning. Have you ever met any of her family?"

Charlie shook his head.

"Well, she has three boys, nice kids, fourteen, twelve and eleven. The eldest plays in a football team on Sunday afternoons and on his way home this Sunday he was beset by a group of older boys – bully boys – in Victoria Park. They threatened to beat him up and taunted him, calling him an effing German Yid immigrant, poor little beggar. He managed to run away from them unhurt, but he was in a state about it when he got home. But then he would be, wouldn't he? He's a sensitive boy."

Charlie nodded slowly, frowning.

"I expect the gang was from Bethnal Green. There's a lot of anti-Semitism around there."

"Oh?"

"The B.U.P. is getting a lot of support in that area and out towards Leytonstone. I see it on my rounds. You see signs and slogans chalked on walls. I get the impression, from general customer chat, there's a lot of resentment of immigrants working for low wages and taking their jobs. With what's going on on the continent, particularly Jews being persecuted and forced to leave Germany, they migrate here. Then it's easy for these groups to point the finger."

"But those boys were all born here in Stepney!"

"Yeah, but you know how it is, Laura. He probably looked Jewish. He'd probably been playing with a Jewish team. Then he left the group and was on his own. Bullies always pick the easy target. They're just out looking for trouble."

"You are right, of course. We shouldn't get emotional about these things, but Shayna Dekker is lovely, she's a brick. She hurts no one and she's the first to offer help to anyone who needs it."

Charlie shrugged; Laura sighed.

She thanked him for the coffee and returned to the china department. Charlie went to gather his required stock for the day and bumped into Walter Habisch at the basement stock counter. They exchanged greetings, then Walter burst out:

"Ha-ay, Charlie! Wotchoo been doin' getting' my customers all of a doodah?" He broke into his big, beaming smile. "Alice Pensell was drooling over you! She said you was gorgeous and she was yours whenever you wanted to take over her account!"

"Alice Pensell? Wilf Tattle's sister? I only saw her for a few minutes at the Tattle house! Her husband's waiting to be sent down for the Dalston Empire job, isn't he?"

"Yeah, yeah! Bert's a bad lot, 's'a shame. Alice is a lovely girl. She deserves better than him an' those two boys, but you can't say nothin' to her. She won't hear a word against him. But I gotta say she was very taken with you! 'Ooh,' she said, 'I could eat him up, all six feet whatever of him!'"

Charlie shrugged helplessly.

"You'd better make sure you keep her away from me, then, Walter. I'll need your protection."

"Thass alright, I'll protect you, son! You're safe with my protection!"

Walter giggled as he walked off, a case in each hand. Charlie collected his goods and set off on his Tuesday round.

* * *

The anxieties that assailed Charlie after the Bank Holiday Monday trip to Southend had not been greatly relieved when, a week later, he had arrived at Armagh Road to find an excited Lottie Cutter alone in the house. She had greeted him warmly as usual.

"Oh, I'm glad you're here, Charlie! Do come through. It will be just us two for lunch today, the family has deserted us. Tom is taking a packed lunch for a couple of weeks because his boss is on holiday and he has to deputise. He gets all worked up about it and insists on taking a packed lunch. And Sally is having her lunch at work as well!"

"Oh?" Charlie was not sure whether he felt disappointed or relieved.

"Well, this is the first day back after the factory holiday closedown and it's a busy time as they start to get the new autumn fashions out. She's still working in that office all on her own and I think it's a cheek! There should be another person to share the load, shouldn't there?"

"If you say so, Mrs Cutter, although I should imagine if Sally felt it was unfair she would tell them."

"Mmm, probably, but she's been a bit down this last week. Women do sometimes, of course. She'll buck up now she's active again."

"Yeah, I suppose so."

"Yes, of course." Lottie Cutter dismissed the subject. She was obviously too excited about something else.

"But you won't have heard our good news yet, will you? Our Cissie is going to have a baby!" Her eyes were bright with the thrill of her announcement. "We are going to be grandparents!"

Charlie grinned. "Congratulations!" He opened his arms and hugged her. "That's wonderful news. You and Mr C must be absolutely delighted. I expect Cissie and Harry are too. I shall look forward to seeing them tomorrow."

Regardless of the excitement in the Cutter family, Charlie was not to see Sally again for nearly two months. Although Mr Cutter resumed his normal routine, Sally did not come home for lunch on any Tuesday during the rest of August and most of September.

It was on the Tuesday on which Margret had left for Paris in the last week of September that things changed dramatically. Charlie arrived at Armagh Road at the usual time. The door was opened, not by Mrs Cutter, but by Sally herself, looking as beautiful as ever but pale, with an anxious look on her face. She greeted him with the most fleeting of smiles, saying in an urgent whisper:

"Come in, Charlie. We're all in a rush. Dad's in hospital and Mum's got to get over there to see the doctor at half-past two."

Charlie followed her into the dining room where the table was set for three people. Before he had a chance to ask for more information, Lottie Cutter rushed in from the kitchen, clearly flustered and flushed of face. She was carrying two plates of food. She bade Charlie and Sally sit at the table and she set the plates down in front of them.

"Sorry to rush you, Charlie dear," she called as she disappeared back into the kitchen, "but Tom's in hospital and we have to get the bus by two o'clock."

She re-appeared almost immediately with a third plate for herself and sat down with a sigh.

Charlie watched her until she settled, then asked:

"What exactly is wrong with Mr Cutter?"

The two women started to speak at once, but Sally ceased abruptly at a glance from her mother. Lottie Cutter explained:

"Tom has had this irritating cough for a long time. He's always said the wood treatment at the timber yard made him cough. I've been at him to see the doctor but he's kept putting it off. He's been taking a cough syrup from the chemist to ease it, but last night he started coughing after supper and didn't seem able to stop. Then he suddenly started coughing up blood. Sally phoned for an ambulance from the box on the corner and they were here in no time. They took him straight to Hackney Hospital. We were told to stay here and to go over at half past two this afternoon, when they will have had time to examine him and we can learn what's what."

"Oh, I see," said Charlie. He shrugged. "Well, you don't have to rush for the bus, do you? It's only five minutes in the car, so I can take you when you've had your lunch. You'll let me do that for you?"

"Oh, Charlie you are so kind! Are you sure it's not putting you out at all, though? We can manage on the buses, you know."

Charlie grinned. "You've got enough to worry about without concerning yourself with my round. Any way, it will only take a few minutes. It's the least I can do."

"Bless me, Charlie, you're a treasure! Thank you very much."

They concentrated on the food in front of them for a few minutes, then Mrs Cutter said:

"Yes, of course it is all a bit of a worry, but I expect things will turn out alright in the end."

Charlie nodded encouragingly, his deep blue eyes giving away nothing of his thoughts. Coughing up blood… They did not need him to express what they were all thinking. He glanced across at Sally. Other than when opening the front door to him, Sally had not spoken since her mother had begun to explain the situation. Now, she returned his glance with a nervous smile.

"You been okay, Sal?" he asked. "This business with your dad will have been a shock for everyone, but I mean apart from this. I've not seen you for ages."

"Yeah, I'm okay. Life's been a bit hectic at the factory. We've been busy and I've been out a lot. I ran up there first thing this morning and they let me come home to be with Mum till we know Dad's alright. Cissie and Harry will come over after work."

She smiled again, slightly easier, but not a Sally smile. Charlie nodded. They returned their attention to the food.

When they reached the hospital, Charlie offered to wait for them and to take them home but Mrs Cutter, not knowing how long she may be detained, insisted he leave them and resume his normal routine. They would get the bus home and Cissie and Harry would probably be waiting for them, she explained.

Charlie reluctantly accepted that he could be of no further help at that time and so moved on to his next customer.

* * *

His day's calls, completed; Charlie called at Amhurst Road to take tea with his mother. With Billy and Sally Walters now running a successful business from the lower ground floor at Amhurst Road and not needing her guidance, Millie was spending four mornings per week in the little church office. This was a busy week, she explained to Charlie. Father Peter, now well into his sixties, needed all the assistance she could offer to manage his heavy workload. The congregation had grown hugely with the building of the new church but he had been reluctant to accept the bishop's offer of an assistant priest.

Recently, though, he had conceded that he could not cope satisfactorily, and the young and innocent-looking Fr. Thomas Maine had been appointed to the new post the previous week. Father Peter had introduced him to the full congregation on Sunday.

Millie's judgement was that the appointment was a sound one. The young priest brimmed with sincerity, energy and optimism. However, while she fully approved of his energy, she could not stop herself from comparing him with her beloved Fr. Peter.

In appearance, Thomas Maine was the absolute antithesis of the old priest. Poor Peter was worn and tired, but still, as ever, effusing his gentle warmth to all. Whereas Fr. Peter was short and wide of girth, the new man was tall and thin. Fr. Peter's visage was round and rosy red, and Fr. Thomas was pale, and angular.

"Nevertheless, the odd couple seemed to work well together from the very first day," admitted Millie.

"He'll do well if he proves as popular as Father Peter," said Charlie. "He's been a remarkable priest all these years."

"Yes, he is very special to me – to us – but time moves on, Charlie. I think dear Peter feels his time is past. It is time for him to rest now."

Charlie shrugged. "I suppose that's reasonable enough," he replied.

His mother sighed and abruptly changed the subject.

"Did Margret get away alright, yesterday?"

"Yes. I took her to Charing Cross and saw her onto the train."

"Mmm. Are you going to stay in that house on your own?"

"Yes, in the main. I shall no doubt spend a lot of odd nights here, though. That okay?"

Millie Stoker tutted. "Of course, you foolish boy! Your room is always ready for you, you know that. You look tired, how's your work going?"

Charlie studied his mother for a few moments. He was a bit tired; the last few days had been particularly stressful; but he could see that she herself had heavy black shadows under her eyes. She did not look as sprightly as usual. He decided it was not the time to load his anxieties upon her.

"It's okay, Mum, I keep busy. But are you sure you're not overdoing things? What with managing this place and running the church…"

"Don't be silly! I don't do too much at the church, although, I must say, the arrival of Father Thomas will change things a bit. And I do worry about Father

Peter. He has given so much of himself for so many years. He needs to rest, but I'm not sure that he can. He'll die in that cassock!"

Charlie wondered if that thought may not actually please the old priest, but he refrained from saying it. Instead, he changed the subject slightly.

"One thing that does bother me a bit at the moment is the amount of anti-Jewish and anti-immigrant feeling that's beginning to show up around the area. I meet a lot of people who seem to support the ideas of the B.U.P. Bobby's mentioned it several times to me. He worries about Daphne and her family – her dad goes on about it a lot.

"Then, yesterday morning, Laura at Collick's told me about a crowd of bullies threatening Shayna Dekker's son. You'll remember Shayna Dekker? Mrs Dekker from the curtain department."

"Yes, the little Polish woman, nice woman."

"Yeah. A really decent woman, and her family's the same, Laura said, nice people."

"Mmm, yes, I'm sure."

Millie nodded thoughtfully. When she spoke again, her words surprised Charlie.

"The trouble is, you see, Charlie, a lot of people worry about their jobs. You know times have been hard. A lot of people are still living in poverty, either without work or working for very little reward. Many of these people think that the incomers are stealing their livelihoods, their chances of progressing. They get frightened, fear the worst. It's a fact of life that people tend to react badly when they are frightened."

"Yeah, but we can't turn the other cheek. We can't condone these things. If you condone it, you're condoning the law of the jungle. That road leads to chaos!"

"The seeds of discord are always with us, Charlie. It is our responsibility as good Christians to see that they are not allowed to grow."

Charlie breathed deeply. He shrugged.

Chapter Fourteen
God's Finger

The house at Woodside Way was not welcoming when Charlie reached there on that Tuesday evening. Margret had been living at home for most of the last three months, and Charlie had become accustomed to the company. Now she was gone, and she would be gone for two years. Although he was accustomed to finding an empty house, it seemed at that moment more deserted, more uninviting than ever. He felt more alone than ever. He poured himself a whisky and lit a cigarette.

There was nothing to be gained by feeling sorry for himself. Briefly, he considered going out. He was anxious to know the situation at the Cutters' but rejected the idea of making another visit that night. It would be intrusive of him. Instead, he pottered about in the garage for an hour or two.

The next morning, he made a small detour from his usual route and called at Armagh Road, Bow. He found only an empty house. No doubt Sally had gone back to work, and it was likely that her mother was out shopping. Nevertheless, he felt uneasy about the situation. He was due to call on the Batesons later and might learn something there. If not, he decided, he would return to Bow before his evening swim with Bobby.

As it happened, Charlie found Harry Bateson waiting impatiently for him to call before rushing off to his mother-in-law's. Harry's brow was drawn. He had seen the family the previous evening and the news was bleak.

"Mother-in-law was alright, considering the shock," said Harry. "So was Cissie. Sally and her mum got a chance to speak to my father-in-law last night and he was in good humour, like always, but the x-ray result was bad. It showed a large white mass on his lungs, and they had it explained to them that that almost certainly indicated a carcinoma. The surgeon is going to open him up to examine the situation thoroughly, but he wants him to rest for a day or two before any surgery, so that his body can settle down after the to-do with the coughing blood."

"That doesn't sound good, Harry," said Charlie sombrely, "but he's in the right place and we must hope for the best. I don't want to intrude, but if I can be of any help, running errands or taking people to and from – anything at all – will you leave a message at Collick's? I'll give you the phone number and I'll check with them every day."

"You're a good man, Charlie, thanks. As things are, I don't think anyone can do anything, but I'll tell my mother-in-law what you said. She'll be grateful for the thought."

* * *

The following Tuesday, having heard nothing more from the Cutter family in the intervening days, Charlie again called at Armagh road. A troubled-looking Lottie Cutter welcomed him.

"Hallo, Charlie dear, do come in. I'm glad to see you. You always bring a bit of happiness into the house!"

Charlie gave her a big smile. "I do my best, but it's not easy!" He followed her inside. "How are things?"

"Well, Charlie, it's not good I'm afraid. Tom is very ill. Harry told you about the x-ray, didn't he? Well, they did an operation on Saturday and the chief doctor told me they are starting a course of radiation treatment to kill off the cancer. He explained that the latest x-ray equipment can be used to kill cancerous tumours, and he thinks that's Tom's best chance. They're giving him a week to get over the operation and they are starting the treatment next Monday."

Charlie nodded gently, his brow drawn. Lottie Cutter continued:

"He was very nice, but he said quite bluntly that if they do nothing Tom will die; but if this treatment works like they hope, he will recover and be fine. He said Tom is otherwise healthy and that is in his favour. We just have to be patient for a couple of months."

"Well, that sounds encouraging, anyway," said Charlie. "If the consultant said that, that's great news. Is it okay to visit him? What did he say about visiting?"

"There's nothing to stop us going, he said, but Tom may not feel like having visitors for a few days when the radio treatment starts. I'll tell you more in a minute. Let me get the food on the table first while you do the books."

The three Collick's account books were on the mantelpiece with a ten-shilling note protruding from the top one, and Charlie took the note and filled in the week's entries. He had not expected to find Mr Cutter's payment included, but there it was, as usual.

The table was laid for three people and Sally came through the front door while Mrs Cutter was still the kitchen. She called a greeting to her mother before, seeing Charlie smiling at her, she greeted him with a pained smile as she removed her coat, a stylish woollen model, mustard-coloured and three-quarter length.

"It's turned chilly, hasn't it?" she said, feeling the need to justify her choice of apparel.

"Yeah, it can do that at the end of September, can't it?" he replied disarmingly. "It catches you out. Although, to tell the truth, I hadn't really noticed it today."

"Well, it's alright for you. You've got a three-piece woollen suit on!"

Charlie shrugged. That was a little more like Sally. Her mother entered with two steaming plates.

"How's Cissie doing?" asked Charlie.

"Very well, considering," said the proud grandmother-to-be. "She's still at the sick in the morning stage but quite well on the whole. Now come on, eat!" she urged. She disappeared, returning with her own steaming plate and resuming her conversation with Charlie as if it had not been broken off.

"General visiting is allowed each day between two and three o'clock, or between seven and eight o'clock, no more than two people at one time. I've gone each afternoon and the girls have shared the evenings. Cissie and Harry went last night and Sally's going tonight, aren't you, dear?"

She turned towards her daughter as she spoke. Sally nodded her confirmation. She had not spoken since her opening words.

"Would it be okay for me to visit?" asked Charlie. "I should like to if possible."

"Yes, of course, Charlie dear. Tom will be pleased to see you. When do you want to go?"

"I could take you on Thursday afternoon, if that suits? I'll pick you up at 1.45 pm sharp. Actually, to save you from rushing, would you like me to drop you off this afternoon? I shan't be able to stay but I can certainly take you there."

"Bless you, Charlie. You are an angel!"

* * *

The weather had turned warmer with the arrival of rain the next morning, but it was nevertheless a quiet night at The Chequers, the current pub of choice for the two friends after their Wednesday swim. The only other occupants of the saloon bar were an elderly couple playing cribbage at a table by the window and a bearded, but otherwise nondescript lone drinker at the end of the bar.

Bobby was again showing concern about the news dribbling in from Europe. He reported it to Charlie as distilled from Daphne's father's apoplectic outbursts.

"He was s-saying that in Na-azi-land – that's what he calls Germany now – the latest official announcement was that Jews are 's-ub-humans' – I can't pronounce the German word, something like 'u-undermention' – and they're not allowed to mix their blood with Aryans. He reckons that if a Jewish boy is seen with a non-Jewish girl, they are both hauled off to a concentration camp! It's h-hard to believe, i'n't it?"

Charlie shrugged. "I don't think I understand what's going on anywhere anymore—"

He broke off, failing to complete the comment. He drew on his cigarette, the tip burning brightly for several seconds. He slowly exhaled, and crushed the stub into an ashtray. Then he smiled at Bobby's concerned expression and shrugged again.

"Bobby, the world's only a problem for those who need to worry about it. There's no point in our concerning ourselves. You've got enough problems worrying about repairing motors and looking after you and Daphne. Leave running the world to those who can, or think they can."

Bobby was shaking his head.

"It's all p-part of the same thing, Charlie. Daphne s-sees her old man in a state and sh-he gets in a state. She was telling me the other day that he was on again about it all starting here, now. His cousin lives in the East End and her son was set on by anti-Semitic hooligans on his way home from football."

Charlie looked up sharply. "What's his name?"

"A-Alfie, Alfie Dekker. Why?"

"His mother works at Collick's."

"Sh-Shayna? Does she? I didn't kn-know that! You know her?"

"Yeah, I knew about the boy as well. He wasn't hurt, though."

"No, by the grace of G-God!"

"Yeah, maybe."

The last word was uttered almost inaudibly but Bobby heard it and his reaction was half way between surprised and quizzical.

"W-what d'you mean? Y-you alright, Charlie? That doesn't sound like you."

Charlie sighed. "I'm beginning to doubt that God's got any grace, Bobby," he said in a tone of guilty doubt.

Bobby's look was now purely quizzical.

Charlie went on:

"No God who cares would allow the world to carry on as it does. You don't have to think of the world picture, the rise of dictators: Hitler in Germany, Mussolini, charging through Africa. You don't have to look beyond our daily life."

He stopped abruptly and lifted his glass, then slowly replaced it on its mat without sipping from it. Bobby waited. This was a rare speech from Charlie and he was sure there was more to come.

"You know I went to Southend at the Bank Holiday with the Cutter family," said Charlie.

"Yeah?" Bobby couldn't stop himself from adding, "The blonde's family?"

"Yes! Well, the point is they are really nice people, a lovely family, mother, father and two daughters. Sally is the younger. Her dad's a smashing bloke, assistant buyer in a timber company. Last week, he came home from work, collapsed and got taken to hospital. Now they've said he's got cancer in his lungs. He's dying. Just like that. No real warning, nothing! Just that God's finger picked him out. That's God's grace for you, Bobby!"

"Oh, Charlie, I-I'm s-sorry! That's b-b-b—"

Bobby stuttered to a stop. He went to place a consoling arm on his friend's shoulder but Charlie immediately stiffened. Bobby withdrew the arm. This was a different Charlie; one Bobby had never seen before. This was a Charlie stripped of the veneer of shrugs and smiles. This was Charlie hurting badly and speaking from the heart.

"Th-that's bad, Charlie, but th-that's not all, is it? You're hurting bad, I can see. What is it, mate? Wh-what else is eating you? You know you can tell me. Y-you know I'm here for you."

Bobby was almost in tears in his anxiety to help his friend, but Charlie's response was pure Charlie. After a deep sigh, he shrugged and gave his friend a reassuring smile.

"No, I'm alright, Bobby. It's just that, sometimes, sometimes when you think you've got life worked out, it suddenly throws you all out of joint. There have been a few things happened all at once just lately and I suppose I'm still trying to steady the ship, as my grandfather used to say."

He lifted his glass and drained it. Bobby watched, then said:

"Anything you want to t-tell me about, Charlie?"

Charlie stared at him over his empty glass.

"Yeah, it's your round!"

* * *

Elsie Philpott had produced her second child, a girl, just before the end of the heat wave, two weeks after the August Bank Holiday of 1935. Her mother had been on hand to assist her through a tiresomely difficult few days, but by the middle of October she was a round-faced and round-bodied mother of two, bustling around happily at 34 Barlow Street.

When Charlie arrived, Elsie greeted him with her usual big, blushing smile. He was carrying a couple of ladies' afternoon dresses and when she caught sight of them she uttered a cry of delight.

"Oh, Charlie! A new dress is just what I need!" She giggled. "If I can get into one!"

"We'll find one to fit you, Elsie. You're looking very well, I must say."

"Oh, you! You'll say anything to flatter a girl!"

"No, I mean it. You're looking great. Having kids seems to suit you!"

"Oh, Charlie! Now come in and sit down. Alice, my sister-in-law is here, so you can chat with her while I just finish making some tea."

She pointed him towards the small front parlour and scuttled on to the kitchen. He found Alice Pensell standing, rocking the new baby gently in her arms. She explained that she had popped in to visit her youngest niece and to share a cup of tea and a chat with her sister-in-law. Her eyes, though, were drawn at once to the dresses.

"They look nice! Are they mid-calf or ankle?"

Charlie grinned. "I only bring shorter ones to Elsie. They'll all be too long!"

"Oh, I expect so. Not for me, though!"

Alice was an impressive woman, at least five or six inches taller than Elsie and with a well-shaped figure.

"No, I think they'll be too short and too wide for you!"

"Yeah!" She gave a short laugh. "They do look like nice dresses, though. Have you got that green one in my size? Probably a 38" hip for comfort."

"As it happens…" said Charlie with a grin. "I've got one in the car. Would you like me to give it to Walter to bring along to you? You're on his books, aren't you?"

Alice appeared momentarily discomfited, but then she smiled wickedly.

"Well, yes, but is that a reason for not opening an account with you? I can leave the money with Elsie if you don't want to call at the house."

"It would be a pleasure to call on you, Alice, but I wouldn't want to upset Walter, and I wouldn't be able to call on Fridays. It would have to be a Monday afternoon call."

Alice Pensell broke into a wicked smile.

"That suits me just fine. I'll tell Walter. He'll be annoyed, but it'll keep him on his toes!"

* * *

Charlie Stoker was enjoying considerable success as a tallyman towards the end of 1935. In his nearly four years as a salesman, he had built the business to such an extent that he had become one of Aitch Harrington's so-called 'gold-standard members'.

When he had first taken over Round 3, in February 1932, he had inherited fewer than two hundred accounts in about one hundred and fifty homes, collecting a total less than £30 per week. By the end of 1935, Charlie was collecting between £70 and £80 every week from nearly four hundred accounts, but the number of actual weekly calls was no more than one hundred and seventy.

There were, including Charlie, four 'gold standard members' – men with rounds whose collections exceeded £60 every week. Each Thursday, Aitch would call out the name of the week's top man, and if by some chance it was someone other than the golden four, the sales manager would delight in berating all four as slackers.

Three of the four had developed businesses from the roots established during the early nineteen-twenties by Harrington himself and two of the men who were now his supervisors, Messrs Spafford and Grieve. The fourth was Round five, which Walter Habisch, under Harrington's guidance, had built from 1926. All four 'golden' rounds had been developed organically. That was Harrington's method.

As soon as a customer's children began to earn, so each was encouraged to open their own account. As the children married and set up their own homes, so they developed new family groups, all with a bond of loyalty to the salesman/collector who visited each week and who found ways to furnish them with their requirements at a price that they could afford to pay.

That goodwill was spread to friends and neighbours and to their families. If the growth became unmanageable for a salesman, then accounts would be re-allocated on a geographical basis to form the basis of new rounds, the transfers carefully monitored by the supervisor.

To become a 'gold standard' member, a man must achieve and maintain the 'golden' level for a minimum of three consecutive months. On achieving the standard, he was invited to enjoy a glass of champagne with the Managing Director in his third-floor office, after which, on the raised dais of the salesmen's room in front of the whole sales force, he was presented with a set of crystal glasses engraved with the company crest. He would also receive a bonus of £15.

Charlie qualified for the award at the end of September 1935. So it was, therefore, that he entered the top floor office for the first time in almost five years, on the second Thursday of October in the company of both Mr Harrington and Mr Spafford.

Stephen Collick greeted the three men cordially with a handshake and a glass of champagne for each. His attitude to Charlie was exactly as he had promised it would be at their private meeting in January 1931. He was the charming company boss who was introduced to, and warmly shook the hand of and chinked glasses with, Collick's newest young star.

Stephen complimented him on his exceedingly rapid progress and reminded him how fortunate he had been in having two such remarkably good tutors in Messrs. Harrington and Spafford. Turning to the manager and the supervisor, he emphasised to them how well they had done to find and to develop such a fine young star. Just before releasing them to go to the general meeting in the basement, he surprised Charlie by saying, with a beaming smile:

"One more thing, young man. You are probably aware that the position of supervisor in our company requires qualities other than those required of a salesman. Not all men are suitable. Mr Harrington is planning to make the next supervisory appointment early next year. He has told me that he believes you have the qualities to fill that position and he would like to offer you the post when it comes to pass. What do you say?"

"Thank you, sir," replied Charlie, his blue eyes, as always in such situations, betraying nothing of his thoughts. "That's a great compliment, and very flattering of Mr Harrington."

He said no more. The hint of a smile remained in place, but his mind whirled. He loved his work. He loved the freedom of setting his own daily schedule and the joy he experienced in the relationships renewed each week with so many customers. He did not want to change the state of things he had so carefully built. He was not yet twenty-five years old. He was not ready to move on. He was doing what he was good at and he did not intend to give it up.

* * *

After four weeks of calling at the Pensell home on Monday afternoons, Charlie had learned that Alice Pensell was a woman of unpredictable mood. If he had hoped to find Alice in one of her more subdued moods this week, he was sorely disappointed. She greeted him wearing a peach-coloured negligée over a matching nightdress.

"Thank God you're early Charlie," she greeted him with a wicked smile, "I need you!"

Charlie response was a raised eyebrow. He followed her into the little sitting room, where she abruptly stopped, turned, and reached for the back of his head with her two arms, pulling him down into her embrace. She kissed him hungrily, then, equally abruptly, sat down on the two-seat settee and dragged him down next to her.

Charlie had still not uttered a word. The Stoker smile was hinted at in his eyes. Alice was wearing a seductive perfume. She deliberately began to stroke his thigh.

"Okay, Alice," said Charlie, now openly smiling but not looking at her, and conscious of the beginnings of arousal, "you can stop just about now!"

"Cha-arlie, I can feel you don't mean that, and I need a man, a bi-ig man!"

Charlie stood up. "That's enough, Alice. Stop, now!"

But Alice was not in the mood to be chastened.

"Charlie, my husband is in gaol for a year and I am desperate. You know we light each other up, it was obvious from that first minute at Elsie's. Make love to me, take the ache away and make me feel like a woman!"

Charlie stood, facing away from Alice. He lit a cigarette.

"You are every bit a woman, Alice. You don't need the negligée or the perfume. You are a damned attractive woman. But I am not the man for you. I am a married man and I do not stray."

He turned his head towards her and grinned suddenly.

"Any way, what would Walter say?"

"F*** what Walter would say!"

Charlie drew on his cigarette and blew several smoke rings. Alice said:

"Walter's a good pal, but you're a big man! Come on, Charlie, be the big man."

"I can't do it, Alice. No matter how much you stir me up, it's not going to happen. I'll always be here if you need a friend, but I will not be your lover." He shrugged and inhaled.

"Let's have a cup of tea, eh?"

"You're a bastard, Charlie Stoker!"

"I'll wait while you get dressed."

Alice rose from the settee and swiped her arm across the side of Charlie's head, causing his ears to ring. She swept out of the room.

Chapter Fifteen
God's Holy Law

Charlie's twenty-fifth birthday fell on a Wednesday that year, and he celebrated it in a small Soho restaurant with Bobby, Daphne and Jennifer. Birthday gifts were handed to Charlie, a bottle of Jameson's from Jennifer and a box of cigars from Bobby and Daphne. Then, they spent the first part of the evening happily reminiscing. It was the first time the four had enjoyed what was, in effect, a reunion dinner.

Having come together as a group almost from Charlie's first day at the Northern, the four had remained firm friends. It was through this friendship that he had met Margret, whose absence was noted rather sombrely – the only disappointment of the evening.

Both Charlie and Jennifer were in regular mail contact with her and both understood that she was thoroughly enjoying the excitement of living in Paris and the challenge of lecturing in French. Daphne expressed concern that Charlie now had to look after himself, but he laughed it off. Margret had simply exchanged Clare Market for Paris, he said casually. He imagined that Jennifer, who had been close to Margaret for most of her life, was as much used to seeing his wife as he was, and would be sorely missing her friend. Jennifer coloured slightly.

"Yes, of course we miss her," she said, "but she is doing what is right for her."

"Yes, I'm sure that's right," said Daphne. She looked at Bobby, who found it necessary to clean his glasses at that moment.

Charlie shrugged.

Daphne had pre-arranged for a small birthday cake to be brought to the table with the coffees and liqueurs. Charlie blew out the one candle and everybody laughed at his display of strength. The rest of the evening passed pleasantly, with Jennifer chatting mainly to Daphne, and the two boys talking to each other.

Jennifer's chemist shop had been open for a year and was a thriving business. Since her move, the girls had seen very little of each other. Most of their contact was by telephone or by messages carried by Jennifer's father between the two pharmacies. Naturally, they had much catching up of gossip to do.

During the evening, Bobby tried more than once to raise the subject of his friend's anxieties. Charlie avoided all such discussion with either a shrug, a smile, or a change of subject.

At the end of the evening, Daphne suggested they should not wait until birthdays or other special occasions before getting together again. Instead, they should have a monthly dinner out at a restaurant. She thought they could take turns to choose a venue, and she would undertake to plan the next one, in December.

The idea was well received, Bobby nodding vigorously. Jennifer cried out "Yes, of course!" and Charlie, amenable as always, shrugged.

* * *

At the end of 1935, having spent three months in Paris, Margret returned to Chigwell for a two week stay at Christmas. She was excited about her life in France, and stressed at every opportunity how much she was relishing the 'intellectual stimulus' gained from her interaction with her peers at the Sorbonne.

Early in the New Year, Charlie once again took her to Charing Cross station for her return to France. Before leaving, she summed up her feelings about the trip. She had 'tolerated' the necessary socialising with the Mabeys and their friends; she had 'enjoyed' a Christmas lunch at Amhurst Road with Charlie, Millie, Stephen and Father Peter; and she had been relaxed by a couple of days at home in Chigwell with Charlie. But she left her husband with the clear impression that her happiest days were the ones spent with Jennifer at the Bounds Green flat and at the Lacey New Year party.

Charlie accepted the farewell peck on his cheek without comment and drove back to work. He had certainly found the atmosphere at Clay Hill, when they had taken lunch with Margret's parents, if not exactly tense, then certainly not relaxed. The whole Mabey family had been present, and the relationship between Margret and her brothers was as icily antagonistic as always.

Harry, whom Charlie had not seen for a couple of years, and who now preferred to be called Henry, had put on some weight. His appearance had become much more like that of his father, burly and florid; but it was his voice, shrill and lacking a shred of warmth, that more truly disclosed his character.

Terence, Margret's younger brother, had completed his university course and was now working under Henry's guidance at Cavendish, Brigham, Mabey. He was slight of build, quite unlike the other two Mabey males, and of a clearly nervous disposition, with irritating hand movements and darting eyes. He was also clearly dominated by his brother.

Their father, Herbert Mabey, had been his usual surly self until he had drunk sufficient alcohol to make him for a time overbearingly sociable, then sleepily maudlin. His attitude towards his sons was as dismissive as ever, and even towards Charlie it was far more acerbic than in the past, although as the day progressed it mellowed.

This coolness was apparently a consequence of his failure to develop a business relationship with Stephen Collick and the Collick Estate. He appeared unaccountably aggrieved that Charlie had not been able to influence 'the Collicks' to appoint his company as legal advisors, at least to one or two of the companies in the group. Charlie had shrugged helplessly at the ludicrousness of the suggestion. The idea that a mere salesman from the smallest division in the Collick family's affairs could influence company policy was beyond amusing.

The day at Amhurst Road had been, in contrast, a truly delightful experience. They had arrived on Boxing Day at eleven o'clock in the morning to find both Stephen and a smiling Father Peter there ahead of them. After a joyous exchange of Christmas gifts and some sparkling champagne, they had all eaten too much, drunk too much and played silly games until late in the evening. Charlie marvelled at how his mother had blossomed into the perfect hostess in the few years since she had first taken tea with Stephen Collick. She had found happiness and contentment after years of tragedy.

Even more remarkable was the relationship that had developed between Margret and his mother. Margret always looked forward to visiting her mother-in-law. When in Millie Stoker's presence, Margret became a different person. There was none of the sneering superiority, the disregard of good manners. She was a respectful, sensitive, warm and understanding daughter-in-law.

It bothered Charlie not at all that elsewhere she may appear a harridan. He and Margret had reached their understanding in their marriage. Providing they did nothing to disturb the harmony of life at Woodside Way and providing each was always available to fulfil any joint family obligations, then what they did with the rest of their life was their own business.

The situation should have suited both well, but the more time passed, the more Charlie became discontented. For six years, they had lived their strange married life. On one level it was a success. Both parties had bricks and mortar to come home to and freedom to pursue their careers.

For Margret that was enough; but, although he had been the driving force for the union, Charlie believed in his heart of hearts marriage should mean more. There should be love and there should be children. That was what marriage meant. That was at the centre of everything he had been taught from childhood, a belief enhanced by his own parents' sad inability to grow their family beyond their only son.

The drawback was that the marriage oath was sworn 'till death do us part.' There was no exit clause for choosing recklessly. He and his wife had sworn that oath, and they must live accordingly. He recalled the words: *for better, for worse, for richer, for poorer, in sickness and in health, to love and to cherish, till death do us part, according to God's holy law…*

Well, he reflected, in self-righteous mitigation, he may be deficient in love, but he still honoured most of those commitments.

The truth was that Charlie was having to re-think much of his attitude to living. For the first twenty-five years of his life he had learned, then practised, a life of strict conformity to his mother's rules, except for smoking and drinking, both of which she had come to tolerate. The adherence to the teachings of Father Peter O'Rahilly and the Catholic Church, however, were inviolable.

As interpreted in the language of the two young men in the saloon bar of The Chequers on a cold January night in 1936, those teachings boiled down to: if you lived a decent life, a life of probity and hard work, then God would take care of you.

The problem for Charlie was that he had come to doubt that God was keeping his share of the bargain. Not that he could complain about his own progress in life. In spite of his sins – his smoking, his drinking, his college fornicating, he was doing better than most people of his age in terms of health and wealth. But that morning, he had attended the funeral of Tom Cutter.

"Tell me what Thomas Cutter, of all people, has done to be deprived of his life?" he demanded, raging directly at the Lord. He stared ferociously at the half-empty glass in front of him, as if to see there an image of the target of his question, and seeing instead the compassionate eyes of old Father Peter.

"Tell me, explain to me why could I not be allowed to see my son born with a beating heart? Tell me what my father had done to merit his years of agony and to be trampled to death? What had my mother done to lose her whole family, one after the other? What are the sins of all those I love that they deserve this punishment? For pity's sake, tell me, how is all this the work of a benevolent God?"

Chapter Sixteen
The B-Blonde

Sally's father had succumbed to a particularly aggressive form of cancer less than four months after that first episode of coughing blood. Charlie had visited him in hospital on several occasions and had seen for himself the rapid deterioration in the man's condition. The whole sixteen-week experience, heartbreakingly stressful for all those near him, had taken a terrible toll on the health of his wife, Charlotte.

Charlie had watched the tragedy unfold and wept inside, powerless to be of any real assistance beyond providing a taxi service. In three years, he had come to hold the Cutter family very dear. He had formed a close attachment not only to Sally, but to the whole family; a bond as strong as that he treasured with Bobby and with Stephen Collick.

Not only had the Cutter family shown him love, but they had succeeded in showing him how to reciprocate that love. They had, in a sense, replaced his own lost family. They had pierced his shield. He had planned to have them meet his mother at Christmas time, but that had inevitably to be postponed for the time being.

He had kept his promise to be available for Lottie Cutter at any time, and had taken her to and from the hospital every Thursday and on a number of Sundays. On the Sunday visits, Cissie and Harry had usually been with them, but he had seen very little of Sally. She had accompanied her mother on one Sunday trip but had been extremely subdued and had avoided having any real conversation with him.

At the funeral, she had looked painfully beautiful, dressed all in black with a complexion as colourless as her mother's. After the ceremony, Charlie had attempted to comfort her. Sally had not exactly rebuffed him, but her whole manner had suggested a sense of despair, a sense that her life was worthless.

The situation with her father had arisen suddenly and was no doubt reason enough for her to be emotionally stressed; but the odd fleeting looks that had passed between the two of them told Charlie that what they felt for each other could not be ignored. It was a major issue to be dealt with when the sad business of the day was concluded.

After the morning's funeral, Charlie had been invited along with a number of attending well-wishers to share a tea and sandwich buffet with Lottie Cutter and family at the Tudor Tea Rooms, near Victoria Park. The party included a number of cousins, several old friends of the family and a small group of Cutter's work colleagues.

Charlie, of course had given his usual public performance, smiling, shrugging and generally leaving a good impression with all. Unfortunately, he had found no opportunity to speak more than a passing word with Sally, who made only a very brief appearance before disappearing.

When it was all over, Charlie had felt the need for a strong drink. He had made his way to The Three Kings, where he was joined by a few friends from Collick's. Several drinks later, he had called Bobby and asked him to forego their regular swim on this particular evening. He had asked his friend to go, instead, straight to The Chequers, where he would join him. An hour or more – and several drinks – later, Charlie had left the Three Kings to meet Bobby.

At The Chequers, his deep blue eyes fierce with the alcohol-fuelled anger of impotence, he dragged his attention up from the fading vision in his half-empty glass to his speechless friend, demanding an answer to the unanswerable question within his questions.

Bobby, watching anxiously through his thick tortoiseshell spectacles, was at a loss as to how to help. This was all wrong. Everything was topsy-turvy. This was Charlie! Charlie having a drunken rant! It should be him, Bobby, who got drunk, not Charlie. Charlie never got drunk. That was the way things were, how they'd always been.

He removed his glasses, wiped them and replaced them.

"S-s-steady on, old mate!" he said, surprising himself with the authority of his tone. "Th-this is not like you, Charlie. Y-you don't go on about things. And, you're not the chap to l-lose your way, ever, w-whatever you're on about…"

He paused, gathering the courage to say more. Then, as calmly as he could, he said:

"Charlie, you kn-know I'm not really the one to speak to about G-God and all that. But there's s-something else b-bothering you deep down. It has been for m-months now. You've g-got to tell me. You've gotta get it off your chest!" His face turned scarlet as he exclaimed in utter exasperation: "Whatever it is, for C-Christ's sake let it out!"

At the sound of the shouted oath, all conversations in the saloon bar went silent. Bobby's scarlet face became puce. Charlie's gaze was again fixed on his half-empty glass, his expression, as usual, telling nothing. He sipped at his ale, then pushed it away in distaste. He shrugged, a reflex movement. He looked at his wide-eyed friend. He shook his head. Eventually, he spoke.

"You're right, Bobby," he said. "You deserve more. You are the nearest thing to a brother I can ever have" – a fleeting hesitation – "or could ever want. You deserve better, and I'm really sorry."

He hung his head. When he spoke again, it was as if he were sober.

"The truth is, last summer, quite suddenly, I found myself in a situation. I became involved with someone, the girl I should have married."

"The b-b-blonde!" exclaimed Bobbie in a loud whisper.

"Yes, the blonde. For me, she is the perfect woman. She has every quality I could ever desire. But I am a married man."

"B-But y-you've always s-said—"

"Yeah, I know, I can take it or leave it." Charlie shrugged. "This is different. It's not sex. You know why I called you today, you know that a customer died. And you know I've mentioned the Cutter family to you before, the family I took to Southend."

Bobby nodded.

"Well, it was Tom Cutter, Sally's father, who died."

"The man who coughed up blood and you went to see in hospital? You said he was dying."

"Yes."

"B-Bloody heck! S-Sally, that's the b-blonde!"

"Yes."

"And y-you've been seeing her?"

"No, not like that, Bobby. We've never been properly out together, unless you count that one day with her parents in Southend. There hasn't been any physical contact, other than one brief kiss. In fact, apart from chatting at the house on Tuesday afternoons and one trip to a tea room, we've never been alone together."

Bobby snorted.

"W-Well, that's n-nothing, then, is it?"

Charlie shrugged.

"No, I'm afraid it's not nothing, Bobby. It's the opposite of nothing. I've never cared how good-looking a girl is, or how sexy she might be, and I have never chased after one. I like people for all sorts of reasons. Friendships happen or they don't. Like ours. It just happened." He laughed. "Like my marriage! It just happened."

Bobby was listening intently, not quite sure what he was hearing. Charlie went on:

"When Sally walked into her house a year ago last May, I hadn't seen her for a couple of years. I remembered her as a skinny schoolgirl, but almost as soon as she came in that room, I experienced something remarkable. She smiled at me and my heart dropped. Like a lump of lead. You read it in books and it happens to other people, but that's what happened, Bobby."

"I knew then. She came into that room and smiled. But that smile was an arrow to my heart. Cupid's arrow! For the first time in my life, I knew what it was like to fall in love. More astonishing, though, was that Sally felt the same way about me. When we were at Southend last August she told me she had worshipped me from afar since she was fifteen!"

"B-B-Bloody heck!"

"I tried to ignore it, to carry on as usual, confident I would get over it, really. It was just an infatuation: but it wasn't. I saw her at her mother's every Tuesday lunchtime for over a year and that was almost our only contact. When we went to Southend in August, we went for a walk together and it all came out. Suddenly, she was in my arms and I was kissing her."

He shrugged.

"I realised the situation was impossible and I sat her down in a café and told her so. I told her she would find someone else in time and that I would always watch out for her and be her friend."

He stopped speaking and proffered his cigarette case. Bobby said:

"D-did she g-go along with that?"

"I don't know. I've hardly seen her since, until today. I think she's been avoiding me, but her father's condition has overridden everything. The whole family is in a state and I'm worried about her mother. Her health has not been too good for some time, and now she looks really ill."

They lit and smoked in silence for a while. Bobby ached to be able to help, but with Charlie in such an unprecedented black mood, he hesitated to voice his thoughts. Being Bobby, though, he was unable to hold back what was on his mind.

"Charlie," he said nervously, "y-you are the most ho-honourable man I have ever known. Your f-friendship means more to me than almost anything in the w-world – except Daphne, I s'pose. B-but I've got to ask you, w-why don't you get a divorce? Y-you and Margret don't love each other, you l-live separate lives and now she's even l-living in a different country!"

Charlie stared at Bobby for an hour-long couple of seconds, his face inscrutable. Then he shrugged.

"Marriage is for life, Bobby. You can't throw it away like a broken toy."

"B-But…" Bobby flapped his arms and sighed in resignation.

Charlie had intended to pop into his mother's after The Chequers, but Bobby persuaded him that a pie, some coffee, and then home to bed was a better plan. To make sure the plan was followed, Bobby stayed with his friend until he was on the road, then followed him discreetly on his motorbike. Unsurprisingly, Charlie drove home perfectly well, despite the volume of alcohol in his system.

* * *

The following afternoon, instead of the usual Thursday visit to the Three Kings, Charlie opted for poached eggs on toast at the little café off Bancroft Road. It was his intention to go to Amhurst Road during the afternoon but his first obligation, he knew, was to call on the Cutters.

Lottie Cutter was not alone when he arrived. Cissie and Sally were both with their mother. Cissie, now very pregnant, had given up her job at the paint factory, and Sally had made an arrangement with the goods despatch manager to cover for her. Harry Bateson was not there; he had had to go back to work.

In fact, Mrs Cutter looked much better than Charlie expected. Although still in black, with heavy eyes and hollow cheeks, she had regained a little colour. Cissie, looking very well, was pleased to be able to spend the time with her mother. Sally, in one of her working day dresses, seemed well enough physically, but her expression was a troubled one and she said very little.

Charlie sat with them for about an hour, accepting a cup of tea and a slice of cake and joining in the chat about the events of the previous day. The tone of conversation was never stressful, but did not avoid the fact that Tom Cutter was no longer there. The three women seemed to be coping well with the situation, helped, no doubt, by Cissie's condition and the promise of new life to come. Charlie further brightened the atmosphere with a number of light-hearted stories gathered from his rounds.

Surprisingly, Sally insisted on seeing him out when Charlie felt it was time to leave. She carefully closed both the sitting room door and the front door behind them, then stood on the step to speak to him in almost a whisper. There was tension in her voice, but her words had been carefully considered.

"Charlie, I need to talk to you but I can't do it here. Can you meet me later on at the ABC Tea Room in Dalston? Say, in about an hour? I've got to go into the factory before it closes, but I can get there alright. I'd really appreciate it."

"Yeah, okay, Sal, about four o'clock?" His answer came without hesitation, but he was studying her intently.

"Thanks, Charlie, I'll be there."

"It's okay, don't worry if you're tight for time, I'll wait."

"You're special, Charlie."

Charlie shrugged.

At about a minute past the agreed hour, Sally burst into the little Tea Room to find Charlie sitting at a table by the wall with a pot of tea and two cups and saucers. She greeted him with a huge smiling sigh and sat down heavily.

"Thank you Charlie. I'm so glad you came in today. But that's what you do, isn't it? You always manage to be a comfort when it's needed. I s'pose that's why I love you, why everybody loves you!"

Charlie shrugged, his eyes hinting at a smile. "Tea?"

"Thanks, although I'll probably be weeing all night! I've drunk so much tea today." She gave a little laugh. Charlie filled her cup.

"You're alright, Charlie, really? It's fantastic of you to be here for me. You've got enough problems in your own life without worrying about mine."

"I'm fine, Sal, and there's nowhere I'd rather be than anywhere you are. I told you I'll always be here for you and you don't have to doubt that."

Sally blinked several times and made a point of sipping her tea before speaking again.

"Charlie, the fact is, I'm in a terrible mess. I've been an awful fool and I need you. Not just a shoulder to cry on but I need your clear head to guide me. Up till now, there's always been Mum and Dad, but all of a sudden Dad's gone and Mum's not well. She's got enough on her plate. She's not in a fit state to know my problems."

She lifted her cup again and sipped at it. Charlie watched and waited patiently. Sally spoke from behind the cup.

"After that day in Southend I had a bad few weeks. I couldn't get my head around the fact that you'd said you loved me but that we could never be together. I stopped going home on Tuesdays so I wouldn't have to bear being so near to you."

She replaced the cup on its saucer. "At work, people were saying 'What's wrong with Sally?' Then a couple of the girls persuaded me to go out with them to a club on a Saturday night. They said it would take me out of myself a bit. And it did, I suppose. We got pie-eyed and laughed a lot. We said we'd make it a regular thing every Saturday till Christmas. We made friends with a lot of people there. Some of 'em were foreigners. There's a bunch of Danish sailors that were nice chaps. They carry cargo from Denmark to London and stay in London every second weekend."

She looked into Charlie's eyes and seemed to draw confidence from the empathy reflected there.

"When Dad wasn't getting better, I told Mum I'd stop going out till Dad was alright, but she said I was to do nothing of the kind. There was plenty of opportunities to see Dad, she said, and Saturday night was the time for young people to get out and enjoy themselves. Anyway, she said, Cissie and Harry would do Saturday visits.

"So, I kept on goin' out. It was quite fun and we had no trouble. Usually, some bloke or other would try it on a bit with one or other of us, but we could handle ourselves and we had a lot of fun.

"Then, at the end of October, four of us got invited to a private party by a bloke attached to the Danish Embassy. It was a very posh place in Mayfair and the party went on all night. We all got terrible drunk. We were drinking some Scandinavian stuff that looks like gin but it's much more powerful. We were drinking it straight, with these big Danish blokes. I don't remember anything after about eleven o'clock. I must have passed out. When I came to in the morning, I was stretched out on a big bed with one of the other girls asleep next to me. She woke up and we got ourselves together, and she said, 'Weren't they great!' and I said, 'Who?' and she said, 'Anders and Sven!'"

"Honest truth, Charlie, I haven't the faintest idea who Anders and Sven were. I remember chatting to a big chap named Hans, at least I think it was Hans. He reminded me of you. He was about your size and just as blond but his English was not good. We were having a decent time and smooching a bit, like you do at parties, but after that I just don't know what happened."

"After that night I stopped going out with the girls. Dad was getting worse and, although we didn't say it, we knew he was dying. Mum was beginning to have a bad time. She's never been really well since she was in hospital a few years ago, and Dad being in that state was breakin' her up. Cissie was a great support, and her bein' in her condition was a good thing in a way, 'cos it took Mum's mind off Dad.

"By the time December came, the hospital had already told us we must prepare for the worst with Dad. The cancer was everywhere."

Sally paused. Charlie had refilled her cup. She sipped some more tea. She took a deep breath and looked up at him, her eyes brimming. She said:

"It wasn't a time to tell them that I was going to have a baby as well, was it?"

Her words flung out in a tone of utter self-contempt, Sally was terrified of Charlie's reaction. She had ruined her life and was confessing her shame and seeking support from the one man she had dreamed of giving herself to, of sharing her life with. Now, what could he feel but anger and disgust? Tears trickled down her cheeks.

Charlie reached across the table. He took her hand.

"Sally, my poor love," he said softly.

"Why isn't it yours?" she cried in an irrational whisper. "Why isn't my baby yours?"

The trickling tears became a flood of sobs.

* * *

After that confession, Sally somehow pulled herself together at the tea room. As delicately as he could, Charlie raised the possibility of terminating the pregnancy. She dismissed the idea peremptorily and reprimanded him for suggesting it.

"I may have been a silly cow, Charlie, but I'm not a murderess. Why should the baby die because its mother didn't know what she was doing? It's not the baby's fault, is it?"

Charlie had no answer. He was ashamed of himself for introducing the subject. He, of all people, had no right to make such a suggestion. Seven years earlier, in vaguely related circumstances, he had blithely told Margret that their baby must live. The only difference now was that Sally was not being asked to go through a sham marriage.

He crushed out the cigarette he had been smoking and moved on to the next problem created by the situation:

"Sally, with losing your dad, your mum's going to be tight for money and you will have to give up your job. How are you going to manage?"

"I dunno. I haven't discussed anything with Mum yet. I'd have thought she would guess, but she's never said a thing. Maybe her mind was too much on Dad to notice."

She thought about what she was saying and her apparent self-composure crumbled. More tears ran down her cheeks.

"It's all a mess, Charlie. Everything is shit!"

Charlie shrugged and squeezed her hand.

"We'll get through this, Sal. You know I'll be here for you, whatever you need."

"Why? Why d'you say that, Charlie? You don't owe me anything. I love you and I'll always love you but you don't owe me a thing!"

"I do, because I love you, Sally, and I'll always take care of you."

Before leaving her to explain her situation to her family, he kissed her softly on the lips. There was no point in hiding his feelings any more. They loved each other. Her child would be born lacking a father. Well, he was a father who lacked a child. He would be a father to her child.

Chapter Seventeen
A Remarkable Man

Aitch Harrington's office was on the second floor of the Collick's building, and Charlie was instructed to report there at ten o'clock in the morning on the first Monday of February.

Since receiving the Gold Standard Award, Charlie had had almost no direct contact with the Sales Manager. There had been the usual Thursday accolades and the odd pleasantry when seen in passing, but otherwise it had been business as usual. Ivor Spafford, always the soul of discretion, had given no indication that anything was afoot, but it was he who informed Charlie of the instruction, when the young star arrived at the supervisor's table that morning.

"Oh? Any idea what for?" asked Charlie.

"No, but I'm sure he has!" replied the cryptic Spafford, who immediately changed the subject. "Have a good weekend?"

He held out his hand for Charlie's books.

Charlie handed over the two books with his weekend's collection totals entered on the back pages. It had been stormy on the Friday night, with snow settling a couple of inches deep by Saturday morning. Driving the motorcar had been rather perilous but Charlie had managed to complete his rounds.

"Not bad, considering the weather. Not nice to get about in, though, was it?"

"No." Spafford smiled in guilty sympathy. He had had a rare Saturday off, with all his men being fit and active. He glanced at Charlie's totals and at the sales slips enclosed, and passed the books back with a nod and a sharp "Good job, Charlie!"

Charlie dealt with his stock requirements and handed his takings and books into the office before presenting himself to the Sales Manager promptly at ten o'clock. Aitch was his usual informal self, and he rose from behind the desk to greet Charlie with a warm handshake.

"Hallo, laddo, come in and sit down. Glad you could make it. Fancy a coffee?"

The office was just large enough for the two small wooden armchairs in front of the desk, on which sat a tray with two cups and a pot of coffee.

Charlie grinned. "Dying for one, sir."

Aitch nodded. "Yeah, me too."

He poured coffee into the two cups and passed one to Charlie.

"So, how did you manage out there this weekend? Pretty tough going in that storm, wasn't it?"

"It was a bit tricky to drive around in, but things worked out well enough for me, considering," replied the salesman.

"Good for you. I think it was worse for the boys a bit further out, where there was probably less traffic to clear the roads. I don't suppose working on the new estate at Becontree was much fun!"

"No, probably not, sir. Nor was driving to Chigwell."

"Ooh! That's right, you live out there, don't you?" Aitch laughed without embarrassment. "You'll have had enough problems getting home and back!"

"Yeah."

Aitch Harrington drank some coffee and studied Charlie's big frame over his cup.

"So, the king is dead. Long live the king, eh? What do you think?"

The newspapers had been full of speculation for weeks. King George V had died the previous week, after a long illness, and Edward, the Prince of Wales, had now acceded to the throne. The old king had been an austere, but greatly respected monarch, but opinion was split throughout the country about King Edward VIII. Very popular with the common people, the handsome, dashing Prince of Wales was known for living life to the full and having many affairs. However, he had recently announced his intention to marry the twice divorced American, Wallis Simpson. Such a match for a king was quite unacceptable to his family, to the Church and to most politicians. Charlie agreed.

"To be honest, sir, I think he is irresponsible. I think to suggest that a twice-married American divorcée should be made Queen of England is an insult to the crown. I think he should recognise his responsibilities and find a suitable wife."

Aitch smiled. "You don't think he would be a popular king, showing his free-thinking individuality?"

"He would be degrading our monarchy and insulting our empire. I do not think it will happen, sir."

"You're quite a boy, young Charlie. You have a remarkably clear head. That is why you are here this morning. You've achieved everything I hoped you would when I spoke to you at the Three Kings. Now you're one of our golden boys. How do you feel about it?"

"I love it, sir. I'm doing what I always dreamed of doing. I'm building a business and making a lot of friends."

"That's right, Charlie. That's the secret! Just make a lot of friends and life gets easy. Ivor Spafford said to me after your first three days, 'The boy's a natural,' and you've proved us both right.

"Now, I think the time has come to take the next step. We've reached the stage where we need a fourth supervisor, Charlie, and I think you are the man for the job."

He raised his cup and saucer again and drained the cup. Charlie followed suit in lifting his cup, but drank only a little. He did not speak and his face gave away nothing of his reaction. Aitch continued:

"You can train a new man on your round and he will become your first salesman-collector. Then we'll build a new group for you. What do you think about that?"

Charlie did not rush to reply. Stephen Collick had hinted at this move before Christmas, but his own feelings on the subject were unchanged. After a long pause, he said:

"I feel greatly honoured to be presented with this opportunity, sir, and I have thought about this moment carefully; but the truth is I don't think I am ready for such a move."

"Oh? Why's that?" Aitch appeared genuinely puzzled.

"Sir, I am just twenty-five years old and I've been doing this job for barely four years. I love my work, but I am still learning. There is still much development to come on Round three and I don't want to leave the job half done."

Charlie wanted to leave it at that but he realised he must say more.

"The time will come when I shall be ready and keen to accept the challenge of building a group, but I know it is not here yet. I mean no disrespect, sir. I hold both you and Mr Spafford in the highest esteem, but I would ask you to trust my instinct at this time."

Aitch Harrington looked steadily at Charlie for some seconds. Then he broke into a smile. He said:

"You really are a remarkable man, Charlie Stoker. I've had a lot of men turn down job offers over the years, but that was the most considered rejection I've ever heard. I'm not going to press you on this, I think you know exactly what you are doing. Go ahead, boy, build us the best round we'll ever have! This job will be here for you when you are ready for the challenge."

Charlie left the office with a firm handshake from the Sales Manager. Harrington sat down at his desk, shaking his head slowly with a smile on his face. He would have to settle for second best, and that was not the way he liked things. Yet this time, he told himself, the boy was right. He was not ready for the step up, but how many people in this world would have expressed it like that, with that maturity?

He shook his head again and summoned his secretary. The Group A supervisor, Jack Grieve, had a man who was keen for promotion and would have been Aitch's choice for the job had not Charlie's star shone so brightly. The day would prove to be Bert Cox's lucky day.

Cox had been with the company almost as long as Jack Grieve and was keen to become a supervisor. Grieve had been the first to be appointed, and Cox's disappointment at being beaten to the post had been assuaged by Harrington's good management. He moved Cox into Grieve's group as a support for the new supervisor. When Ivor Spafford was given the next group, Bert had again been forced to swallow his disappointment.

The truth was that Bert Cox was a conscientious trier, a man who was fiercely loyal and prepared to work as hard as possible. The one thing he lacked was flair. He would never be the brilliant salesman that Charlie was, or Walter Habisch, or the other gold standard men. Bert was the company's 'Steady Eddie'. Perhaps that was not such a bad thing, thought Aitch.

* * *

Walter Habisch had been understandably put out when Alice Pensell told him that she had bought a dress from Charlie Stoker, and he was not mollified by Charlie's offer to transfer the account.

"No, you can't. She tol' me she wants you to call on Mondays. Iss not right, Charlie!"

Charlie grinned and shrugged.

"I'm sorry, mate. I tried to tell her you should have the business but she laughed at me. That's some woman, Walter!"

"Yeah, she's some woman, alright. Lovely girl but she's strong-willed and she likes to stray a bit, you know. No surprise, with no man in the house for a year. She has needs."

Charlie's grin grew wider. "And you've been supplying those needs!"

Walter blushed. "My Esther, I love her with all my heart, but she's not well, and a man…" – he gave a helpless shrug – "… a man also has needs."

"Don't worry, Walter, your secret's safe with me. We're still friends?"

The little man broke into his sheepish grin. "Yeah, we still friends, Charlie!"

For the next few months, Charlie carefully avoided the ever more blatant efforts of Alice to get him into bed. The weekly visit fitted nicely into his Monday round. It was an early afternoon call. He arrived at about two o'clock and made a point of not staying too long. After the New Year, however, he found it safer to re-organise his round so that he arrived later in the day, after four o'clock.

Alice's two boys came home from school at that time and in their presence, their mother was a little more discreet. Walter had warned Charlie about the two boys, as had Elsie Tattle. They were, according to Elsie, an unpleasant pair of troublemakers. While not doubting the truth of that assessment, Charlie himself had found both boys quite respectful whenever he saw them.

On about the third or fourth week of his reorganised schedule, he was sitting in his car making entries in his book a little way from the house, when he saw the two boys in a cluster with three or four other youngsters in the street. The Pensell boys were not tall but the elder, Rick, who was about ten years old, was solidly built and easily recognisable with his square head and black curly hair.

There was some jostling and a lot of noise in the huddle, then suddenly fists started flying. One boy went down holding his face, a second went down in a heap, and two more ran off. Rick, the elder Pensell boy, nonchalantly kicked the kidneys of the boy holding his face, cursed, then swaggered off towards his home, his younger brother excitedly following.

The moment they reached their front door, however, both boys tidied their clothes and bent down to remove their boots before stepping over the threshold. When Charlie approached the house a minute or two later, Alice greeted him as warmly as ever and led him seductively into the front room. The boys were not to be seen.

* * *

Much though Charlie yearned to see Sally after their ABC meeting, he made no attempt to contact her before his next call at the Cutter house. Lottie Cutter, despite looking pale and unwell, appeared to be coping with the practical problems of settling her husband's affairs as well as the daily housekeeping routine.

She had made a point of telling Charlie that he would still be expected for lunch every Tuesday. On this occasion she had set the table for three but feared it may be just the two of them. Sally had been taking lunch at the clothing factory for the last few days and she wasn't sure if she'd get home today. She looked closely at Charlie when she said this but saw only a nod and a smile. She held his look for a moment, then sighed.

"Has she told you?" she asked miserably.

"Yes." Charlie shrugged.

"Are you the father?"

"No."

"I'm sorry. I had no right to ask. I'm not suggesting – but she wouldn't tell me, Charlie!"

They were still standing by the dining room door. Lottie Cutter was very close to tears.

"Shall we sit down for a minute?" said Charlie, guiding her to her usual seat. She dropped onto the chair, finding a quick smile for him.

"Oh, yes, of course, bless you."

He took a seat. She resumed in the same shocked tone:

"I'm her mother and she wouldn't tell me! All she kept saying was that it doesn't matter. How can it not matter?"

She paused, but Charlie offered no answer. She went on.

"The only thing that matters, she said, is that she is going to have a baby. Then she got upset and didn't come home for her dinner the rest of the week. She settled down at the weekend, and it blew over, but, I don't know, Charlie, everything's going wrong. And it's not only us, is it? You hear the news on the wireless and it seems the whole world is upside down!"

Charlie reached across the table and took her hand in his two hands.

"It has to be her decision, Mrs Cutter," he said gently. "She said more or less the same thing to me. She is a brave girl, Sally. She will yet make someone a wonderful wife. You have to trust her."

She looked at him quizzically. "A girl with an illegitimate child? Who will take that on?"

"Any man with the sense to see what is there. In other circumstances I would be first in the queue."

"Oh, Charlie!"

Now, tears fell down her pallid cheeks. After minutes, she withdrew her hand and said: "Let me get the dinner."

No sooner had she served him, a huge plate of braised lamb and vegetables, than the front door banged and Sally came in, looking much more like herself.

"Sorry I'm late," she called to her mother in the kitchen, "there was a rush of stuff to get out and I had to log it all. Hallo, Charlie, you alright?"

Charlie smiled and shrugged.

"Always!" he replied. "How about you?"

"Yeah, you just gotta get on with it, haven't you?"

"That's the girl!"

Lottie Cutter re-appeared with two plates of food. She placed one in front of Sally and set the other down for herself.

"That's alright, you're just in time, eat up! Unusual for work to cut into your lunch hour, isn't it, Sally?"

"Yeah! The foreman of the packers, that's the blokes who pack the orders and see them through the despatch office and onto the vans, he left. They've promoted a chap from in the factory. He's a nice bloke but he doesn't know the job yet and he got in a terrible muddle this morning, so I stopped to help him out!"

"They'll miss you when you leave that office," declared Lottie Cutter.

"I reckon so, but I'll miss the job too. It works both ways, doesn't it?" Sally made the comment without looking up, her eyes fixed on her plate. Then she suddenly lifted her head and smiled.

"I'll miss mornings like today, you know. You should have seen the state that Percy got himself into. You'd'a thought it was the first time anyone'd ever messed up! He's a really nice bloke, and he tries so hard, but I think the foreman's job's a bit much for him. Still, we'll see. He may grow into it."

"With a little help from his friends?" suggested Charlie, laughing.

"Yeah, probably!" Sally laughed. She and Charlie exchanged glances – glances that told each other a thousand truths.

The conversation moved on to discuss Cissie's condition as she grew closer to her time. She had spent most of the days with her mother since the funeral but felt the need to rest today. She was becoming heavy, and was needing to rest more. Her baby would be due in a few weeks' time. Lottie talked eagerly about the coming baby. Could it be that there would be a boy in the family at last?

Before leaving, Charlie dealt with the weighty business of the weekly accounts. He had refused to accept payments on Tom Cutter's account as long as his customer had been in hospital, and he now told Lottie that the account would be deleted and the balance of £1.4s. 8d. written off by the company. The £4.5s.6d outstanding on the main account, on which she was unfailingly paying six shillings per week, remained payable, but the weekly payment would now be reduced to three shillings a week until it was below two pounds.

Lottie Cutter explained that, although their financial position would obviously suffer a bit, Tom Cutter had been a very careful man. The mortgage had been insured so that she would now own the house, and other investment would secure a small income for her.

Charlie smiled. "That's good," he said, "but we'll still make these adjustments."

Lottie Cutter kissed him.

Sally accepted Charlie's offer of a lift back to work, so they left together at a few minutes to two. It was only a short trip to the factory.

"You look better, today, Sally," said Charlie as he settled in the car. They looked at each other through the little reversing mirror.

"Yeah, I've got over the shock. I'll be alright now. It's like I said, you have to get on with it."

He nodded.

"Yeah, but you'll need your friends. Sal, I know you can always get me through Collick's, but I'm going to give you two, other 'phone numbers'. One is mine, the other is my mother's. You can always reach me through one or the other. Whatever you need, whenever, Sal. You know that?"

"Yes, Charlie, I know, I love you." She smiled at the mirror.

"You'll also know I don't give these numbers out."

She nodded and looked away. They arrived at her work and Charlie stopped the engine and climbed out. As Sally came out of the rear door, he pulled her to him and hugged her. He whispered into her hair: "It's you who is special, Sally."

* * *

Bobby Bruce was bursting to share his news with Charlie when the two men met for their regular swim, the next evening.

"W-w-we're moving out!" he declared proudly. "Y-you know that w-we've been s-saving hard since we got m-married for our own p-place. W-well, just l-lately D-daphne's s-suddenly g-got the urge to have a b-baby! W-we were w-working things out the other w-w-week and w-w-we w-w-worked out that w-w-we'd—"

"Hold on, mate!" Charlie interrupted his friend, laughing. "Now, take a deep breath and start again slowly!"

Bobby stared open-mouthed for a moment, then burst out laughing. "Y-yeah! S-sorry, I do get excited, don't I?"

He resumed his story with almost no stammer. "W-we worked out that we'd saved enough so that we could afford our own house now. We've been crowded into Daph's p-parents' for four years and we n-need some space. They're good people but it's a small house. W-we need our own space, especially if we're goin'o have kids!"

He took another deep breath. Charlie grinned. Bobby went on:

"We w-went and looked at a semi-detached, it's actually an end-terrace, in Hillfield Avenue, in g-ood condition and we b-both loved it! It had quite a wide alley way at the side and a good bit of garden at the back, s-so I s-said we'll buy it. The B-building Society m-mortgage won't be bad, about fifteen bob a week, s-so it's all been agreed."

Charlie clapped his friend on the back. "Good for you! Congratulations. You deserve it, you both work hard. When will you move?"

"A couple of months, I should think. We're w-waiting for the official acceptance and settlement date, but w-we won't rush."

After the swim, they enjoyed a celebratory pint or two. Charlie said:

"You'll miss Daphne's income a bit if she has a baby, won't you?"

"Yeah, but we can m-manage! I'm doing pretty well at the workshop now. We'll do fine!" affirmed the elated Bobby. "How about you? Have you seen the b-bl—have you seen Sally again?"

"Yes. She'll be okay. I think we've got a decent understanding now."

Bobby mulled this over for long enough to take a drink, then said:

"Th-that's a t-typical Charlie answer. It tells me n-nothing!"

Charlie laughed and shrugged.

"Life's what it is, Bobby."

Bobby stared at his friend's blond hair and veiled blue eyes.

"Ch-Charlie, sh-she may be okay, but it's you I'm worried about. Are y-you okay? R-really okay? Don't mess with my brain, t-tell me the truth!"

"Yes, Bobby." Charlie looked openly at his bespectacled friend. "I'm okay. I know you care, and I love you as a brother, but I'm okay!"

Bobby shook his head, frustrated and perplexed.

* * *

Millie had expected Charlie to visit and to stay at Amhurst Road more often once Margret had moved to Paris, but the change had not occurred. The fact was that Charlie had settled into a weekly routine that was comfortable, and he had no inclination to disturb it. In effect, he was living the life of a self-sufficient bachelor and it suited him. He made a point of visiting his mother at least once a week, usually Wednesday, but sometimes Thursday, and that suited them both.

About once a month, Charlie accompanied his mother to church. At first, he had made excuses for the missing weeks but after a time she stopped asking. She accepted that he did not gain the same strength from the church as she; he did not need its support as she did. If she was disappointed, she at no time showed it, believing that he would find true faith in his own time.

Millie's birthday was on the twenty-seventh of February, and in 1936 this was a Thursday. She had intended to celebrate it on the following Sunday with Stephen and Charlie, but a few days before the actual birthday Charlie surprised his mother by announcing that he was taking her out to dinner on the Thursday and that there would be a special extra treat.

On the day, he reached Amhurst Road at about three o'clock, having spent the usual Thursday morning in Collick's and enjoyed a pie and a couple of pints at the Three Kings. They drank a pot of tea together and Millie updated Charlie on the goings on at the Church. Father Thomas was now rather running the show, as Father Peter's health was not as good as in the past, but the old priest was still clearly the most significant presence at major ceremonies.

Charlie nodded and shrugged his acknowledgement of her words, but carefully refrained from any comment. He admired and respected Father Peter. He was a fine man, an exceptionally good and wise priest. But it was an almighty struggle for Charlie to understand why the priest's Good God should have caused or permitted the tragedies and disasters that constantly reshaped his own life. If there was a purpose, he concluded, it was one that would never be revealed. In which case, what was its point?

After tea, Charlie drove Millie into Soho to the same restaurant that he had visited with Bobby, Daphne and Jennifer three months earlier. 'Le Billet' had, as far as he could guess, an authentic provincial French atmosphere. It served French dishes that were quite new to Millie and which she found absolutely delicious. She sipped a little red wine and was very happy.

Following the dinner, Charlie walked with his mother through the Soho streets to the grand movie theatres of Leicester Square, where they joined the throngs going to the pictures. They watched Charlie Chaplin and Paulette Goddard in 'Modern Times'. Millie was ecstatic, it had been a perfect day, and to complete it, Charlie stayed the night in his old room.

Chapter Eighteen
Life Renews

Just three days later, Charlie was back at Amhurst Road for his mother's planned birthday treat, the Sunday lunch. She had invited Billy and Sally Walters, as well as Stephen and Charlie.

Billy had now been managing the shoe shop in the basement for ten years and had matured into a strong-minded and successful businessman. He was now responsible for all aspects of the business, and Millie no longer needed to look after the accounts. Billy was fiercely loyal to the Stokers and was proud of the fact that he now provided a considerable income for the house. For her part, Millie had come to regard Billy and Sally as part of her extended family, and as such they were welcomed into family celebrations.

It was the first time Charlie had seen Stephen Collick since his meeting with Aitch Harrington, but Stephen gave no indication that he knew anything about it. He was his usual charming social self and regaled them all with a stream of delightful tales of doubtful origin. Charlie had long ago come to appreciate that Stephen, once he had drunk a couple of glasses of wine, was a compulsive story-teller, much like Bobby.

Billy sprang the surprise of a lifetime after lunch, when he disappeared very briefly to the basement only to return with his accordion strapped around his shoulder. Red-faced with embarrassed pride, he played a couple of well-rehearsed pieces, then they all spent the next hour or more singing favourite songs along to Billy's accompaniment.

Charlie was amazed at the shoemaker's competence on his instrument, which had never before been seen in public! Billy and Sally left at about five o'clock.

It was only later in the evening, when Millie went downstairs to organise a little supper for the three of them, that Stephen mentioned work to Charlie. Placing his cigar in an ashtray, he said, in that tentative manner of his that indicated a serious subject:

"Charlie, we have an agreement not to talk business here, but I feel an exception is warranted. You have done remarkably well in your progress, my boy, and I—" he almost stuttered, "I felt great pride when I was asked to confirm your induction into the Gold Standard Group at the end of the year."

He looked away, then quickly looked again at his treasured protégé. "This week, in his report, the Sales Manager has informed me that on Monday he offered promotion for you to a supervisory position and that you declined the promotion. He has instead promoted another. He was somewhat bemused by the situation, as am I. Is something wrong, Charlie?"

Charlie shrugged.

"No, sir, there's nothing wrong. Mr Harrington is a first-class man and manager. He has appointed the right man, Bert Cox. Cox will do an excellent job."

Stephen was unable to hide his amusement. "I'm sure he will be gratified at your accolade!" He chuckled. "I have no doubt of Mr Harrington's abilities, Charlie. It is yours I am questioning."

Charlie created a pause by lighting a cigarette. Then he repeated the words used to Aitch.

"It is too soon for me, sir."

He inhaled, then leaned forward in his chair, breathing out smoke. He spoke earnestly but calmly.

"I'm glad you've broached the subject because I have wanted to speak to you about it, and I have no way of reaching you without others knowing."

Stephen frowned. Charlie ploughed on.

"I'm pleased that I haven't let you down and that my progress so far has been in accordance with your vision. To be honest, I am beginning to believe in my potential to do what you have in mind for me; but it will take time. In reaching my present level, I have come to realise how much more can be done. The fact is, Stephen, the horizons are too low!"

Stephen Collick's frown was replaced by a slightly raised eyebrow, but he made no attempt to interrupt. Charlie charged on.

"I am one of only four men producing the Gold Standard, and that standard is not high enough. I think there've got to be other levels. If instead of the 'Gold' standard, we introduce a 'Bronze' at say sixty pounds per week, a 'Silver' at eighty and a Gold at one hundred, then we shall see some real progress. All men will work harder if they see competition for those awards. But, someone has got to set the pace! That's what I can do now. In a few years' time, I can take the responsible step up and lead others to achieve those levels, but I've got to do it myself first."

Charlie drew smoke down into his lungs and crushed out the cigarette. Stephen reached for his cigar. When he looked up again, there was a gleam in his eyes.

"Charlie," he said almost reverently, "you are Charles reincarnate. You are your father's son. That speech takes me back thirty years. I knew I was right about you, just as you are right about your future, now."

He drew on his cigar and broke into a wide smile.

"I think Harrington sensed it, you know. He recognised that you could achieve greatness as a salesman. He was quite happy to promote Cox."

He chuckled in delight, then said, "By the way, you have a point about contact. I have a private telephone line in my office and I shall give you the number. If ever you need to contact me, you will call this number."

From within his jacket, he produced a small pocketbook and pen, wrote the number in it and tore out the page. He handed it to Charlie.

"We are getting there, son," he said softly.

* * *

Back in his own home at Chigwell, Charlie poured himself a whisky and reflected upon Stephen's words. He felt honoured to be likened to his father. That was an immense compliment, and the granting of direct access to Stephen at Collick's was an indicator of his progress in his career. He had much to be pleased about in his life. He had worked hard to perfect the public image of Charlie: big, blond, easy-going, ever reliable Charlie, everybody's friend and problem solver.

He shrugged. Then why did he feel so miserable? It was ironic that his career should be going so well when his life was chaos. But nobody saw the other Charlie, the private Charlie hidden so deep within him; the Charlie who hungered for a loving wife and a son.

Nobody had ever seen that Charlie but Sally, whom he had instantly rejected. For what? For loyalty to a false commitment; for strict adherence to a set of laws that made no concessions for love or good intentions; for the God of conformity.

It was not Margret's fault. Margret was not a bad person. She had been misunderstood, unloved and abused throughout her childhood, and her teenage behaviour had been a reaction to that abuse. Then she had grasped at Big Boy Charlie's gracious offer to take her away from all that and to set her free. Now she was free, and he was in hell, a hell of his own making, Big Boy Charlie's private hell. He finished his whisky and went to bed.

* * *

The spring of 1936 proved, as miraculous spring always does, that life will renew regardless. In the early hours of the last day of March, Cissie Bateson gave birth to not one, but two baby boys, to the confounded surprise of herself, her husband Harry and her sister Sally; and to the unbounded joy of her mother. A rather frail and very tired looking Lottie Cutter, after three months of mourning, wept from happiness. The gift from God for which she had fervently prayed for so many years, she now saw granted through her daughter.

The births had been wonderfully easy and smooth. When Cissie had recognised the first signs of labour, in the morning of the preceding day, Harry had been sent to fetch Mrs Cutter. Sally had not yet given up her job, although by this time she was showing signs of her own pregnancy. Nevertheless, she insisted on accompanying her mother and assisting. It necessitated a telephone call to the dispatch manager, who gave her cover for two days together with a warning that she'd now used up her favours. The two women had gone straight to the flat in Bentley Road and had remained with Cissie throughout the long labour to the birth at 2.00 am.

The on-call doctor, a youngish man new to the family, had been called in mid-afternoon and he had examined Cissie and pronounced everything as being fine. He instructed them when to call him again and left. During the evening, he called again and once again gave the thumbs up. Then, when he returned after midnight to actually deliver the baby, he received as big a shock as everyone when he found a second baby boy hiding in the womb.

Harry Bateson had smoked a whole packet of cigarettes pacing the living room of the flat, chatting with his in-laws and taking short walks around the block to fill the hours of Cissie's labour. After the doctor left, he sat at the bottom of the bed, utterly drained of energy, staring in wonder at his exhausted beloved and at the twin miracles she had wrought, now asleep in the cot crammed between the bed and the wall of the small room. They had agreed that if a boy, the baby would be named Thomas; but they hadn't thought of the possibility of two boys. James would be nice, he thought, after his own father who had died at the Somme in November 1916. He would talk to Cissie when she woke up

In order for everyone to get some rest, Sally stretched out next to her sister on Harry's side of the bed, while Harry and his mother-in-law slept for a few hours in the two armchairs in the living room. When the babies made themselves heard between eight and nine in the morning, Harry rushed off to work leaving the others to look after things.

The space problem had been worrying Harry for some time, but the birth of the twins had concentrated his mind considerably. The flat was simply not big enough for them to raise two boys in. They would need more space.

He arrived early at the drapery store, hoping to spend a few minutes alone with his employer, Mr Levitt. Levitt was a decent man, approachable and generally not difficult to deal with. He had a formal manner that invariably became relaxed after a few minutes' conversation; but on this occasion he immediately beamed his delight and pumped Harry's hand in congratulation. Then he listened carefully as Harry tried to find the best words to convey his message. He needed a larger home and in his present situation he could not afford to move. He desperately needed help to find a solution. Mr Levitt nodded as Harry talked, then stroked his chin pensively.

"I understand exactly what you say, Harry," he said slowly, "and I want you to leave it with me. You are a good man, and I will help if I possibly can. Leave it with me. Maybe, you never know…" He waved his hands in the air and raised his head to heaven, "You never know…!" He wandered off into his office, leaving the bemused Harry none the wiser at the sales counter.

At the flat, Sally and her mother had breakfast while Cissie, having fed the babies, was sleeping.

"Had you thought, Sally?" exclaimed Lottie suddenly. "It's Tuesday today, and Charlie will go to the house for his lunch! There'll be no one there!"

Sally looked up from her bowl of corn flakes, laughing at her mother's consternation.

"It's Charlie, Mum! He knows Cissie was close, he'll know straight away that we're over here. I bet he turns up at five past one!"

"Well, we'd better prepare for him, in case. I'll pop over to the butcher's and pick something up."

Sally's judgement proved to be accurate when, just after one o'clock, a knock at the door signalled Charlie's arrival. She opened the door to find the big man standing upright and wearing a serious frown.

"Is it due?" He asked anxiously.

"You're too late!" she retorted, laughing. "*They* are already here, and hungry!"

The Stoker grin reflected his immediate grasp of the significance of the pronoun.

"Twins? Boys, girls or both?"

Sally led the way into the living room. "Two boys, Tom and I'm not sure yet. They're beautiful! And Mum's in the kitchen getting your dinner!"

"Hallo, Charlie!" called Lottie from the kitchen. "Be with you in a minute."

"OK!" Then to Sally:

"How is Cissie? Can I congratulate her?"

"She's fine, tired of course, but at the moment she's just started feeding them, so she'll be busy for a while. When she's done the first one, we can bring him in to let you meet him!"

Charlie was relieved to see Sally so obviously happy and relaxed. She had clearly drawn strength from his commitment to support her, expressed in that unexpected embrace outside the factory when he had taken her to work from Armagh Road. At that time, she had not shown much reaction, but in the weeks since it had helped her to regain her zest for life.

Lottie Cutter appeared from the kitchen carrying two plates of lamb chops with chips and peas.

"Now sit and eat, you two!" she commanded, laughing. "Isn't it wonderful news, Charlie? Two beautiful boys!" She put the plates on the table and looked at him excitedly.

"It certainly is, wonderful news," agreed Charlie, noting her sunken cheeks and the deep black rims beneath her eyes. "I think you'll be ready for a good sleep now it's all over, won't you?"

"Yes, but I'm too excited to think about that yet. When Cissie feels she can get up and deal with two babies, we'll see."

She revisited the kitchen to collect her own plate. "Cissie will eat when she has finished feeding the boys," she said, the proud grandmother, sitting down.

Sally, seeing her mother collapse onto a chair with a big sigh, suggested:

"Mum, I got more sleep than you through the night, and you look as if you need some! Why don't you go home with Charlie when we've eaten? I can stay here and be with Cissie 'til Harry gets back."

"Well, yes, I'm tired, but we can't put upon Charlie like that."

Charlie looked up sharply. "Nonsense, Mrs C. You know I'll be delighted to help out in any way I can. Driving you is a pleasure! Anyway," he added mischievously, "the books will be at Armagh Road!"

* * *

Cissie Bateson, although not blessed with the beauty and vivaciousness of her sister Sally, was nevertheless a fine, healthy woman. She had now given birth to two beautiful boys, two male grandchildren for her so recently bereaved mother. After the depressing months of tragedy and sadness for the whole Cutter family, the new-born twins signified a restoration of faith in life going forward.

That was not to say that life going forward was without its problems. Their one-bedroomed flat could not realistically house their new family and Cissie knew that Harry had asked his employer for help. The response, when it came, surprised them.

When the twins were just three days old, Mr Levitt called Harry into his office and bade him sit on the wooden chair in front of the desk.

"Harry," he said in his usual slow manner, stroking his chin, "I think you're a good man. You work harder than the others and you're no fool. I have a proposition for you."

He removed his hand from his chin and sat upright.

"You know I have another shop?"

"Yes, sir, over the water somewhere, I think." Harry was immediately nervous.

"Yes, Lewisham. In the High Road. My wife's cousin was managing it but he is ill, he is dying. But the business must still run and I need a new manager. I think you are the man for the job."

He stopped and looked at Harry enquiringly. Harry was speechless.

"Eh? What do you say?"

"But, Lewisham?" were the only words to come from the astounded Harry.

"Yes, yes, but you see, I own property. I have a house in Adolphus Street in Deptford. It has two floors and three bedrooms. 's a nice house! I'll pay you a manager's wage, extra £1.10s.0d per week, and I charge you only ten shillings each week for rent for the house."

Harry was dumbfounded. He fought back the tears of shock. He mumbled words of thanks for the generosity and for the obvious indication of confidence in his ability. They shook hands and agreed that they would go together to Lewisham on the following Monday morning.

"There's only one thing," said Harry hesitantly before leaving the office, "I don't know what my wife will say about Lewisham. It's a long way from her mother."

"So go home and tell her at lunchtime!" Levitt gave a dismissive shrug. "I don't think she'll have a better offer!"

To Harry's relief, Cissie was delighted. Her actual words in reply to his news were: "Harry, it's Lewisham, not Birmingham!"

* * *

Charlie had side-stepped Lottie Cutter's observation about the world 'being all upside down' but he was very much aware of the validity of her concern. He kept abreast of affairs in both local and world news. Apart from its actual news value, he found it of great advantage to be well informed when chatting to his customers. Throughout 1936, the reports he read in his morning papers certainly indicated that the world was 'all upside down'.

During the first eight months of the year, it became manifestly clear that the leading countries of the old world were in turmoil:

In contempt of the Versailles Treaty, Hitler's troops had reclaimed the Rhineland for Germany without any opposition.

In Africa, the forces of Italy's fascist leader, Mussolini, crushed the stubborn resistance of Abyssinia with mustard gas.

In Palestine, while Zionist Jews were busily buying land wherever they could, the Arabs declared a general strike that lasted six months, during which they attacked British and Jewish targets.

In Moscow, Stalin was exhibiting his total control of Soviet Russia with show trials and executions to eliminate any opposition.

In Spain, in the far west of Europe, a civil war had split the country into two. The Republican forces of the left-wing government fought the fascist-leaning Nationalist army under General Franco.

British newspapers and B.B.C. wireless broadcasts faithfully reported these momentous happenings. At the same time, they always made clear the official government stance that non-interference in other countries' affairs was imperative to maintain world peace.

As the seasons passed, however, the rumbles of discontent grew ever louder and ever nearer home. In the East End of London, Communist cells were stirring unrest among workers, unrest fermented by Mosley's anti-Semitic fascist gangs.

The subject of anti-Semitism was beginning to pre-occupy Bobby Bruce and, naturally, he expressed his fears to Charlie. In spite of Charlie's conviction that the fascist movement would not succeed in Britain, Bobby reminded him one summer evening, "Oswald Mosley has not gone away, has he? His B.U.F., with its thousands of members, looks like it's building a solid base among the working class, doesn't it?"

Indeed, in speeches and pamphlets aimed at winning the support of local workers, Mosley had repeatedly highlighted the questions of unemployment and housing, and cunningly linked them to his racist arguments against Jews and immigrants. An anti-Semitic campaign in the East End of London had become a major focus of his drive.

"D-aphne's dad was telling us he'd heard there've been groups of B-Blackshirts smashing windows of Jewish shops and hurling bricks into places, causing f-fires and stuff in around where all the im-m-migrants and refugees are living," claimed the bespectacled engineer. "That's not right, Charlie, is it?"

Charlie shrugged and lit a cigarette. After so many years, it was automatic for him to hide his reaction behind his protective shield of casual detachment. Every day, he heard similar sad stories from his customers; but he also regularly heard the arguments from the other side, from the discontented youth of families resident in the East End for generations. He saw the anger of those who had served their country, or had lost their kin in the Great War, and who yet struggled to find or keep a job; the frustration of the dockers and the redundant workers from the cotton mills of Lancashire who had travelled south with their families in the forlorn hope of finding work.

He recalled his mother's words of a year earlier about the seeds of discord being always with us. It was true. These people all felt hard done by. They were resentful of those with limited English, or strong foreign accents, or strange religious beliefs: people who appeared to be able to find work more successfully than they could.

"No, it's not right, Bobby," he said. "The trouble is, there's very little that is right in the world just now. Luckily, most of it doesn't concern us. Here, in England, we're doing okay. Yeah, there are pockets of discontent, but most people tend to ignore it. Why turn a small fire into a conflagration?"

He drew on his cigarette, the bright burning end aptly illustrating his metaphor. "As for Mosley's strutting and sabre rattling," he added disdainfully, "if he seriously steps out of line the powers that be will squash him flat." He tapped out his ash.

"It's my round, I think."

* * *

Originally opened as the Ivy house Maternity Hospital for Unmarried Mothers in Mare Street, Hackney in 1884, the Mothers' Hospital of the Salvation Army was a large establishment in Lower Clapton Road. From the time of the Great War the hospital had ceased to distinguish between married and unmarried women, and by 1936, it was capable of handling some 2000 births each year.

Its proximity to Armagh Road meant that Sally was able to gain admittance without any fuss when her time came to give birth. Thus, in the heat of a sunny July day, Sally Cutter brought into the world, trouble free, a male child, Lottie Cutter's third grandson. The well-formed baby boy, weighing nearly nine pounds, was born with his mother's blond hair sprouting above a rosy face. The birth presented no particular problems for mother or child beyond the physical and emotional stress caused to every woman in childbirth.

After a well-earned rest and having fed her baby, Sally greeted her mother and Charlie Stoker late in the afternoon with her lovely face pale but wearing its customary beaming smile. Charlie had been assumed by the hospital staff to be the father. He made no attempt to disillusion them. He leaned over the bed and kissed Sally gently. The large bunch of flowers he had carried in were taken by a nurse and arranged in a vase on the window sill by the bed.

Mrs Cutter sat herself on the small chair by the bed and Charlie stood back to give mother and daughter room to chat. Lottie Cutter was elated, but to Charlie she still looked ill. Her cheeks were hollowed and her eyes dark with strain. She had lost considerable weight in the year since her husband had been taken ill and to date showed no sign of regaining it.

During their visit, the nurse needed to fuss round Sally for a few minutes, so they were taken to the nursery, where they were able to see, through the window, the new baby exercising his vocal chords in a cot, watched over by the duty nurse.

Sally had given thought to the naming of her child for some time before the birth. If it were to be a girl, she liked the name Shirley, she explained to her mother. It was a name that hinted at both Charlotte and Sally, but was more up-to-date.

Should it be a boy, she did not want to use the name Thomas so soon after her sister had. Instead, she thought it would be nice to use her father's second name, Henry, although she thought Henry was a bit stuffy. It was usually shortened to Harry, though, and she liked the name Harry. This pleased Lottie, as did Sally's next words.

"If it's a boy, Mum, I shall give him a second name. I want to call him Harry Charles. Charles was your father's name and you were named after him, but also big Charlie has become so important in our lives, hasn't he? He's so super special."

Lottie had nodded with a big sigh. "Yes, he's very special."

Chapter Nineteen
Cable Street

In July of 1936, Bert Pensell was released from gaol. All the fitter for his enforced absence and a full year of abstinence, Pensell resumed his crooked career as if it had not been interrupted. On the Monday after his release, Charlie called at the house to find Alice at home with her younger son, Paul. Alice handed Charlie her book to mark up and sent Paul outside to play.

"Everything okay, Alice?" enquired Charlie.

"Yeah, Bert's back. Fitter than he has been for years, but he won't be for long. He's gone straight back into the old routine. He's down the Ace of Spades now. He's a bastard, that Bert, but I knew it when I married him. He's even got my young Rick running for him now. The boy's only ten but he's a sharp little bugger."

"Why do you put up with it, Alice?"

"I do okay. I married him for better or for worse, didn't I? I knew what I was marrying. Give him his due, he's always been good to me. And it's not as if I don't have a life, is it?"

Charlie shrugged. "Anything I can do for you?"

"Yeah, I want another dress, Charlie, something showy. Bert wants to take me out on Saturday to celebrate. Can you sign a note so I can get one from the store tomorrow?"

"Why didn't you ask Walter?"

"Don't worry yourself about Walter! Walter's being looked after. He's bringing stuff for Bert and the boys on Friday."

Charlie filled in the order form and signed it. The fact was, Alice had never missed a payment on the account. He had no reason to refuse her. As he handed over the form, he asked:

"Does your husband know about this account?"

Alice laughed. "Bert's not interested in my accounts. He gives me money to run the house and that's that. As long as I don't ask him for more he couldn't care less what I do with it."

Charlie shrugged.

* * *

The plan for the monthly reunion dinner of the four college friends had not been forgotten, but neither had it been keenly followed up. There had been only two since Christmas, and at the end of July Charlie arranged a third dinner, this time with an extra attendee. Margret had returned to Chigwell for the summer vacation.

Margret being Margret, there was no detectable change in her appearance or manner from when she had left them a year earlier. Tall and slim, with her hair in a tight bun, she looked in good health and quite unaffected by Paris life.

"Everybody in Paris is exactly what one expects," she declared to the table, "all very French, although some are quite intelligent. My student group is surprisingly cosmopolitan, though. They are, mostly, fluent in English, of a sort. Otherwise, one must converse in French. A number are from America. Those are usually keen to learn, but argumentative, in that American way, you know."

It was pure Margret, and the others were happy to let her bathe in her glory as an internationally recognised academic. Jennifer, looking as stunning as ever, sat, entranced. Her hair was shining, with a short fringe and fashionable loose curls; and she wore a bottle green velour velvet dress, softly gathered under the bust, with short puff sleeves. A fashionable art deco brooch in silver with faceted round and baguette rhinestones made a brilliant contrast.

As the evening progressed and the wine did its work, the table became louder and louder and ever happier. Four voices fought to be heard, and Charlie watched them and nodded contentedly, the hint of a grin in his blue eyes.

Jennifer, Bobby and Daphne had all come to the West End by underground and when the time came to close the restaurant doors, they were delighted to accept Charlie's suggestion that they all crowd into the Ford to be driven home. Daphne and Bobby were the first to relieve the crush at Crouch End, then Charlie drove on to Bounds Green. As they arrived at Jennifer's, Margret said:

"I think I'll stay with Jen tonight, Big Boy. I've been at Chigwell all week and tomorrow is her only day off. Perhaps you'll come over and join us for tea in the afternoon?"

Charlie shrugged.

They all climbed out of the car and Jennifer gave Charlie a hug. Margret pecked his cheek and said:

"Thanks, Big Boy."

* * *

Increasingly, during the long, warm summer days of 1936, one of the warmest recorded to that time, Charlie, on his rounds, witnessed evidence of Mosley's campaign to win the support of the workers in London. Racist slogans were splattered on walls and windows; there were many cases of violence against individuals in the streets; and a number of fire bombings of Jewish premises.

It was difficult to remain impartial as the callousness and immorality of the acts became so apparent. Customer after customer mentioned 'the goings on'. Many were frightened and many were angry. Shayna Decker was both. On a Wednesday morning in August, Charlie called at the curtain department to leave an order. He found her red faced and agitated.

"Things are not right," she whispered in reply to his expressed concern. "On Sunday, there was a brick through Levy's window and 'JEWS GET OUT' was painted on the door. Levy was in a state and my Aaron's terrified for his job and his life!"

Levy was her husband's employer. He was a good tailor and a good employer, but he was getting old and his wife was in poor health. It would not take a great deal of pressure for the old man to close up shop. It would be hard for Aaron to get another similar position. There were plenty of young men looking for jobs like tailor's presser.

"It must seem a rough ride to you, Shayna," replied Charlie sympathetically. "Just you hold on tight, you'll be okay. It will all calm down when we get some rain. Aaron's a good man and so is Mr Levy, and the police will catch the vandals soon enough."

"Hmm. Maybe, but what about my boys? They hear things from the other boys. My Alfie's talking about demonstrations. 'All Jews uniting in protest against Hitlerism' is what he came home with. We don' want protests! We want to be left in peace!"

Charlie gazed intently. He squeezed her shoulder gently and repeated his advice, "Just hold tight, Shayna, you'll be fine."

Leaving Collick's, Charlie put the troubled thoughts to the back of his mind. He was Charlie Stoker. He must remain detached.

He completed his Wednesday calls, which no longer included Bentley Road, by just after three o'clock. The Batesons, complete with four-month-old twins had settled in Deptford. Their account, after a word with Jack Grieve, who supervised all business south of the Thames, was transferred to Ray Parsons, a gold standard man who covered Lewisham and Deptford.

Consequently, Charlie arrived at Amhurst Road early enough to enjoy afternoon tea and a light meal with his mother before his evening swim. Millie Stoker brought her son up to date with all the news and gossip gleaned from the church office during the week, duly acknowledged by Charlie with regular nods and smiles.

Eventually, though, Charlie felt impelled to take the conversation to a more serious level.

"From all you say, things appear to be fine in Stoke Newington, but tell me, Mum, when you go shopping, or just walking along the High Road, do you sense the unease in the air?"

"Unease?" Millie looked up sharply.

"Just here, you seem to be beyond the range of it, but walk a few hundred yards south or east and you enter a different world. There's an edginess to everyone. A mile down the road there are broken windows and ugly graffiti. There's tension in the air and I'm not sure anyone is doing much to stop it building. To what, who knows?"

Millie studied her son for some seconds before replying.

"That is most unlike you, Charlie. You are agitated about something. What is it? What exactly have you seen that has so upset you?"

Charlie shrugged, sighed and smiled.

"Yes, it's not like me, is it? The fact is there's a lot of political troublemaking going on in the East End this summer. It's unpleasant, Mum. This morning Shayna Dekker was wound up fit to burst!"

"That's the lady in the curtain department?"

"Yeah."

"Why?"

"Fascist vandals put a brick through the window at her husband's workplace and scrawled anti-Semitic insults on the door."

"Oh dear!"

"Quite. As you know, I usually remain pretty detached from these situations, but all over my area, I'm hearing conflicting arguments from house after house about what is essentially politics. They spout either the fascist arguments or the workers' mostly communist ones. When you think it through, neither side is right, but neither is particularly wrong. The government has to steer a middle course. But it also has to stop them starting a civil war. This is not Spain! That pumped-up Hitlerite, Mosley, has a lot to answer for!"

Once more, Millie Stoker stared at her son. "I don't think I have ever before heard you utter a political speech, certainly not an angry one, Charlie!"

"No, and I shall try not to do it again!"

He opened his cigarette case with a grin.

"Do you mind?"

"No, dear, if it calms you down."

Charlie lit the cigarette.

"I expect Bobby will be full of it tonight," he reflected, as much to himself as to his mother. "He gets stirred up by Daphne's father. I don't know if I've ever mentioned it, but David Hipstead and Shayna Dekker are cousins."

"Are they? No, you've never mentioned it. By the way, did you know that Sally downstairs is expecting?"

"Sally Walters? No! Are they still living at Billy's mum's?"

"Yes, but I have been toying with the idea of letting them take the top two floors here. It would make it much more convenient for the business."

"That's a great idea if you've thought it through, and knowing you, I expect you have."

Millie raised an eyebrow but then smiled.

"I think so. I talked the plan over with Stephen and he thought it was sound. We'll convert the two flats into one maisonette with the living accommodation below and the bedrooms above."

"Good for you. Does Billy know?"

"Not yet. I shall tell him this week. The young couple are moving out of the top flat this weekend, and Mr Bannister, the bachelor on the first floor, is emigrating next month, to America."

"That's excellent planning, mother. You don't miss many tricks, do you?" Charlie grinned broadly.

* * *

The Olympic Games of 1936 had been awarded to Berlin before Hitler had come to power, but the dictator planned to use it as a spectacular showpiece of Nazi organisation and Aryan supremacy.

His plans were dented to a great extent by the star of the Games, Jesse Owens. Very non-Aryan, very black, and an athlete from the United States of America, Owens won four gold medals. Hitler, rather than shake the hand of the undisputed champion, left the stadium. The incident was noted by the world, but it really changed nothing. Fascism ruled most of Europe.

At home, Oswald Mosley's B.U.F. had become more vehement in their anti-Semitic stance. Jews were described as 'rats and vermin from the gutter of Whitechapel.' A march was announced for Sunday, 4th October. It would be a show of strength for the British Union of Fascists.

The plan was to march thousands of his supporters in their Blackshirt uniforms through the heart of the East End. The march, Mosley believed, would intimidate not only the Jewish community but all the unionised working classes. Such a show of strength would cause workers to rethink their loyalties and to succumb to his fascist arguments.

Many in the East End were very unhappy with this, and their reaction was fierce. A petition signed by a multitude of people was submitted to the Home Secretary, seeking to ban the march because of the likelihood of violence.

A few days before the event, Bobby called Charlie:

"D-daphne's in a state! Her dad's joined a J-J-Jewish P-Protest group! He's going down the East End on Sunday to d-demonstrate against the march! Her mum thinks he's crazy and she's not talking to him. D-aphne wants me to g-go down there and l-look out for him. W-Will you come with me?"

"Yeah, 'course I'll come if you need me." Charlie responded without a second's hesitation. "What time d'you want me to pick you up?"

Bobby explained that his father-in-law was going on Saturday evening to his cousin Shayna Dekker's. Young Alfie's enthusiasm had evidently transferred itself to his father Aaron and most of his associates. All those broken windows had initiated a reaction far more intense than that expected by the fascists.

When Charlie and Bobby arrived at the Dekkers' on Sunday morning, they walked with David Hipstead and Aaron Dekker to where a road block had been built at the beginning of Cable Street. Shayna Dekker had forbidden the children to leave the house, but Alfie defied his mother and ran off to join the others.

As they walked, they mingled, talked and joked with dockers from Limehouse and Poplar – men known usually to be anti-Semitic. There were also miners from Wales mixing with furniture makers from Bethnal Green. And, of course, there were the tailors of Whitechapel. All were united on this remarkable day.

They reached the impressive barricade, but even more impressive was the sheer number of people. Something like twenty thousand demonstrators against fascism filled the streets east from Gardiner's Corner.

Officialdom had dithered. The petition to the Home Secretary had been refused. Instead, a police escort had been authorised for the marchers, and the massive crowd of demonstrators was met by between six and seven thousand policemen. Mounted police led the attempt to clear the road so that the march of three thousand Blackshirt Fascists could proceed. As a consequence, what followed was not a conflict between anti-fascist demonstrators and fascist marchers, but one between demonstrators and the police.

As the police drove forward into Cable Street, they were met by an onslaught of sticks, bricks, chair legs and whatever else was to hand from the workers. At the same time, they had to contend with an attack from above. From the roofs and the upper floors of buildings, ordinary housewives were throwing down milk bottles, rotten vegetables – and every other kind of refuse – onto the police.

Charlie and the three men with him were hearing rather than witnessing much of the happenings. They were part of the dense crowd but well away from the front line. Charlie, several inches taller than the others, suddenly caught a glimpse of the Dekker boy through the crowd. He instinctively yelled:

"Alfie! No!"

Young Alfie, fourteen years old and small for his age, had run on ahead of them and met up with some friends. They had squeezed through the crowd to where they could throw stones at the horses of the mounted police, causing the horses to rear and their riders to fight for control. However, Charlie instantly realised that they could just as easily be trampled to death. Ten years earlier, his own father had lost his life, crushed in a similar, if far less momentous engagement.

He barged his way through the crush of shouting demonstrators, Aaron Dekker tucked in behind him, desperately holding onto the back of his jacket. As they neared the front, the nearest horse reared wildly and one of the boys screamed in pain. Although still two rows from the front, Charlie lunged forward and with his long arms grabbed Alfie Dekker by the shoulders. He hauled him backwards, and Aaron dragged his sulking son back to safety.

As the battle went on, there were many, many injuries and the police arrested more than a hundred and fifty people in their attempts to clear a path, but the crowd refused to give way. After a series of mounted charges, the police accepted that it was impossible to clear a route for the marchers. Mosley was compelled to cancel his planned march and public address.

Charlie, Bobby and Mr Hipstead did not stay for the raucous celebrations of the victorious anti-fascists. It was enough to know that the home team had won. Once back at Smithy Street, Aaron Dekker was again effusive in his thanks to Charlie for the rescue of the four-foot ten-inch Alfie.

Having lectured Alfie on the difference between demonstrating and attacking the police with weapons, Aaron told Shayna the whole story, swearing that God's hand had guided the blond giant. Charlie said nothing more than that his action had been an automatic reaction to an obvious danger. He was embarrassed, aware that by the next day a glamorised version of events would be all over Collick's.

When they reached Crouch End, Daphne and Mrs Hipstead insisted Charlie stay to eat with them. Conversation throughout the meal was mainly about the events of the day, as triumphantly related by David Hipstead. Bobby was content to tend to everyone's liquid needs, and Charlie nodded and shrugged without saying much.

After they had eaten, Charlie made his excuses and drove home. He said he needed to plan for the week ahead, but really he wanted time to himself, to reflect. Everyone was deliriously happy about the outcome of the day's events: everyone except Charlie Stoker. Charlie was troubled. He poured himself a large glass of whisky and sat down in his favourite armchair.

For several years after 1926, he and his mother had lived with the shock, and the aftershocks, of his father's death. Gradually, both had put the pain behind them; but it could never be forgotten. Now, on this October Sunday in 1936, it had all been brought vividly back to him. He had personally witnessed – no! He had actually experienced – an event identical to the skirmish that had killed his father, albeit magnified a hundred times.

He knew that he would never forget the sight of the uncontrolled fury of those fighting the battle of Cable Street. What had taken place earlier that day had been a war, no less. He had no idea how many people were hospitalised, or how many, if any, had lost their lives. He swirled the whisky in his glass. What was it, he asked himself, what was it that turned decent people into barbarians?

* * *

The battle of Cable Street, as the demonstration was triumphantly named, forced the government to take action. A Public Order Act was rushed through parliament. The act banned the use of political uniforms and gave the police the authority to prohibit marches that threatened public disorder. It was a massive blow for Mosley and the B.U.F, although the act did not proscribe the B.U.F. itself.

Charlie was in and out of Collick's quickly the following morning. He knew that he would be the subject of many of the exaggerated stories of the previous day's exploits that would be flying around the building all day. He preferred to be a subject in absentia.

Throughout that year, Charlie had been putting in extra hours on his rounds. To achieve the target standards that he had proposed to Stephen Collick, he needed more customers. He estimated that he would require to add one new address each week, and so he established a routine of calling on potential new accounts for one hour on each of his three short days. He badgered established customers for the name of a neighbour or friend not known to Collick's. Then, using all his charm and sales techniques, he called upon the named person, and kept calling until a new account was opened. His success rate was high, but it took time and patience.

Towards the end of the year, he was beginning to see his success translated into figures. His weekly collections total was averaging in excess of eighty pounds per week. Within two years, he calculated, he could hit the hundred-pound target.

Two days after the Cable Street affair, Charlie reached Armagh Road on his regular routine at one o'clock. He found Sally apparently alone in the house with her baby son. The baby was in his pram in the hall, crying loudly.

"Hallo, Sal, where's your mum?" Charlie's query was automatic. Mrs Cutter always opened the door on Tuesdays.

"She's not well, today, Charlie." Sally replied in a lowered tone, a mark of concern. "She was up all night and now she's in bed, sleeping."

"Oh! I'm sorry. Anything I can do? Do you think it's just something she's picked up?"

"I don't know. I don't think so. She hasn't been really well for some time. If she doesn't look any better by tomorrow, I think I'll call the doctor. Anyway, it's just us two together today."

"I like that. Have you managed alright on you own?"

"You silly lump! You think I can't manage to cook a dinner?"

"No, of course not, that was stupid." Charlie was suitably abashed. "What are we eating?"

"Braised steak, mashed and cabbage. Be a few minutes, 'cos I had to feed Harry first."

The baby had stopped crying but had not yet gone to sleep. Charlie could see a pair of eyes staring at him through the open door, big and blue, like his own.

"How is Harry? He looks fine. He's a big lad for five months, isn't he?"

"Yeah, he's coming on well. Got a nasty temper, though!"

"Really?"

"Oh, yes. When Harry's upset, the household is upset. You should hear him! He's got a great pair of lungs has my Harry." She disappeared into the kitchen, Charlie's gaze following her.

Sally was looking very well. She had recovered her figure, and her blonde hair was shining. She was as beautiful as ever; motherhood had done her no harm. She reappeared with two steaming plates. They sat and ate together.

"Have you heard from Cissie this week?" asked Charlie.

"Yeah, they came over on Sunday. She said the road was blocked around Aldgate and they had to come a different way, across Bishopsgate and through Hoxton. That was a big to-do at Cable Street, wasn't it? Sounds like it was a big punch in the belly for those Fascist beggars!"

"Yes, it was. An amazing affair altogether. The barricade was massive. One of my customer's boys nearly got trampled on by the police horses!"

"Yeah? I'm not surprised. There were a lot of injuries, according to the paper."

"Yes. I'm surprised there weren't a lot more, from what I saw."

"You saw? Were you there?"

"Yeah. My pal Bobby asked me to go with him, to look out for some of his wife's family. They live right in the middle of the East End."

"Oh! It must have been exciting to see it." Sally forked some mashed potato. "D'you know, Charlie, apart from what you told me about your marriage, that's the first time you've ever talked about your private life. It's nice. You know you can always tell me anything, don't you?"

Charlie stopped eating and stared. Then he nodded.

"I suppose you're right, Sal. You are the one person, except Bobby, that I feel I can talk to about anything. He and I have been close since college. We're not really alike. He's five foot eight, red hair, thick glasses and a stammer. I'd trust him with my life, and vice versa."

"A bit like me and Cissie, 'cept we're sisters."

"Yeah. Bobby's the nearest thing to a brother."

"Does he know about," she hesitated, "does he know that…"

"He knows about you Sal. I don't say a lot, but I have told Bobby about us."

"That's nice." Sally's eyes glowed. "What did he say?"

"I think his comment was 'Bloody hell!'"

Sally burst into laughter. "Really, was that all?"

"As far as I can recall, yeah. He may have said it twice."

They ate in silence while Sally pondered. Then she said:

"He didn't give you any advice, then?"

"No. Bobby's not strong on advice. He just listens. I'm the one who's supposed to give advice. I'm good at giving advice to others. I'm just incapable of keeping my own affairs straight."

"That's not true, is it? The only thing wrong in your life is me. Otherwise, everything is perfect, if you allow for a marriage with no love in it."

Charlie sighed, a deep sigh.

"Talking to you, Sally, is like talking to my soul. You understand everything instantly. You knew me from the first moment you saw me. No one else has ever seen through me as you do."

They stared at each other. Then they ate in silence again. Sally reached for Charlie's empty plate but he lifted it and rose from the table. Sally did likewise. He walked around the table to where she sat, put his plate down and removed hers from her hand. He took her in his arms and whispered:

"Whatever we do, wherever we go, for the rest of our lives, I shall always love you, Sally. You will always be my only love."

"And you are mine, Charlie."

They kissed, tenderly, passionately. Their tears met, married and died together as they remained locked in the embrace.

They washed up the dishes and Sally said:

"Have you time for a cup of tea?"

"Yes, I'll make time." Charlie passed her the kettle.

When they were both seated again, he asked:

"Do you hear anything from your friends at the clothing factory these days?"

"Yes!" Sally laughed. "The girls come in to coo at Harry, and Percy pops in regularly. I've told you about Percy before. He's the foreman of the packers. I think he's sweet on me but he doesn't dare say so! He's a really nice chap but quiet, you know what I mean?"

Charlie nodded. "Maybe you should encourage him more."

"Charlie! You're disgusting!"

"Nothing disgusting about being sensible, Sal."

Sally stared at the only person in the world she wanted to encourage. He was right, of course. There was nothing disgusting about being sensible.

Chapter Twenty
The Darkening Skies

The four friends' so-called monthly reunion was held in December, for only the fourth time in 1936. It was the usual thoroughly enjoyable, noisy evening. The wine flowed and the tongues wagged.

The announcement had just been made of the abdication of the popular young king Edward VIII. The king had chosen to marry his American divorcée lover rather than accept the responsibilities and privileges of the crown of Great Britain and the British Empire without her as his queen. Jennifer, after dinner and a glass or three of rosé, was keen to defend the now Duke of Windsor.

"I think he's marvellous! It's absolutely wonderful that he was brave enough to abdicate. To relinquish the British monarchy, the highest ranked position in the world, to give it up for the woman he loves is beyond anything; it is beyond any great deed I can think of. It is the ultimate example of love triumphant!"

Daphne looked blankly at her friend, Charlie sat with a smile playing at the edges of his mouth, and Bobby snorted derisively.

"H-He's a no-good playboy! He's had l-loads of women and th-this is about the worst of 'em! Sh-She's been married twice before already! I-I say good riddance to 'em both!"

"What do you think, Charlie?" asked Daphne.

Charlie shrugged, and puffed at his cigar before replying.

"I think he's a weak and selfish man. He's handsome and popular, but soft. If he were not the king, he would have been ignored as just another spoilt rich child. The decision he has been forced into is good for the country. I think King George VI will make a far better king than Edward VIII."

"Charlie! How can you be so callous?" Jennifer's eyes were afire. "How can you be so cold-hearted? Everyone is entitled to find love, even a king!"

Charlie grinned sardonically. "Yes, everyone is entitled to find love!"

"Well, then," the sardonicism had sailed past Jennifer unnoticed, "why are you so against him?"

Charlie tapped his ash slowly, his eyes fixed on his finger.

"Because I believe duty and honour come before self-indulgence."

* * *

If any period of Charlie Stoker's life could be called a quiet period, it would be the year following the Cable Street War. While much of the world appeared to be politically troubled, with all major countries either at war, threatening war, or, like Great Britain, energetically trying to avert war, Charlie was able to devote his life to building his business.

Throughout the year, his relationship with Sally remained unchanged. The young couple no longer needed to hide their feelings from each other. They embraced fondly and confided in each other, although there was perhaps a degree of restraint when Lottie Cutter was present. Quite regularly, Charlie took Lottie, Sally and little Harry for country drives, and Charlie and Sally went to the Regent cinema at Stamford Hill on half a dozen occasions, leaving Harry in the care of his grandmother.

There was never any question, however, of what at the time would have been called hanky panky. Charlie, disciplined through more than seven years of married celibacy, was well able to control his desires. For Sally, it was hard to accept, although she had plenty to keep her busy most of the time, caring for both her sick mother and her fast-growing baby son.

In May, they all joined the thousands of people who thronged the centre of London to catch a glimpse of the Coronation procession. Albert, Edward's shy younger brother, now King George VI, was crowned with his Queen, Elizabeth.

In July, Margret completed her attachment to the Sorbonne. She left Paris and returned to England, fluent in French and laden with presents for the two people in her life who mattered. For Charlie she brought a large bottle of the best French Cognac and a huge box of Cuban cigars; for Jennifer, she brought a presentation box of the exclusive Chanel No.5 perfume together with a set of lingerie in rose pink silk, trimmed with lace.

At the end of that month, a monthly reunion dinner was held at Le Billet. Arranged as a welcome home party for Margret, the evening did not disappoint her. Everyone ate well and drank freely, and Margret was encouraged to tell all about her time in France. As usual, she took the opportunity to deliver a lecture. Her subjects were the excellence of French food and the weaknesses of the French political leaders. She was also flattering about the Sorbonne, declaring that her two years there had greatly expanded her understanding of world economics as well as broadening her outlook upon life.

In September, Margret returned to the London School of Economics as a full-time lecturer. She did not, however, return to her College accommodation. Instead, she surprised Charlie by choosing to commute daily from Chigwell. She wanted her independence, she explained: she wanted to be able to be free of the place when she was off duty. To facilitate that freedom, she had decided to purchase a motor car, something sporty, she said, like an MG TA.

Charlie grinned and shrugged. A two-seater MG was absolutely the right choice for Margret. She could comfortably afford it, and Jennifer, he thought to himself, would absolutely love it. To accommodate both cars, though, they would need to widen the garage. Charlie arranged, through Stephen Collick, for that work to be done.

Charlie's own career was also progressing well. At the end of each year, at his Thursday morning meeting, Aitch Harrington read out the average weekly collection totals of the 'Gold Standard' men. The figures were calculated from the September, October and November results.

In December 1937, the average weekly collections from Round three were £88. 0s. 0d. This was comfortably more than any other salesman at Collick's. The next highest was Horace Darbyshire, who was, by the end of the year, collecting about £10 less. He was followed by Ray Parsons, just a pound or two behind. Both of these men, and Walter Habisch, had been comfortably collecting between £60 and £70 for some years. The new averages showed that Charlie had been the spur he had hoped to be to the other men.

Aitch was careful to announce that the totals for the fourth 'Gold' man, Walter Habisch, were unchanged at £70. This was despite the fact that Walter was losing hours each week because of his wife's illness. It should be noted, Aitch roared across the room, that Walter's figures had not dropped by one penny!

Charlie met Walter in the store the next morning and they took coffee together.

"Six years ago, I showed you the bizness, now you're the top man! I show you right, eh?" The little man was beaming with pride.

"Yes, Walter, you certainly did. I learned a lot in those three days and I've never forgotten it." Charlie was smiling but his words were meant seriously. "You're still the best, Walter. I mean that."

Walter's face was a picture of embarrassed pleasure. Charlie went on:

"How's your wife now? Is she getting better?"

"I do' think so, Charlie. I don' see much change. She never been really well since she had my Maria, bless her. My Esther gets tired so quick, every day. I try to help her, but she wants to do things hersel'. She's a good girl."

He looked round furtively, then up at Charlie with a sheepish grin. "She deserves a better husband than me."

Charlie shrugged.

"Somehow, I don't think she'd agree with you on that, Walter. You've made her a home and a life here; you are a good provider. You're a good man. We've all got our weaknesses; we've all got our crosses to bear. Just never forget what's important to you."

"Thass right." Walter nodded fiercely. "The home and the job, thass what matters!"

They left the coffee shop and Walter went off to collect his stock. Charlie said a quick hallo to Laura Matthews and to Shayna Dekker before going on his way.

* * *

By 1938, the world had become a darker place. For many people throughout Europe, it was an uncomfortable time in which to live. Hitler's Nazis annexed Austria and immediately set about what the Nazi newspapers called a 'spring-cleaning' of Jews. In Spain, the rebel General Franco was winning the civil war, with the aid of Germany and Italy. Further afield, Japanese troops were murdering their Chinese neighbours, and in the Soviet Union Stalin continued to annihilate all opposition with his show trials.

In England, pressure was at last building against the appeasement policies of Prime Minister Neville Chamberlain. Recognising the need to take a stand, Anthony Eden, the Foreign Secretary resigned in protest at Chamberlain's dealings with the Italian Ambassador.

In Armagh Road, by the spring of the year the most recent addition to the Cutter family, Harry, was toddling about and needing constant surveillance, a little boy of nearly two, with blue eyes and a mass of yellow-white curly hair. Lottie Cutter had recovered considerably and, although still thin and pale, she was once more involved in the running of the home. In fact, she felt well enough to look after her grandson, and thus allow Sally to return to work.

The despatch manager was delighted to welcome Sally back to the clothing factory. He admitted that her presence had been sorely missed in the intervening two years. None of the six girls who had held the position during that time had been able to properly handle the job.

Even more excited to see Sally back was Percy Spence, the foreman packer. Percy had visited Sally at home regularly through the whole period of her absence. Having eventually mastered his job, he swore that had it not been for Sally's support in his first months he would have been sacked.

Charlie Stoker had met Percy only a few times. Percy lived with his mother in Malmesbury Street. Mrs Spence had been a customer of Charlie's for two or three years, also on his Tuesday round, an early morning call. Percy, a quiet, unassuming man, was always at work when Charlie called, but his mother had bought shirts and shoes for him, and Charlie had made a point of calling back on those evenings to meet him and to ensure the goods were suitable. Percy had been nervous and rather timid in the presence of the big blond salesman, but Charlie gained a clear impression of the man nevertheless. He was filed away in the big man's mental ledger as honest and sensible. He reminded Charlie a little of Harry Bateson, a man he knew instinctively to be trustworthy, a man who would never let you down.

Sally came home for lunch every day, and on Tuesdays, Charlie collected her and delivered her back to the factory. It gave them an extra few minutes together, time relished by both. Sally chatted about everything and Charlie nodded and smiled.

After a couple of months, Sally had just finished telling Charlie of an incident that morning involving Percy, when Charlie said:

"Has he asked you out yet?"

"Charlie! Course not! It's not like that. You know better than to ask!"

"Why? The bloke's crazy about you and you know it."

"Charlie, you know there's no man in my life except you."

Charlie stopped the car. They were still a few hundred yards from the house. He turned to face the passenger seat.

"We know how we feel about each other, Sal. We also know that nothing will change. We have to face the facts. Your mother is in poor health. If the worst should happen, you would have to give up work. You are barely twenty-two years old. You need a husband, but I can't be that. I will always love you, I will watch out for you, but you must find a husband and a life."

Then he added: "You could do a lot worse than Percy Spence."

Turning away to discourage any reply, Charlie started the engine and drove on to the Cutter house. He wanted Sally to think carefully before replying.

* * *

At the London School of Economics, Margret's year had not gone as planned. Promotion at the L.S.E. was strictly hierarchical. Progress to a professor's chair would be painfully slow. The esteem in which she had been held in Paris did not transfer itself to London. Encouraged as a bright young thing before she had left in 1935, she now found herself to be just another lecturer, a junior one and female.

The situation did not suit Margret, and as always when a situation did not suit Margret, she reacted. When, early in the academic year, applications were invited for departmental posts at the new South West Essex Technical College, to be opened at Forest Road, Walthamstow in September 1938, Margret was quick to apply for the position of head of the mathematics department.

The selection process was slow, but by early summer she had been offered the post of assistant head of department. It was explained to her that the man appointed to her preferred position was fifty years of age and had twenty years more experience than she. At the tender age of twenty-eight, she had plenty of time to develop her career.

Infuriated by what she considered short sighted stupidity, her immediate reaction, as explained to Jennifer and to Charlie, was to refuse to accept. In the end, however, common sense prevailed. The choice was years of daily commuting to the city to lecture, or a comfortable position at a college situated midway between Chigwell and Bounds Green, in which she would hold a position of authority with good prospects.

And so began Margret's life at Walthamstow College. Inevitably, it also began the way of life that was to become her norm. She spelled it out to Charlie:

"Dear as you are to me, Big Boy, Jennifer needs me more, and, in truth, I need her more. Naturally, I shall always honour our agreement. We remain a married couple. That farcical state will remain as it is for the rest of our lives. But you know, you have always known, that my first love is my little pearl. I intend to spend my nights with her, although I shall always be available to honour our marriage commitments."

Charlie shrugged. He was not sure quite what her last few words meant but could not be bothered to ask for clarification. He realised he no longer cared enough to ask.

* * *

The Spanish Civil War raged on throughout 1938. Many Liberal and Communist volunteers formed brigades to fight for the Republic against Franco's rebels, but with Nazi German and Italian Fascisti support, the Nationalist forces had become stronger. The British and the French governments remained officially neutral, although our ambassador to Spain believed that a victory for Franco would be in Britain's best interests. He worked to support the Nationalists.

In September, Prime Minister Chamberlain returned from Munich, where he had signed an agreement with Herr Hitler. He proudly waved a piece of paper to a cheering crowd and proclaimed 'I believe it is peace for our time'.

Many people, however, regarded the agreement as a sell-out to Hitler, one step too far in appeasement. In parliament, the out-of-favour ex-minister Winston Churchill made a powerful speech expressing his fears for Czechoslovakia now that Austria had been absorbed into the Nazi net. The mood of the country was changing and, at last, serious re-armament had begun.

In the saloon bar of The Chequers, September 1938 was significant to Charlie and Bobby for entirely different reasons.

"Do y-you realise it's exactly ten years since we m-met in the ph-ph-physics department?" Bobby reminded his friend.

Charlie lifted his glass from the table. "Let's drink to it!"

He was as proud of that relationship as was the excitable motor engineer. The friendship with Bobby was the one constant, the one aspect of his life that had remained utterly reliable and unchanged since his first day in college in 1928. Except for the times when each had married and taken honeymoons, they had met every week to swim together, drink together and generally support each other.

They touched glasses. Bobby said:

"D'you fancy g-giving me a hand to d-deliver some leaflets?"

Charlie raised an enquiring eyebrow.

"For Daph's dad, e-election stuff."

"When?"

"Tomorrow afternoon? Ab-bout half-past three at the h-house?"

"Thursday? Yeah, okay."

David Hipstead, by this time a local Labour councillor in Hornsey, was vociferous in his efforts to bring pressure upon the government to change its appeasement policy. As part of his campaign for the local elections late in the year, he wrote a fiercely anti-fascist election leaflet for distribution throughout his council ward. With daughter Daphne not being available, he recruited his son-in-law Bobby to be the delivery man.

Daphne was expecting her first baby within a few months. She had given up her job at Highgate reluctantly, and Lionel Lacey, fully appreciating her urge to be a mother, suggested that she become a relief pharmacist for him in the future, when she felt free to do so. She was, he said, too efficient to lose forever.

Bobby was happy to help out with the leaflet delivery. Delivering the leaflets was a healthy relief for him from the grease and grime of the workshop, and he could easily spare the time. His seven years of hard work in building the motor cycle repair business was now being rewarded. His reputation had spread and the volume of work had increased significantly in the last few years. He now employed an assistant and an apprentice, both good workers.

When Charlie arrived the following day, Bobby had split the leaflets into two equal piles and had placed them in two shoulder bags. He arranged for each of them to cover half of the designated area. They would meet when they finished and enjoy a pint at the White Hart, a pub standing on the boundary of the council ward.

Charlie set off on foot, starting his deliveries near the house, and Bobby took his old BSA, parking it near the pub. The White Hart had a side entrance at the end of a narrow side street in which he left the BSA and sidecar.

When Bobby finished his deliveries, he returned to the vehicle to find his exit blocked by a large butcher's van parked broadside across the street, its rear doors open towards the side entrance of the pub. On the other side of the street, a lamppost prevented him from riding over the pavement. He was not too concerned, since he was meeting Charlie for a drink and realised the road would be clear when he came out.

Instead of going to find his friend as intended, therefore, Bobby decided to have a glass of ale and wait. He strolled over to the pub entrance, intending to squeeze past the open door of the van. He was forced to make a sudden stop. From out of the building, at head height, came a sharp cornered metal meat tray held by a pair of outstretched arms.

"Whhh-oops!" Bobby screamed to a halt just sharply enough to avoid the corner of the tray hitting him in the face. Instead, he lost his balance as it whistled past his eyes. He stumbled backwards and fell, landing on his backside. "That w-was t-t-too b-bloody close!"

"Yer wanna look where you're goin, yer dozy sod!"

The harsh accusation infuriated Bobby. He blurted out a riposte as he dragged himself upright:

"You could kill someone rushing out like that, you b-bloody fool! You should be more careful. You should come out backwards!"

"Fuck off!" The dismissive insult came from behind the opened rear door as the person carrying the tray threw it into the van, and at that instant Bobby recognised the coarse-toned voice.

"A-Alec Chapman, you buggar! I should have known!"

Chapman's burly figure came into view as he slammed shut the van door. Standing, arms on hips, looking to Bobby like a red-faced teapot, he sneered. "Well, sod me, it's the yid motorbike man!"

"Y-you can cut ou-out that nonsense, Alec. I'm not J-Jewish and your l-language is insulting!"

"Whether you was born Jew or just married Jew is all the same to me. When we get in power, you'll all be thrown out!"

"Y-you bloody f-fascist!" exclaimed Bobby, now himself red in the face.

Without warning, Chapman's fist flew into Bobby's face, sending him reeling backward and quite unprepared for the follow-up blow to the chest. He went to the ground, where the butcher gratuitously kicked him in the ribs.

"That's how we'll deal with yids," scoffed Chapman.

"As long as they're caught unawares, eh?" said a voice behind him.

Chapman spun round to see the huge figure of Charlie Stoker standing by his van.

"What d'yer mean? He—"

Whatever was to follow was stifled by a lightning-fast blow to the solar-plexus that bent the butcher double, and an uppercut to the chin that sent him flying through the air to land flat on the ground next to Bobby, not quite unconscious but completely dazed. Charlie glared at him for a moment to ensure that he still had his full attention.

"The only difference," he said very deliberately to the much-shaken butcher, "is that I don't need to kick a man when he is down."

He turned to Bobby. "You okay, pal?"

"Yeah, just embarrassed. I should've been r-ready for him."

Charlie put his arm around Bobby's shoulder and guided him into the pub, leaving Alec Chapman lying on the ground.

Chapter Twenty-One
Perfect Planning

At the end of February 1939, the British Government officially recognised General Franco as the new leader of Spain, albeit to cries of 'Shame' and 'Heil Chamberlain!' from the Opposition benches. Barely two weeks later, Germany invaded Czechoslovakia, as forecast the previous year by Winston Churchill.

Throughout Britain, people were now anxious, fearful that, regardless of the Munich Agreement so proudly announced by Prime Minister Chamberlain a few months earlier, war was imminent. The bombing of Guernica by German and Italian aircraft in 1937 had shown the world what was now possible in an air raid. At the beginning of 1939 the Home Office began to issue air raid shelters to city dwellers likely to be targets of bombing raids.

With an Anderson shelter newly erected next to her beloved vegetable garden, Millie Stoker celebrated, one day early, her fiftieth birthday. She had been insistent that she would not enjoy a big celebration (Stephen Collick had wanted to arrange a smart catered affair), but instead she wanted to prepare, with Florrie Brown's loyal assistance, a traditional lunch at home for those dear to her heart. Charlie, accompanied by Margret; Stephen, of course; Billy and Sally Walters and their two-year-old daughter, Sarah Mildred; and Father Peter O'Rahilly. All happily attended to help her spend the day in the way she most enjoyed.

During the years of her friendship with Stephen, Millie had come to enjoy the taste of good wine with her meals and on this occasion, the distinguished man provided a case of Dom Perignon champagne in addition to the fine claret they usually enjoyed together. The house was quickly filled with the joy of good conversation and of song, to the accompaniment of Billy Walters' accordion.

It all became a bit overwhelming for little Sarah Mildred, and Sally took her upstairs to their flat for an afternoon nap; but Father Peter, regardless of his failing health, stayed the whole day and joined in all the fun. He also made a short but eloquent speech in honour of his hostess, his most treasured parishioner.

Millie had never demanded a great deal from others and was usually content to live her life quietly. However, to be able to spend the day in her own home on this special occasion, surrounded by and catering for the small group of people she held most dear, was her idea of heaven. To see her son, the image of his dead father with the Stoker smile playing about his eyes, sprawled in an armchair with a cigar and a brandy, and chatting with her friend and benefactor, Stephen, gave her more joy than she could ever express.

And Margret, as always in Millie's presence, was the loving, respectful daughter-in-law. As Charlie studied his mother across the room, he took great comfort from the fact that she, at least, had now found complete peace in her life. It was ironic, he supposed, that much of that peace of mind rested on the false impression she had of her son's life.

At twenty-eight years of age, Charlie Stoker was the undisputed top salesman at Collick's, with a fine home, his own motorcar and a solid balance in the bank. He gave the world the impression of an easy-going achiever, a man contented with his lot. In his own eyes, nothing could be further from the truth.

Masked by his veil of casualness and his remarkable self-discipline, Charlie's heart and soul were tortured. His life was in chaos, and the chaos was entirely of his own making. For the most part, he lived alone, the life of a celibate. He yearned for a child, yet insisted upon remaining married to a woman who had declared that she would never have one, who despised marriage, and who spent most of her time living elsewhere with her lover, Jennifer Lacey. He himself loved another, a woman he would not allow himself to possess, no matter how much they both desired that union. Instead, he had driven her into having a fatherless child and was now actively encouraging her into marriage with a man she did not love. So much for the great Charlie Stoker! He dropped his gaze into his brandy goblet, then swallowed the contents in self-disgust.

* * *

Sally Cutter was a young woman of exceptionally quick and sound mind. She was capable of adjusting quickly to circumstances, and after the emotional upheavals of the previous two years, she had done exactly that.

When Charlie left her to contemplate the possibility of encouraging Percy Spence, she neither lost her temper nor dismissed the idea. Instead, she reflected. Her father had died and her sister had had twins and moved away. She had given up her job and she had given birth to an illegitimate son. She had watched her mother's health seriously deteriorate, and once, or occasionally twice a week she suffered the torment of seeing the man she loved and who loved her but who could never be hers. Their love would never mean more than a hug or a kiss.

Until the summer of 1938, the only relationship she had had with Percy Spence was contact at work and his polite visits to her home. That Percy was in love with her, she had no doubt. Of the fact that she was not, nor ever would be in love with Percy, she was equally certain. But did that mean she should not marry him? She would be a dutiful wife and mother, she was sure. She could be the strong partner a man like Percy needed in marriage. But could she be happy? Sally thought about it, then giggled to herself as she came to a conclusion. In *those* circumstances, she thought, perhaps she could. Her first task was to get Percy to ask her out.

Gently, over the next six months, Sally encouraged Percy to take her out, at first just walking across the park, then to the pictures, and then to Saturday evening dances at the Royal Ball Room in Tottenham. Gradually, she grew very fond of Percy. There was, quite simply, nothing about him not to like. Percy Spence was a thoroughly decent man. He was not in any way a romantic. He was what her recently departed father would have called 'the salt of the earth'.

At the end of the year, after the firm's Xmas party, Percy actually stuttered a proposal of marriage to Sally, who said she would think seriously about it, but she told him she needed time. She knew that Percy would make a husband with whom she would be safe. He would provide support for her at all times.

During the winter, she discussed the matter with her mother, who was clearly in favour of the idea. Lottie considered Percy a nice enough chap. "A bit shy, but that's not a crime, is it?" she said with a shrug.

"And if," she added, "he is so in love with you to want to take on the responsibility for both you and Harry, good luck to him. The little monster is proving more than a handful for me!"

Lottie was indeed finding the highly active child almost too much to handle during the hours Sally was at work. Sadly, the pernicious condition that had troubled her for some years was now getting the better of her. Her strength was lessening with each month that passed. Having ignored her poor health for several years, she had recently visited the doctor. A blood test had confirmed the condition to be chronic leukaemia. She understood she had only a limited time left, but she had not yet told Sally. She did not want to precipitate a false move by her daughter.

Sally sighed. Reliable and undemanding Percy certainly was, but he was also unexciting. He was quite incapable of stirring her emotions, of rousing her to anything beyond simple companionship. Never would Percy, nor any other man, she confessed to herself, be able to remove or replace the ache in her heart for Charlie Stoker.

The Collick's man duly appeared at the clothing factory at lunchtime on the Tuesday after his mother's party and drove Sally to Armagh Road. They took lunch with Lottie as usual, dealt with business and chatted about everything and nothing, as usual. Then Charlie took Sally back to work. As soon as they moved away from the house, Sally said:

"Stop the car, Charlie, I want to talk to you."

Charlie pulled to the kerb and switched the engine off. He lit a cigarette and turned to face Sally, raising a questioning eyebrow. Sally took a deep breath.

"I told you that Percy had proposed after the firm's dance at Christmas, didn't I?"

Charlie nodded.

"Well, Charlie, you know he's about as exciting as mince and potatoes, but he's a decent man, and I know I should settle for that. But... and there will always be that *but*, Charlie, unless you agree to two things."

"Oh?" Charlie raised both eyebrows, eyes twinkling, and he inhaled.

"Charlie, this is serious! Now listen to me! If I say yes to Percy it will be for life, and I'll be a good wife to him. But... But two things. Number one, I will never tell him what or why about Harry."

Charlie nodded.

"Number two is you. Two things. First, your promise to always be there for me. The marriage won't change that?"

"Nothing will ever change that, Sal."

He reached for her hand. Sally's tense tone vanished and she smiled at him.

"I love you, Charlie."

They looked at each other for a few seconds. He gently squeezed her hand.

"The second thing is the heart of the whole matter, Charlie," said Sally softly. He looked at her steadily without speaking.

"I intend to have your baby. You are to promise me you will make love to me just before my marriage. Percy will never know, and I shall make him a good wife. But at the same time, I'll give you the child you so badly miss, and that will tie you to me for life."

Charlie's gaze remained steady. Then he whispered, half to himself:

"Bloody hell, Sal. You don't go halfway to anywhere, do you?"

He inhaled deeply, then exhaled, a huge explosion. It was Sally's turn to remain silent. He nodded.

"OK. It's a deal."

He raised her hand to his lips and kissed it. "Your servant, ma'am," he said admiringly.

* * *

Walter Habisch was not smiling in the basement that Thursday morning. His face wore a stricken look, he was almost tearful.

"Walter! What's the problem?" Charlie asked.

Walter looked around anxiously. "Not here, Charlie. We go to your motor, iss private!"

Charlie led the way to the Ford, parked in front of the store, and they both climbed in. Immediately, Walter began to pour out his story.

"You know – I don' haf to tell you – that Bert Pensell got hisself in more trouble the end of the year?"

Charlie nodded. Pensell had stolen some cash from the publican at the Ace of Spades. It was a questionable offence, because the publican, a man named Aspinall, was himself a known crook, involved in the same betting racket that earned Pensell's income; but Bert's record told against him and he was sent down for another three months.

"See," said Walter, "at the beginning of the year, my Esther took a turn for the worse and needed to rest a lot. I haf to work, to earn our keep, so there was no one to look after my Maria. So, Esther took her with her to stay for a few weeks with her aunt (Esther's aunt), who's been over here a long time and lives in Hammersmith. So, I bin livin' alone."

Charlie shrugged sympathetically.

"Well," said Walter, his head bowed, "I started again with Alice. I know! I'm meshuga, but we were both lonely. Only for a couple weeks, then I stopped. I come to my senses. Anyway, last week, Alice tells me she's expecting, and it's mine! Then she says, 'You don' have to worry. Bert thinks it's his and he's happy as Larry!' She doesn't care! But I do worry, Charlie, I do worry. Now, I muss watch out for Alice, she carryin' my child, and I muss earn my wages, but I gotta have time to look after my Esther and my Maria."

The little man was on the brink of tears. He looked plaintively at Charlie, desperate for some guidance. Charlie lit a cigarette and inhaled smoke. He opened the window and exhaled.

"Walter, could you manage if you only worked Friday Saturday? You don't collect too much on your other days, do you?"

The little man furrowed his brow.

"About sixty, seventy percent weekend. But I need the other accounts too."

"Yeah, I know, I meant caring for the family. Could you find the time to work your Friday and Saturday rounds?"

"You mean if I stay home on Mondays, Tuesdays and Wednesdays? Yes, sure. But I can't lose those accounts."

"How long d'you think this situation will go on?"

"I dunno, Charlie. My Esther, I think it's bad. I don' think she got long." The tears began now to fall slowly down the little Czech's face. "She's dyin', Charlie."

Walter started shaking uncontrollably. Charlie placed his hand on the little man's shoulder. The shaking eased.

"Be strong, Walter, what will be, will be, but you still have your daughter to care for. Anyway, there's a way through this. Will you be able to manage if I collect your weekday rounds for you? You can hand them in on Thursdays."

The little man wiped his tears, blew his nose loudly and pulled himself together. He looked at Charlie in awe.

"You mean you… you collect yours, and mine for me?"

"Yeah, of course that's what I mean. There's plenty of time on the weekdays. Every now and then, you could pop in to see the ones who might cause difficulties, we can handle it okay."

"How much I pay you? I need…"

"Don't be daft. You don't pay me. I'm repaying you for teaching me how!"

Walter Habisch stared absently for some seconds as he mentally searched for possible problems. Then he broke into a huge grin. He grabbed Charlie's hand and pumped it furiously up and down.

"Charlie, you, you're a special man. You make everything right! I love you like a brother."

* * *

In the second week of March, Daphne Bruce gave birth to a baby daughter, Helen. Bobby, the proud father, was far too excited to work for the next few days, although he rushed around madly to ensure that mother and baby had everything they could possibly need. As Daphne gradually took the reins of the house again, Bobby relaxed. He and Charlie enjoyed a celebration night at the Chequers. There was an upright piano in the saloon, and with a regular who played to accompany him, Bobby sang his heart out until Charlie was compelled to carry him to the car.

Later in the month, much to the relief of Lottie Cutter, Sally accepted Percy Spence's proposal of marriage. Lottie was desperate to be able to see her daughter married, and although Percy was no Charlie Stoker, he was a really nice man. He would take care of her wonderful, wild, younger daughter, she was sure.

Lottie still looked forward to the company of Charlie every Tuesday. Also, every couple of weeks, he took her, on Thursday afternoons with Sally and Harry, for a drive. Sally had somehow contrived to have Thursday afternoons off. On one of these trips, when they were sitting on a bench in a park at Brentwood, while Sally was riding on a playground roundabout with Harry, Lottie told Charlie about her medical condition.

"I don't know," she said, in answer to Charlie's direct question, "but I suspect I shall not be here next year, Charlie. That's why I'm so anxious to see Sally married. It will settle things; you know what I mean?"

Charlie nodded. "Yes, I understand, it's only natural, you're a loving mother. You, of all people, deserve peace of mind."

He paused, then added quietly, "I shall miss you more than I can ever say."

He lit a cigarette. "Have you told Sally?"

"No. I haven't had the courage."

He shrugged.

"It's not courage you lack, Mrs C, it's anxiety about how she'll take it. Tell her. It is the right thing to do. She can handle it."

Lottie Cutter sighed. Sally came back with Harry and the conversation ended. The trip continued as normal.

When Charlie called on the following Tuesday, Sally had been made aware of the details of her mother's condition, and she and Percy had agreed to set a date for the marriage in August. It was to be a midweek ceremony at Hackney register office. Neither had large families to accommodate and the arrangement was easy.

Percy wandered about for most of the intervening time in a state of wonder. He had won first prize in the lottery of life. Sally carried on as usual, laughing, chatting, working, being a capable mother, and spending a few precious minutes each Tuesday lunchtime alone with Charlie.

Late in June, Sally told Charlie it was time to talk about the promise. She had things all worked out.

"The wedding, as you know, is to be on 4 August. My monthly time then will be around 10th to 12th. I want you to take me away during the last week of July. That's when I'm most likely to fall pregnant. I know Thursday is always a good day for you and it happens that Percy always goes to the pub with his fishing mates on Thursdays. Also, I'm finishing at the factory on the previous Friday so I can stay away. Harry will be okay with Mum."

Charlie shrugged but could not stop himself grinning.

"You are something, Sally Cutter. You've been planning this a long time, haven't you? And where exactly am I taking you?"

"I don't care, Charlie, as long as I'm with you. Yes, I have been planning a long time. This will be the most important night of my life. I shall, for that one time, have all I ever want from life. Two weeks after, I begin my penance for my sins, with your present inside me."

Charlie was very rarely stuck for words, but everything was different with Sally, wasn't it? He shrugged. This would be the biggest moment in both their lives. He suddenly had a thought.

"What happens if it doesn't work?"

Sally giggled. "You will have an affair with a married woman!"

* * *

A few days before Sally's wedding, Charlie and Bobby had completed their twenty laps of the pool and were enjoying a refreshing pint or two at The Chequers. Bobby was telling of his father-in-law's latest rant.

"Daph's dad says that b-bastard Hitler is going to force us into a w-war within weeks. He r-reckons I'll get called up 'cos they'll n-need engineers. He's keen to have a go, but he thinks he'll m-miss out 'cos he's over f-forty!"

Charlie shrugged. "D'you think Hitler will back down over Danzig?"

"H-He hasn't backed down over anywhere else, has he? He-He wants to rule Europe. H-He won't stop till he's stopped!"

Charlie nodded. "You're right. So is your father-in-law, I should think. It'd be tough on you, Bob. Your business doesn't exist without you, and Daphne would be stuck at home with the baby. Best not to think about it. If it comes to pass, we'll deal with it."

They both drank to that. Bobby asked:

"Wh-what sort of week you had?"

"Good. Had lunch at my mum's on Sunday with Margret."

"M-Margret? I th-thought—"

"Yeah, but she always joins me for Mum's."

"Aah!" Bobby nodded knowingly. "Your mum okay?"

"Yeah, fine."

"How about S-S-Sally?" Bobby was wearing a cheeky smile.

"She's fine too. She's getting married on Friday." Charlie's face gave away little but his eyes were twinkling. Bobby was wide-eyed.

"R-Really? You okay about it?"

"Yeah, fine. It's good for her and he's a nice bloke."

"You invited?"

"Yeah, but I've got to work. I'll join them afterwards."

Bobby searched for a sign of emotion but there was none. He pushed harder.

"H-How about what you said about her being the one for you?"

Charlie grinned. "Nothing changes, Bobby. The world goes on."

Bobby shook his head, accepting defeat. The conversation moved on. They had another drink.

Under the mask, Charlie had been bursting with feelings. The previous Thursday, he had taken Sally from Armagh Road at about two o'clock. She had looked ravishing in a summer dress he had not seen before, and carrying a small case. Neither were items he had supplied. The dress, in a delicate peach coloured cotton voile, had puff sleeves and a V-shaped under-bust seam. There was a small contrasting bow at the bottom of the V-shaped collar, and her perfect waist was accentuated by a matching belt.

He had complimented her upon it, then added:

"That's not a Collick's dress."

Sally had giggled. "No. this is an Armagh Road dress! Mum made it from a pattern I got from work. I wanted something special for today, something for only today. I shall never wear this for anyone else. The little case is one that Dad had for when he needed to take samples from suppliers. Dad always wanted you and me to be together. So did Mum. She knows what this is about and she's pleased, but she won't talk about it, even to you."

Charlie had been too taken aback to shrug, but he grinned. It was pure Sally, he thought. Total commitment, yet with life compartmentalised and organised. Nothing was ever forgotten, every detail planned, considered and remembered. Yet here she was, carefree as ever, stunningly beautiful, and determined to give herself to him.

Charlie had always felt he could cope with all situations in life. Life came easily to him because he was always careful to remain emotionally detached. At all times, he had his magic shield. But there was no shield from Sally and there was no shield from the sin he was about to commit.

Why, he had asked God a thousand times since he had agreed this tryst, why is adultery different from the other sins I commit daily? Why is it okay to enter a marriage with no love, to live a lie for eight years, to live as a celibate, to condone my wife's ongoing infidelity? Why is it all right to live that life but wrong to take my true love in my arms, wrong to create new life with the one person in this world whom I love with all my heart, who loves me and for whom I would happily give my life?

Of course, he told himself, he had received no answer, because he, the innocent, faith full, college boy, had made that vow: *Until death do us part, I give you all that I have myself, and my love.*

Well, he decided, after a sequence of nights with much whisky and too much self-torture: I now rescind that vow.

"Where are you taking me to?" Sally had asked as soon as they drove off.

"I have given that a lot of thought," replied Charlie, "and I have come to a surprising conclusion. But before I tell you, let me ask, is there any special place that you would really like to go to?"

"No." Sally's answer was instant. "I don't care if we spend the night in a ditch as long as it is our night."

Charlie's heart was pounding. He was aware of feelings more powerful than he had ever known. He concentrated on driving for a few minutes. Then he said:

"Sal, I was going to take you for a drive, maybe a stroll through Hyde Park, on to the West End, to a little restaurant I'm fond of. Then I was planning to take you home. I live in a big house that is cold for lack of love. I have a large bed that has only ever been used by me alone. My wife lives with her girlfriend, except for formal occasions when we must appear as man and wife. I wanted you to share my bed."

Sally did not immediately respond, and Charlie glanced round. She was sitting with glistening eyes, tears on her cheeks, looking straight ahead. He turned his eyes to the road.

"Do we need to go to the restaurant?" The question was asked in a soft, a timid tone.

Charlie smiled. "No, Sally. We can eat each other."

"That sounds good for me." She reached across and placed her hand on his thigh. Charlie took the hand up to his lips and held it there.

They drove straight to Chigwell.

Chapter Twenty-Two
And So to War

"Yes, Charlie, I agree entirely. If Hitler attacks Poland, it will mean war, and many of our young men will be needed to defend the country."

On the second last day of July, a Sunday, Stephen Collick and Charlie relaxed with cigars and brandy in the front room of the Stoker house in Amhurst Road. They had enjoyed a Sunday roast lunch with Millie and Margret, and the two ladies were still downstairs.

"Collick's sales force would be greatly depleted," admitted Stephen, "indeed, the whole country will be severely affected. Of course, a number of otherwise eligible men will be needed to remain in positions essential to keep the country running."

He looked purposefully at Charlie when he spoke the last few words. The big blond man nodded, exhaling the aroma of Havana into the already smoke-filled room.

"I would have to go, Stephen."

Stephen smiled. "Yes. You know what it will do to your mother, don't you?"

"Yes." Charlie paused. "But I would still have to go."

"I thought you would say that. You are your father's son; I expected no other response. Army or Air Force?"

"Army, I think. Flying destroyed my father."

Stephen did not reply at once. He played with his cigar and they sat in comfortable silence for some time. Then the older man said, in his unique soft, aristocratic tone:

"Go if you must, Charlie, but for God's sake, promise me you'll come back whole."

Charlie smiled and raised his goblet. "I promise."

They drank to it and smoked on for a time.

"It's going to happen, Charlie, you know that, don't you?" Stephen said eventually. Charlie nodded.

"Shall I have a word with someone for you?" asked the ever-supportive Stephen.

Charlie became unexpectedly tense as he stared at the man he had come to regard as a sort of fairy godfather.

"No, sir. I need to do this on my own. Whatever follows, there must never be any weight on another's shoulders."

* * *

A smiling Sally Cutter married Percy Spence at 3.00 pm on 4 August 1939. The bride was breathtakingly beautiful in a simple fitted dress of pale turquoise silk crêpe de chine, very slightly flared from below the hips and with a small yellow rose spray by her left breast. She wore matching shoes and a small straw-coloured fedora hat with a turquoise ribbon trailing onto her flowing hair. Attending were her mother, Charlie Stoker, Cissie and Harry Bateson, and the three three-year-olds, Tommy and Jimmy Bateson and Harry Cutter.

The groom, shaking with nerves, wore a navy-blue lounge suit, his first bespoke suit and made for the occasion, with a white shirt, bright red tie and a carnation in his buttonhole. Percy was supported by his mother and by his best man and long-time friend, fellow angler, Brian Smith.

The ceremony went well, and there was a small reception at Armagh Road afterwards. Charlie excused himself quickly as he rushed back to work but the Batesons stayed with Lottie and little Harry for the whole weekend so that the newlyweds could have a honeymoon weekend at Clacton-on-Sea. A taxi took them to Liverpool Street station for the seven o'clock train.

Sally and Percy had discussed thoroughly the question of where they should live, and the problem was solved with Sally's usual efficiency. Both mothers were widows. Whichever they should live with, the other would be left alone. Mrs Spence was a quiet, pleasant-natured woman who had got along very well with Lottie Cutter from their very first meeting. They had become friends. Moreover, both women owned their own homes, the legacy of careful husbands. Surely, Sally suggested, it would be a good idea if the two mothers moved into one house and the young family took the other.

Although both widows were startled by the suggestion, they quickly came to see its merits. Since the Spence home would pass to Percy in due course, while Sally would inherit only half of her mother's estate, it made obvious sense for Mary Spence to move to Armagh Road. And so, it was done. Percy and Sally set up home at 14, Malmesbury Street, less than a mile away.

* * *

After the invasion of Czechoslovakia earlier in the year, it had become clear to all that the country was seriously preparing for war. At the end of March, several eager youngsters from among Charlie's customers had volunteered for service the moment a doubling in the size of the Territorial Army had been announced. One month later, conscription had been introduced for all 20-year-old men.

In August, Parliament was recalled, army reservists were called up and Civil Defence workers placed on alert. On Friday, 1 September, Germany attacked Poland. For the only time in the twentieth century, Parliament sat throughout the weekend. The British army was officially mobilised and ARP wardens enforced the 'Blackout'.

On Sunday, 3 September, the Prime Minister, having forlornly addressed the nation in a broadcast from the cabinet office an hour earlier, made the fateful announcement to parliament at noon:

"This country is now at war with Germany. We are ready."

The threat of war had become a reality. Within a day, an act was passed requiring all males between the ages of eighteen and forty-one to register for armed service, except those with exemption for medical reasons or in key occupations. Just two days later, on Wednesday evening, Bobby and Charlie completed their usual swim and seriously considered the situation.

"W-well, it's h-happened. W-we're at war! Have you r-registered yet?"

Charlie shrugged and shook his head. "Nobody has sent for me yet. They'll take all the youngsters first. I think I'll wait a few weeks to let the dust settle. We've just got to be ready when we're needed, I should think."

"They've started ev-vacuating children, a-and made us all have blackout curtains. They must be expecting air-air raids, eh?"

"Yeah. It's difficult to know what to expect, Bobby. We shall find out in due course. Talking of blackout curtains, have you done anything about them yet? I can always put them on an account for you."

"Thanks, mate. That may be a good idea. We've only just spent a fortune on the c-curtains! I think Daph's goin' to speak to Shayna about the blinds today or tomorrow. B-By the way, did I tell you that Daph's dad joined the Civil Deffence. He's an Air-air Raid Warden! I pity anyone who d-doesn't draw their curtains in his area!"

Charlie laughed. "Does he still have any family in Poland?"

"I dunno. H-he's never said, I should think not. He'd have m-mentioned them, especially now, with the invasion."

They sipped ale.

"I see W-Winnie's back in the war cabinet, a-and Anthony Eden. They'll make a difference."

Charlie made no comment.

"W-When d'you think they'll c-call us, Charlie?"

"I don't know, Bob. It's got to take time to register and to train people, months at least. For now, we just have to carry on as usual. We'll be told more soon enough."

"Yeah, I s'pose. It's f-funny, but I'm not u-upset at the thought of joining up. I'm quite excited ab-bout it, but I'll h-have to close the workshop, I suppose."

"How about your staff?"

"Yeah, it's a pr-problem." Bobby scratched his head.

"I h-had an idea I could let 'em carry on, with Daph watching over the business. Cyril's not a bad engineer, and I don't think they'd take him in the army with his ch-chest trouble."

Charlie looked up. "But?"

"B-But Daph's not keen on me goin'."

* * *

Despite the enormity of the decisions of September 1939, life at home carried on very much as normal for the rest of the year; although one major announcement affecting Charlie more than most people was the rationing of petrol on 22 September. His allocated ration was only ten gallons per month and he was accustomed to using twice that for his business calls. He solved the problem by bringing both the Velocette and his bicycle back into use. The car was reserved for when he needed to carry passengers.

The feared immediate German air attack, the 'Blitzkrieg', did not materialise, however. Instead, Eastern Europe suffered. On 17 September, Russia, having secretly signed an agreement with Germany, attacked Poland from the east. By the end of the month Poland had ceased to exist as an independent nation, the east of the country now controlled by Soviet Russia and the rest under Nazi rule.

Walter Habisch had left Czechoslovakia some fifteen years earlier, but he had family still living there. He had not heard from them for some time and he worried about them. His obvious distress when he met Charlie in the basement of Collick's on a Monday morning at the end of September had a far more urgent cause, however.

"It's Esther, my beloved Esther. She's dying, Charlie. Yesterday she took a bad turn, she bin ill for a long time, but yesterday was diff'ren'. She was thin, and grey, and crying with pain. I called the amb'lance. I just come in this morning to give the books to Ivor. He'll tell you the rest. Now I'm rushin' to the hospital. It's bad, Charlie."

Charlie nodded. "My thoughts will be with you both Walter," he said in a low voice.

"Yeah, you're a good friend, Charlie."

The little man was hopping from one foot to the other. "Charlie, you gonna see Alice today?" he asked sheepishly.

"Yeah. She's had the baby now, hasn't she? I was told not to call last week."

"Yeah, a beautiful little girl. Bert wants to call her Charisse! You know he…"

"Yeah, I know, Walter. I'm not likely to forget it, am I?"

"No, course not!" answered the flustered Walter. "But, to keep my name out of it, Alice wants you to be the godfather. Will that be okay? You don' mind?"

Charlie grinned. "No. I don't mind, Walter. You go and look after Esther."

Habisch gratefully rushed towards the door. Charlie moved on to the supervisor's table, where Ivor Spafford was his usual calm self.

"Nice weekend's work, Charlie," he said after a quick glance at the books. "Now, you don't have to do Walter's rounds from today, I'm going to collect them. I have just told Walter to take the week off. He's in no state to work. The poor bloke's distraught. It sounds as if he may be losing his wife."

"Yeah. It's been coming for months. I'm surprised she's held on this long."

Spafford nodded sympathetically. "I think this really is the end. Poor Walter. And their daughter, she's only eight, I think."

"Yes. He'll have to re-organise his life a bit. But he's Walter. He's a tough little nut. He'll work it out alright."

"Let's hope so." Ivor Spafford's concern was evident. Walter Habisch had been a major strength in his team for more than ten years.

* * *

On a Saturday afternoon in late October, Charlie arrived at 14, Malmesbury Street for his regular weekly call. He was greeted by Sally Spence, looking as beautiful as he could ever remember and with a smile broad enough to light up the entire street. She ushered him inside the door and kissed him lightly on the lips. Then she placed her finger where her lips had been and whispered:

"I am going to have our baby about the third week in May!" She raised her voice to its normal pitch:

"We are hoping to give Harry a little sister next year!"

Charlie followed her through the narrow hallway to the living room, where he found Percy standing by the fireplace in a paint-splattered boiler suit and with a face full of happy disbelief. Charlie grasped him by the hand, smiling warmly.

"Congratulations! Sally's just told me the news."

"Thanks, Charlie. Sally only told me for sure yesterday. It's marvellous, isn't it? As if we were blessed!"

"Well, maybe you were, Percy, maybe you were." Charlie replied. He glanced around. "Where's Harry?"

"He's with his grandmothers," Sally replied quickly. "He likes being with them. Harry and Mum seem to understand each other!"

Percy smiled. "She certainly understands him better than I do! Little buggar!"

"Percy!" Sally exclaimed in mock shock.

"I expect you'll get there in time, Perce," Charlie suggested. "From the experience of most people I know, under the age of six all children are best left with the women!"

Percy shook his head in innocent bewilderment. "I think I've got a lot to learn about this being a father business."

Sally laughed. "You're doing okay, love. A baby is someone different every week! It's only been a couple of months."

"I suppose so, but it already seems a lifetime!"

Sally giggled. She handed Charlie the three Collick's books and Charlie made his entries for the week as she went to the kitchen to put the kettle on.

In addition to their established individual accounts, they had now opened an account for the home and for Harry's needs. Since moving into the house, two months earlier, they had set about making the home the way they wanted it. With their limited budget it would be a big project, the house being dark and tired-looking throughout. With the blackout curtains fitted, Sally was keen to paint the papered walls in lighter colours as soon as possible. Percy was currently spending all his free time on the task, with Sally supervising and giving a helping hand as much as she could.

Charlie had supplied the blackout curtains. He had set the repayment terms as low as he dared to aid their cause. He knew Sally would never miss a payment.

"Did you take Harry to your mum's this morning?" he asked.

"Yeah."

"How was she? I didn't think she looked good on Tuesday."

"She gets good days and bad days, Charlie, but she doesn't like talking about it."

"You can't blame her for that. She's a fighter, your mum. It was nice to see her sharing the housework with Percy's mum. That was clever, arranging the living accommodation like that."

"Yeah, it was," Percy acknowledged with his soft grin, "but I didn't expect to be put to work here so soon. I'd better get on with that ceiling."

Sally patted her husband's arm. "Why don't you relax and sit down for a few minutes, Percy? Have your cup of tea first. Even the best tradesmen take their tea breaks!" Percy obediently sat down in his fireside chair.

"Percy's painting all the upstairs ceilings white. It's surprising how much brighter a clean white ceiling makes a room!"

Charlie grinned. "Yeah, well I suppose it would."

* * *

Alice Pensell appeared to have taken in her stride the problem of giving birth after a gap of some eleven years. She greeted Charlie with her usual smile when he arrived on the following Monday, and ushered him into the front room where the new baby was asleep in a pram.

"Bert's asleep in the kitchen. He's been pissed blind ever since this one arrived. He can't believe he's got such a beautiful daughter."

Charlie shrugged. He leaned over the pram.

"She is a pretty baby. You must be delighted, Alice."

"I'm bloody tired! But she does look like a little angel now she's asleep. Yeah, I'm pleased. 'course I'm pleased. She's a lovely little black eyed beauty, better than I deserve. That's it now, though. I didn't dream I'd fall for this one, but you never can tell, can you? I shall be bloody careful in future. The shutters've gotta go up!"

She laughed, a harsh laugh, tossing her head back. Then she looked at Charlie.

"Have you seen Walter? He was in a state on Saturday. His wife's bad, ain't she?"

"I think she's dying, Alice. Walter's distraught. He won't be round for a few weeks, I suspect."

"Yeah, that's what I thought. Have you got a fag, Charlie?"

Charlie opened his case and they both lit up.

"Poor sod! He wanted to be godfather to Charisse but on Saturday, he said he didn't think he could do it. He can't bear to hurt anyone, Walter. He's such a good bloke, a bloody sight better than mine, but what can you do?"

Charlie shrugged. Alice continued:

"He feels guilty about him and me, although he shouldn't. I always knew what I was doing. He never had a chance, I swallowed him up. I wanted it and he needed it. That's how it always was, for years." She sighed. "Shall we have a cup o' tea?"

Alice went off into the kitchen and Charlie made his book entries. He studied the tiny baby sleeping peacefully in the pram. She had tiny ears and black hair. Over his years of calling on families, he had found that most babies were actually quite ugly, but Charisse Pensell was indeed a pretty little thing.

Alice returned, not with a tray but with two steaming mugs of tea.

"You're drinkin' rough today, Charlie!" she said as she handed him one of the mugs."

"Probably make it taste better!" replied Charlie, sitting down on one of the two armchairs.

"He's still snoring." Alice tilted her head towards the door. "He'll wake up about half past four and go back to the pub at five!"

Charlie made no comment. Alice drank some tea.

"Charlie, I don't want any of Bert's lot as godfather to the baby. Would you consider it?"

Charlie smiled at her.

"I'd consider it an honour, Alice."

Alice drank some more tea. Then, holding her mug with two hands, she said, simply: "Thank you."

They smiled at each other and then she added:

"You know, my sister-in-law Elsie worships you. She always talks about you as if you're some kind of God. Even my Ricky, the wild little sod, is respectful to you. It's only lately that I've begun to realise that you *are* special. You're a pretty remarkable bloke, Charlie. I reckon it's us who's honoured. Thank you."

Charlie shrugged, the hint of the Stoker smile in his eyes.

* * *

Autumn in England was marked not by enemy attacks but by a flood of laws and official guidelines as to how to be ready for the worst. In October, an army of one hundred and fifty-eight thousand men was equipped and posted to France. The British Expeditionary Force was to bolster the French defence and keep the war away from our islands. With the exception of the loss of the battle ship Royal Oak, which was sunk by a German torpedo in the supposedly safe waters of Scapa Flow, 1939 came to an end with the war barely affecting our shores.

Millie Stoker, despite Charlie's and Stephen's eagerness to help, purchased rolls of blackout material from the local drapers. She made blinds for all the windows in the house, including for the Walters on the upper floors. When she completed the job, she kept herself busy for the rest of the year making blackout curtains for the needier members of the congregation.

Stephen Collick, too, found it a very busy time. In spite of petrol rationing, for most of the Collick interests the war meant increased business, but for the department store things were already becoming difficult. Six salesmen-collectors had received their call-up papers, and at least fifteen more would do so in the months to come. From the internal staff, seven men had already gone, and another twenty or so would do so in due course. Sales targets and business plans were on hold and would remain so until the war ended.

Margret always joined Charlie for his monthly Sunday lunches at Amhurst Road, usually driving to Chigwell from Bounds Green in the morning, then staying the night and driving to college on Monday. She had now been at Walthamstow for over a year and had settled, though not comfortably, into her new life.

Most of the time, she was teaching maths to children between the ages of eleven and fifteen, to children who were, in the main, terrified of her. For two periods each week, however, she found relief from the tedium by teaching economics to a few bright sixteen and 17-year-olds. She maintained that this small group, the cream of the College's students, made life worthwhile.

The last Sunday in November, the pair returned to Chigwell and were having a drink together. Margret suddenly said:

"By the way, the Lacey's are throwing a party on New Year's Eve to mark both the end of the decade and the fact that Leonard is going to join the Middlesex Regiment. You'll come, of course, won't you? It will be a great night."

Charlie shrugged. "Yes, I should think so. It's always nice to drink Lionel's Jameson's."

"I don't know how young Lennie will cope with the army, the poor soul. He's really not the type. All he wants of life is to be left to play the piano."

"Has he said?"

"No, it's just the way he looks. I think he's terrified."

Charlie shrugged but made no comment.

"What about you, Charlie? When do you expect to be called up? Your age group won't be needed before the end of next year, will it? If at all?"

"So it seems, but I may go before that."

"Why on earth would you volunteer?" Margret's tone was scornful and, as always, Charlie ignored it.

"Unless someone gets rid of Hitler, it will be a long war. I feel an obligation to support my country."

"Why am I not surprised?" said Margret, resignedly.

Earlier in the day, Charlie and Stephen had chatted. Stephen had asked a similar, if more direct, question.

"When do you want to go?" he had asked.

Charlie had given the same reply as he now gave to Margret.

"I have had a few personal matters to organise. I still have one or two. Then perhaps I'll register."

Stephen had accepted the reply without comment beyond a nod. He knew Charlie's reasons would be sound. Margret, however, retorted:

"Personal matters? What personal matters?"

Charlie smiled at her. "Well, for a start there's this house, Mrs Stoker. We don't want it left empty for years. You will have to stay here for a day or two each week, Margret, to ensure everything is cared for. This is, after all, our home."

"We what?" Margret's eyes flashed. She glared at her husband, then slowly calmed down. Damn him, he was right, and she owed him that. He had let her swan off to France for two years without a murmur. She breathed out with a loud explosion of air.

"Psssh! Blast you, Big Boy!"

Charlie shrugged.

Chapter Twenty-Three
A New Life

The Christmas period, subdued somewhat by the restrictions imposed by the war, nevertheless held several social events for the young Stokers. Margret accompanied Charlie to Amhurst Road on one day and Charlie accompanied Margret to Clay Hill on another. As every year, one trip was relaxed and enjoyable for all and the other a trial to be lived through.

At the Stoker house, for the first time in Charlie's memory, there was no Father Peter O'Rahilly. The beloved priest was not well enough to leave his bed. He had sent his blessings with Millie and assured them that he would be better in the New Year, but Millie said she feared he may be being over-optimistic. They said a heartfelt prayer for him before lunch.

At Clay Hill, the empty seat was that of Terence, Margret's strangely sullen younger brother. He had enlisted in his father's old regiment and was unable to go home for Christmas. Harry, or Henry, as he now insisted on being called, was to be joining his young brother in the New Year. He was his usual objectionable self, but the only clashes he initiated were between himself and his sister. Henry did his best never to address Charlie at all.

That suited Charlie very well, of course, and his ability to remain quite undisturbed by his brother-in-law's indirect insults and general rudeness upset Henry all the more. The result was that Mabey son managed to incur the wrath of Mabey daughter, and as was invariably the case, a fired up Margret was far too much for Henry. He stormed out of the dining room and was not seen again for the rest of the day.

Herbert Mabey, who began the day as the genial host, poured drinks and soon became the worse for wear. He enquired about Charlie's possible call-up.

"I suppose you'll be joining the R.A.F., following your father's footsteps, eh?" he suggested enquiringly.

"No, I don't think so," said Charlie, "I shall join a regiment, sir."

"Oh? Guards?"

"No sir, the Essex Regiment."

"Ha! Really? I see. Hmmph!" Herbert Mabey seemed nonplussed. He inquired no further. Instead, after a heavy meal and too much alcohol he subsided into his favourite armchair and snored most of the afternoon away.

Mairead, like Charlie, seemed unaffected by the performance of her family. She chatted with her guests and enjoyed a festive afternoon of three-handed rummy. After tea and cakes, the Stokers left early.

Margret and Charlie also spent an evening at Hillfield Avenue with the Bruces and the Hipsteads, as well as enjoying one of the four friends' occasional monthly reunion dinners. In between, Margret stayed with Jennifer and Charlie went to work.

Their festive season ended with the New Year's Eve party at Highgate. That year the New Year fell at the weekend. As ever, it was noisy and happy, albeit behind blackout curtains. Bobby and Daphne were not present. The affair was attended less by Jennifer's friends and more by the extended Lacey family and business acquaintances.

Charlie enjoyed the evening, acting as joint barman with Jennifer's father, ensuring all the guests' glasses were full – and drinking a lot of Jameson's. Lacey reminisced as usual and was as entertaining as ever, although Charlie noticed, this year, the chemist was beginning to repeat many of the same stories. It mattered little, he told them well.

Lionel Lacey was now a more contented man. His business was thriving and his children were making their way in life. His only fear, he regretted, was that his son would struggle in the army.

"The boy is willing enough, but he is unsuited to the life, Charlie."

Charlie nodded. He suspected the lad would prove to be tougher than his family feared.

"How about you, Charlie? Which service will you go for?"

"The army. They'll call me when they need me. As it happens, a friend of my boss is the CO at Warley Barracks, and it seems that he wants to talk to me."

Lacey nodded, approving.

Later, Charlie asked himself why he had said that to Lionel Lacey. At Amhurst Road, a few days earlier, he had told Stephen Collick that he may not wait for conscription but would instead enlist as a volunteer in the New Year. Stephen had suggested that Warley would be a convenient place to enlist and that an old friend was in charge there. Would Charlie like to go and have a chat with him? Charlie had replied:

"Yes, maybe, sir. Can I come back to you when I've sorted out a few things and got a clearer mind?"

* * *

Sally Spence was, to all appearances, a happily married young wife and mother. With husband Percy doing the heavy work, they had transformed the inside of 14 Malmesbury Street. It was no longer the rather dowdy home he had grown up in, but rather, a bright welcoming house in which to bring up young children.

Percy Spence was a decent, hard-working chap who strived to be a good husband. He worshipped his wife and was thrilled beyond words that she was already pregnant with his child. Yet, every Saturday, Charlie Stoker called upon them and every Saturday, despite his best intentions, Percy found himself disturbed by the bond, the almost brother-sister intimacy that existed between Sally and Charlie, and from which he always felt excluded.

Percy was jealous, yet at the same time, he was ashamed of his jealousy. Sally and Charlie had known each other for years before he himself had even spoken to Sally. Sally's mother always treated Charlie almost as her own son, and even his own mother, now that she lived at Armagh Road, had started saying how wonderful Charlie was.

Percy knew he had every reason to like the big blond-haired man. Charlie had proved to be a good friend to both families. He always did the right thing and had never done anything to hurt or to offend any of them. Charlie had even encouraged him in his courtship! He had nothing to be jealous about, he knew, but… but when Charlie Stoker entered a room, well, he sort of filled it in a way that Percy knew he could not. He told himself he'd just got to get over it, but it wasn't that easy, was it?

Although Charlie still took Lottie for a drive every couple of weeks, Sally no longer felt free to enjoy the car trips. She did arrange her week so that she visited her mother every Tuesday, however. That meant she still saw Charlie once a week when Percy was not present. They usually managed to get a few minutes to chat together and to embrace out of sight of the mothers, but any other contact was not practical.

Both fully recognised the strength of the bond between them. For Sally, in her daily life, she was Sally Spence; in her heart she was Sally Stoker. Remarkably, she was able to cope with the situation; she was content with her lot and with the secret carried inside her. For Charlie, it was proving to be more difficult.

The war was going to greatly affect everyone for an unknown period of time and with unknown consequences. Stephen Collick had made it clear that all their plans would be put on hold for the duration of the hostilities. Afterwards, he said, they would re-set the clocks.

Alone with a whisky at Woodside Way after the New Year, Charlie assessed the situation and carefully made a list:

1. Sally was now settled down with her husband and her son. She was Mrs Spence. Later in the year there would be a second child, his child. He must be open with her.
2. Margret was settled at Walthamstow College. She was also happily settled with her lesbian mate. Nevertheless, she would take care of Chigwell if Charlie were not there.
3. Stephen would take great care to protect the business and his mother.
4. He must keep his promise to Alice Pensell.
5. He must explain to Bobby.
6. It was time to meet the Colonel.

The following morning, Tuesday, Charlie called Stephen on his direct line.

"I have decided I should like to go along to Warley, sir."

"Very, well. I shall contact my friend."

"As soon as it is convenient, please. I think it may be better not to say anything to Aitch or Ivor until afterwards, in case it doesn't work out."

Stephen agreed and promised to call him back as soon as he could. The return call came within a half-hour.

"You have an appointment with Lieutenant Colonel Sir René Laverton at 3.00 pm on Thursday. René is an old friend of mine. Actually, your mother has met him. You may find him to be a bit of a blow-bag, but his heart is in the right place. He was retired a year or two ago and has now been recalled on a temporary basis. Let me know how you get on."

"Yes, sir. Thank you."

Charlie phoned Bobby and explained that he had some things to do and may not be free in time for Wednesday. They arranged to meet on Thursday instead and Charlie promised to explain the situation then. This manoeuvre left Charlie free to spend Wednesday evening with his mother.

"What a nice surprise!" exclaimed Millie. "Is Bobby not able to meet you tonight?"

"Yes, I've changed the days round. I needed the time. Did you hear me talking to Stephen last week?"

"You mean about the army?" Millie's attention was sharpened. "No, but Stephen told me afterwards. Do you really want to rush into it?"

"Well, I'm going to have a meeting at Warley barracks tomorrow. I haven't told Bobby yet. I'd rather know what I'm talking about before I tell him."

"Oh? I'm not sure I know what you're talking about either."

Charlie shrugged. "Sorry. I'll explain. You knew I'd want to do my bit if the war came. Well, the conscription process is slow. It's age-related – my call may not come until next year, and it may be all over by then! So, I've decided to make things happen. Stephen has arranged for me to talk to someone at Warley barracks. As I just said, I haven't told Bobby what I'm doing. I need to know the facts before I speak to him. That's why I changed the days."

"Why?"

"You know Bobby. He'll want to go with me!"

"You've decided already?"

"Yes, Mum, I've decided. I must go. I can't explain the motivation, I just know I've got to do it."

Millie studied her son with an expressionless face. What she was seeing was the tall, handsome figure of the young Charles. Her eyes moistened as Charles became Charlie.

"Go, son. You don't have to explain why. You are your father's son. If you feel you must go, you will go. I ask only, please, come back to me. Come back in one piece."

A tear ran down each of her cheeks. Charlie looked on in shock. Then he moved to her side and took her in his arms.

"I'll come back, Mum. In one piece, I promise."

* * *

Charlie ordered two pints of brown ale and grinned at his agitated pal. Bobby wore a sheepish smile but his tone was challenging:

"Okay, it's all very w-well grinning, but wh-what's it all about?"

They had finished their swim, showered, and followed each other to The Chequers before Bobby had been able to demand answers from his friend.

Charlie shrugged and proffered his cigarette case. They both lit up. Charlie took a swig of ale and blew a cloud of smoke. He was no longer grinning. He looked his friend in the eye.

"Bobby, I know I've not been saying much just lately, but I've been doing a lot of thinking. As a result" – he hesitated – "well, what it boils down to is this: I am enlisting in the Essex Regiment. I begin training on the 6th of March."

Bobby stared blankly at his friend; his mouth slack, slightly open. He removed his glasses and polished them with his handkerchief.

"I thought we were waiting until we were called," he said without a stammer.

"Yeah." Charlie nodded. He shrugged apologetically. "That is what we said, but the truth of the matter is, I have to make a move, Bobby. I can't go on like this. My life is a mess."

"D-Don't be daft! What d'ya mean, a mess? Y-you've got a m-more organised life than anyone I've ever known!"

Charlie sighed. "Yeah, organised is about right. I'm good at organising. I can organise everyone's life except my own."

Bobby took his time to think about that.

"I-I know what you m-mean," he conceded, "b-but I don't think you're right." He struggled to put his thoughts together. "Y-you're brilliant at making decisions, and y-you always think of other people. You can always see the other person's p-point of view. Th-th-that's why you're the special bloke you are, Charlie. Y-you can always see the way through l-life's pro-problems."

He scratched his head, then picked up his glass and held it in both hands as if searching there for the right words.

"That must—s-s-sometimes, that must—be a w-weight on your shoulders." He looked up at Charlie. "B-but you mustn't change, Charlie. W-We all need you too much."

Charlie's face, as so often, showed nothing of what he was thinking. He crushed his cigarette out and replied in staccato sentences.

"It's not one way traffic, Bobby. I need you just as much. But I've got to go. It's the right thing to do. I owe it to my father's memory. I can't wait any longer."

He took another swallow of his ale, then squeezed Bobby's knee.

"If you hadn't got a wife and baby to look after, I would have asked you to go with me."

"And I w-would, like a shot!"

They both laughed and the tension was broken.

"What are you going to do in the army?" asked Bobby.

"Fight the enemy. Isn't that what it's all about?"

"At W-Warley barracks?"

"Warley is a convenient place to start. It seems I'm going to be training for six months. Basic training is at Warley, then about sixteen weeks at OCTU. I'm not sure where, yet. I think Sandhurst."

"B-Bloody heck! You're going to be an officer!"

"So it seems. But so can you. I asked about the need for engineers and he said the army was in great need of them. But I didn't give him your name."

Bobby shook his head, slowly. "C-Can anyone just go and enlist, just like that?"

"I suppose so. It was easy for me, Stephen Collick knew the CO."

"Oh!" Bobby was not sure what else to say. He drank his ale.

Lieutenant Colonel Laverton had appeared to Charlie very much an officer of the old school, corpulent, with a red nose and weathered features. The colonel received him warmly as 'someone close to the honourable Stephen, brother of Lord Collick'.

"Actually, young man, I have had the pleasure of meeting your enchanting mother, socially, you know."

"No, sir, I didn't know."

"Ha! I failed to make an impression!"

"I don't know about that, sir. My mother is very discreet about her social life. Did you meet her at Parklands?"

"Spot on. Absolutely right. I don't think I ever met your father, though, although Stephen used to speak very highly of him."

"Yes. I believe they were quite close, sir, but that was all before my time."

"Quite, quite. He was a great loss."

They enjoyed a pot of tea together and Laverton talked a great deal about the regiment and its history. He asked a number of questions about Charlie's education and career, but took it for granted that Charlie would be offered a commission with the regiment. He seemed to assume that was why Stephen had sent him to Warley. He asked:

"Tell me, old chap, do you see yourself doing a particular job in the service?"

"I hope to be able to do a useful job defending my country, sir."

"Good for you! Yes, quite." He reached into a tray on the desk and fiddled with some papers.

"Of course, this being the army, everything has to be done properly, you know, with the correct forms correctly filled."

The colonel laughed at his own words and went on to explain that like all entrants, Charlie must undergo a preliminary medical examination, then complete the standard six week basic training course, which would be followed by a shorter pre-OCTU course. On completion of that, he would transfer to Sandhurst for his OCTU training.

Charlie had not considered that he would immediately be selected to train as an officer; indeed, he had been looking forward to starting in the ranks. He had visualised it as more like being with his daily customers. Nevertheless, he was relieved that the decision was made. He had eight weeks to tidy up the loose ends of his daily life, then he could move on.

He left a rather pensive Bobby at the Chequers and returned to an empty house at Chigwell. Before retiring, he gave some thought to the things to be done, but as he mentally went through his list, it occurred to him that it no longer mattered. He had to live through eight weeks of what had become, for some months, a painful routine.

Whenever Charlie thought about his remarkable ability to remain detached from emotional involvement with other people, he told himself that it had its price. In one of those rare moments when his shield fell from him, he had said to Bobby, at the Chequers after visiting Warley, *'I need you just as much. But I've got to go'*.

The cry for love of the first sentence was instantly denied by the decisiveness of the second. That dedication to righteousness, to what was 'the right thing to do', had been the driving force of his life. It had guided him into college and into his career. But it had also led him into his marriage. More devastatingly, it had led him into steering his one true love into a loveless marriage; and now it was leading him into the war.

* * *

At twelve noon on the second Thursday in February, a cold damp day, Charisse Pensell was christened at St. Mary's Church, Bow, in full view of a large congregation of Pensells and Pensell associates; Tattles and Tinkwells; the usual Bow Church congregation; and Charlie Stoker.

Charlie surveyed the scene with a twinkle in his eye. Bert Pensell was wearing a dark grey suit with a shirt and a bright red and yellow tie. It was the first time Charlie had ever seen Bert in a suit, let alone a tie. He was clean-shaven, his black, curly hair neatly trimmed above his narrow forehead, and he was absolutely sober. As Charlie studied the proud father, he saw what Alice had always seen in her husband: a well-built and fine-looking man, albeit, on close inspection, now showing the wear and tear of fifteen years of hard drinking.

Alice, in a green silk dress, looked exactly what she was, an attractive mother, proud of her new baby and surrounded by her loved ones. Their two boys, Paul, aged twelve, and Ricky, now fourteen, were dressed in suits and ties to match their father. Charlie played his part in the ceremony as godfather, but it was Bert who carried the child to the font and proudly named her Charisse.

Afterwards, all were invited to the Pensell home for a small celebration. It being Sunday, there were no open pubs until about seven o'clock in the evening, but Bert had brought home enough beer to start his own party.

It was by now common knowledge that Charlie had been 'called up' and that he would be leaving in a few weeks. The godfather stayed long enough to accept all the good wishes from, and to chat with all the people he knew and a few he did not. Plump little Elsie Tattle beamed lovingly at him, her fourth child in her arms, her second girl, only a few months old. Elsie was thrilled to be there with Wilf and all their children.

Charlie excused himself late in the afternoon and walked the mile or so to Armagh Road, where Lottie Cutter was struggling through another winter. Her health was poor and she had not taken the news of Charlie's impending move well, but she greeted him as brightly as always.

"Hallo my love. Did your christening go well? Did you promise to be a good godfather?"

"Yes, Mother Cutter, I did my duty." Charlie shrugged, laughing.

"I expect you were exemplary!" said Mary Spence from her seat on the other side of the fireplace.

Charlie nodded. "How are you two ladies today? Keeping warm, I see." He nodded towards the fire burning brightly between them. "You are in the best place. It's certainly not a day to be out in unnecessarily."

The ladies agreed in unison. Charlie pulled a chair away from the table and sat between them. He addressed Lottie.

"How are you feeling, Mrs C? You didn't look too well on Tuesday. You look better today."

"That's how things go, Charlie, up and down like the weather."

"Just like all life! What did the doctor say?" The doctor had been sent for during the week.

"He gave me an examination and some more pills. He repeated what he's said before. Don't overdo things and keep warm."

"Well, that's what you must do, then. If the weather's good next Thursday, shall we go for a drive?"

Both ladies lit up with joy. "That would be lovely," replied Lottie Cutter. "Can we say we'll do it, anyway, whatever the weather?"

"That's good for me!" replied Charlie with a laugh. He thought it better not to remind them that it may be the last drive they took together. He had agreed that Ivor Spafford should travel with him for the last week in February to prepare customers for the changeover.

* * *

Charlie had had very little opportunity to see Sally alone since signing his papers at Warley. Every Saturday when he called, Percy was always at home with little Harry, who was more full of trouble and temper than a box full of monkeys.

On the Saturday after the christening, which was the last week that he would be calling on his own, he was surprised to find Sally apparently alone. By this time, she was seven months pregnant. Pregnancy seemed to suit Sally Spence. As beautiful as ever, she radiated good health, and managed to look entirely comfortable with her expanding abdomen. She welcomed him by dragging him inside the door and hugging him in a tight embrace.

"Percy's gone fishing for the day with Brian. It's a nice day and he doesn't often get the chance, poor love" – Sally's smile was as wide as ever – "but it does mean we can spend an hour together. Harry's having a little sleep!"

Charlie removed his coat and hung it on the new hat stand by the door. He followed Sally into the back room. She went on into the kitchen to put the kettle on. He sat down on one of the upright chairs, turning it to face the kitchen. Sally came back into the room and sat on his knee as if she did it every day. She threw her arms around his neck.

"Oh, God, I love you Charlie!" she exclaimed. "Your baby has been moving about a lot lately!"

Charlie held her as if she were fragile, frightened lest he hurt either of the two beings on his lap.

"When is the baby due exactly?" he asked. "Can you work out a definite due date?"

"Well, not exact, but if you put a ring around the tenth of May, you won't be far out."

Charlie nodded. He did a quick calculation in his head. "I think I may have a couple of days off about then. I shall be between courses."

"What courses? All you've said is you've been called up. You've never said a word about what happens after you go in!"

"I think I've got to go to Sandhurst Training College. You know me, Sal. I don't say a lot. It would've been different if I'd seen you alone. I'd've told you, but these last weeks, whenever we've had a minute, we've talked about your mum."

"Yeah, it's true. And she is a worry, but we can only watch and wait. She told me you took them both out on Thursday. That was nice. It always makes her happy. Hang on. Let me get the tea."

She rushed into the little kitchen and came back with a tray of tea and a home-baked madeira cake. She put the tray on the table and kissed Charlie on his forehead. Charlie grinned at the sight of the cake, and felt the kiss as a blessing. As Sally poured the tea, for once in his life, he threw caution to the wind. He spoke the words that burned his soul every day.

"You know, Sally, I have only twice in my life tasted the ecstasy of pure requited love. Once last July, and again today. I love you Sally Spence, and I shall love you till I die."

Sally put down the cake knife she was holding. She turned to him and he took her in his arms. They held each other and they caressed each other, and he caressed the child within her. As Sally's tears wet his cheeks, she whispered, "And I am yours, Charlie, for ever and ever. Nothing will ever divide us."

If, the previous July they had made a miracle, on this February day they were confirming the righteousness of that miracle. This, they both knew instinctively was their secret marriage moment. They clung to each other and remained tied in an embrace for what, to each of them, was a lifetime. The world outside that room would never know, could never understand, but this secret bond of love was strong enough for each of them to face that world and to live a life according to most of its rules.

Charlie left 14 Malmesbury Street that afternoon in a state of peace. Nineteen days later, he reported for duty at the Essex Regimental Headquarters at Warley. Charlie Stoker became a soldier.